A NORMA BERGEN MYSTERY

AN
EQUAL PIECE
OF JUSTICE

Lee W. Doty

Publisher Page
an imprint of Headline Books
Terra Alta, WV

An Equal Piece of Justice

by Lee W. Doty

copyright ©2024 Lee W. Doty

To order additional copies of this book or for book publishing information, or to contact the author:

Headline Books, Inc.
P.O. Box 52
Terra Alta, WV 26764
www.HeadlineBooks.com
mybook@headlinebooks.com

Publisher Page is an imprint of Headline Books

ISBN 13: 9781958914212

Library of Congress Control Number: 2023944996

PRINTED IN THE UNITED STATES OF AMERICA

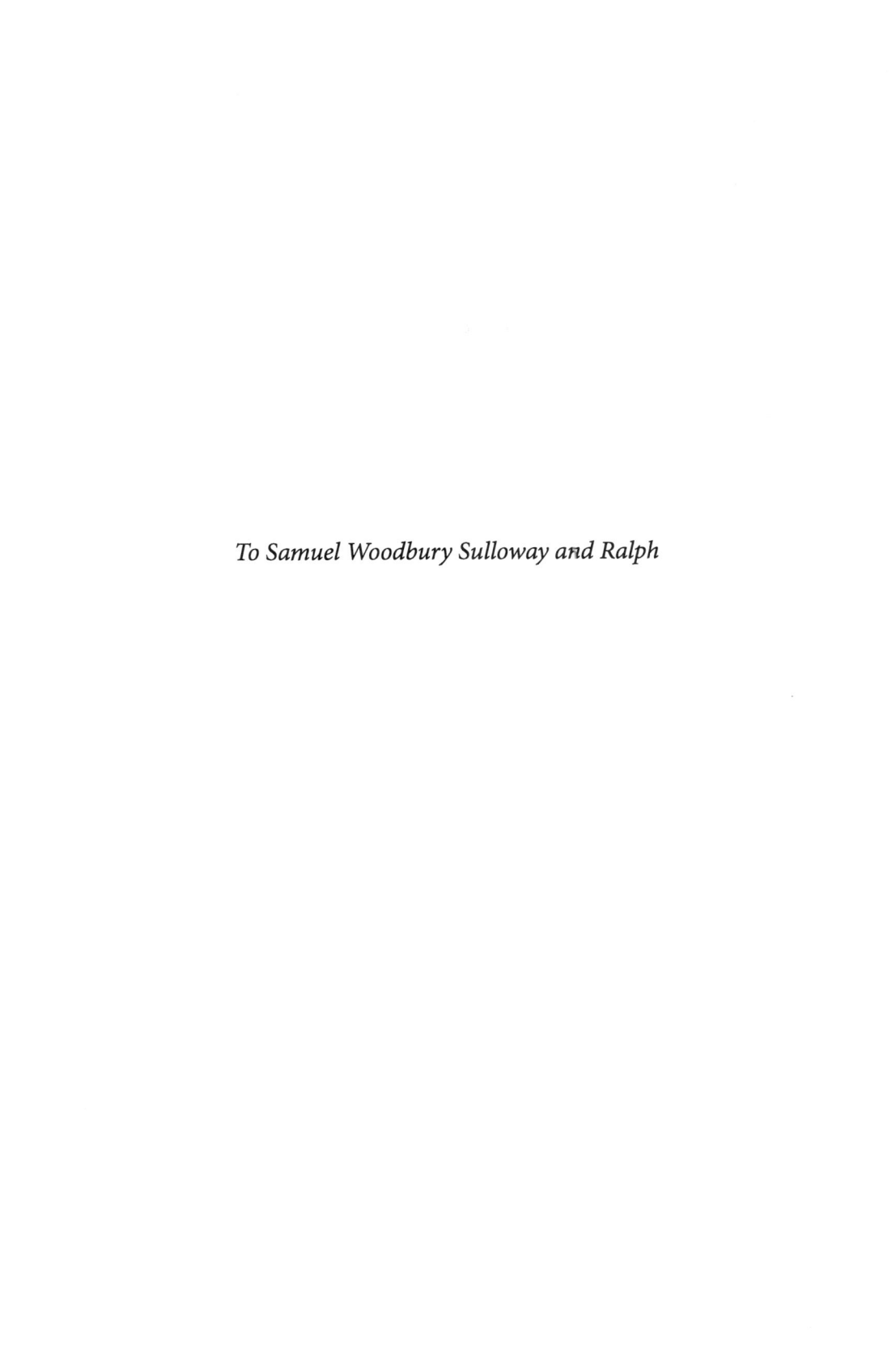

To Samuel Woodbury Sulloway and Ralph

Norma Bergen Mystery Series
Tidal Kin
Last Casualty

Acknowledgments

My thanks to Ruth A. McQuade, former federal prosecutor, and Lyndsey W. Matschat, former Assistant Prosecuting Attorney for Jefferson County, WV, who've shared with me their in-depth knowledge of criminal law and rules of criminal procedure and shown unlimited patience in the process. Thanks also to Sheriff Thomas Hansen and Chief Deputy Victor Lupis of Jefferson County, WV, for educating me in the duties of the Sheriff's Office in a local murder investigation. Any mistakes in these areas of expertise are entirely my own, and I apologize in advance.

I have been guided and cheered on for many months by members of the Spinners writing group, which, during the writing of this book, included Patty Bain Bachner, Pam Clark, John Deupree, D. W. Gregory, Sean Murtagh, Tom Trumble, Ryland Swain, and Lisa Younis.

My beta readers provided incredibly insightful comments and suggestions. They included Eileen Dooley, Mary McCarthy, Han Nolan, and Ruth McQuade.

Many thanks are due to Sandy Tritt for her helpful critique and editing expertise as well as to the hard-working and always cheerful Cathy Teets of Headline Books.

Finally, thanks to Ralph Doty, for never once hesitating to review a chapter—yet again.

"When I take a full view and circle of myself without this reasonable moderator, and equal piece of justice, death, I do conceive myself the miserablest person extant"

Religio Medici, by Thomas Browne, Section 38 (1643), Part I.

1

Norma sat hunched over her office desk, her forehead resting on her crossed arms. She rolled her chair backward and luxuriated in a long stretch as the space between each vertebra expanded. She'd given herself five minutes for relaxation before her client appeared.

Jess Harper, the legal assistant Norma shared with her suitemate, popped her head in the door. "You ought to get rid of that hat of yours when a client's coming."

"Thanks for that unsolicited advice." Norma removed her red fishing hat and finger-combed her hair.

"Who in their right mind covers up long blond hair anyway?" Jess muttered as she headed back to the reception area.

That from someone with pink hair on occasion? Thank God Jess was back to black spikes. Norma should have told her to bug off with her advice, but she liked Jess. She was brassy. Reminded Norma of herself at a young age.

Jess had placed the Fingerhut file on the corner of her boss's desk, and Norma opened it for a last-minute review over a half bottle of Mountain Dew. Norma had only recently "waived in" to West Virginia from Massachusetts, meaning her years practicing law in another state on good terms excused her from having to take the West Virginia bar exam. She'd dilly-dallied about starting a practice when she, husband Will Coigne, and daughter Laney first moved to West Virginia but had finally accepted that she wasn't returning to Cape Cod anytime soon.

Staying put, however, meant starting a new law practice or a new career, and that was a no-brainer. Norma loved the law. Thank God Norma hadn't taken Coigne's name. It was bad enough everyone pronounced it Coy-nee when it's pronounced "coin," like the plug nickel he turned out to be.

Norma's office was just three blocks from the Jefferson County Courthouse on Washington Street, the main drag in Charles Town. She'd been lucky to find a storefront for rent at a price she could afford, but she figured she was owed some good fortune, aside from the award for shortest marriage on record. She'd had to purchase two file cabinets from her suitemate, Drew Fox, a young criminal lawyer. Norma hoped like hell he didn't expect her, as senior lawyer, to help him interpret *West Virginia* criminal law. For one thing, she was a general practitioner and needed time to bone up herself. For another, laws in Massachusetts were as unlike West Virginia laws as imaginable. But her five minutes of rest had come to an end as Jess showed her client in.

"Please have a seat, Mr. Fingerhut," Norma said.

Despite his reptilian features and arboreal height—must have had six inches on her, and she was five-foot-eleven—her client seemed quite human and down to earth, especially once he smiled. He and his wife Hilda ran a dairy farm and volunteered at one of the food pantries. More to the point, he presented Norma with her first adverse possession case. Specifically, the Fingerhuts' cows had been contentedly grazing on land for years that arguably belonged to his next-door neighbor, Marion Chatte, and Marion now objected. Seems she had plans for building a guest house and some additional outbuildings, and her surveyor had brought the boundary line issue to her attention.

"Hilda not with you this time?" Norma asked.

"Not this time. She swam this morning for her bad back, and now she's got some chores to do, but she told me to take careful notes." He smiled and held up a notebook and pen. He removed his cap and took the seat in front of her desk, placing his battered briefcase at his feet and his jacket, buffalo plaid, on the back of his chair. He had to move his chair back for more leg room.

"Let me take that nice jacket. It is rather cool today. Sure beats my raggedy old thing." She nodded toward the red barn coat on the back of her chair, another item her legal assistant Jess wanted her to deep-six.

"Got mine for my birthday." He handed it to her.

Norma allowed herself five minutes of socializing with clients, and his time was up.

It was the Fingerhuts' position that their neighbor, the head librarian at the local university, had never said a word in all the years they'd been neighbors about owning the now disputed land nor objected to the location of his fence between their properties, a fence he and his father together had built many years ago. What's more, the family pets had been buried in the areas she now claimed were hers.

As her opening volley, Norma had sent a letter to Marion Chatte full of legalese that translated into, "In all the years you've been neighbors with the Fingerhuts, you've never asserted your rights to the property by word or deed. You snooze, you lose." She'd hoped for a quick resolution, as the Fingerhuts likely couldn't afford the expense of defending a lawsuit. Of course, putting up a new fence in a different location would be hard on a small farmer's checkbook too.

Mr. Fingerhut pulled from his briefcase his copy of Marion's written response to Norma's letter. "I now see what you meant when you said at our first meeting you two ladies had some history, Ms. Bergen. I don't know what it's all about, but here's my favorite line of hers." He ran his finger down the first page and read out loud: "I should have known your lack of skill, judgment, and principle would find fertile soil in your own law practice. Challenging my rights to my own land is absurd when I have the documents to prove I objected early and often to Fingerhut's trespass." He looked up. "You know, she might have a point, Ms. Bergen. She might have sent us something in writing that we threw out if we were mad enough."

In fact, Norma had asked him about any previous correspondence from Marion at their first meeting, and he'd said he had none. *Clients.* If only she could practice law without them. "Here's the deal. If Marion had something in writing, where is it?" Norma said. "And even if she has it, how long had the fence been in place before she wrote it? Longer than ten years, she's probably out of luck."

Mr. Fingerhut nodded a good while, then read aloud his other favorite part. "Don't think I'm just a librarian with no business sense or clout. I was born and raised here, and, unlike you, I've got connections and influence. So take your letter and shove it."

Mr. Fingerhut raised his eyebrows. "What did you do to her, ma'am? Although, whatever it was, I'm glad you did it."

Norma wiggled her pen between two straight fingers. "I called her boyfriend a murderer. You may know him. He was one of the high school history teachers here for a hundred years. And, just to be clear, it turns out he wasn't a murderer after all. But he left her and left town, and she holds both events against me. Go figure."

Mr. Fingerhut straightened up in his chair. "So what do we do now?" Norma had considered Jerry Fingerhut a gentle soul who'd somehow married a piece of barbed wire, Hilda Fingerhut. But, over the last few minutes, his cheeks had turned an angry red, and his hands had rung the daylights out of each other, adding an interesting dimension to the man's temperament.

"Marion isn't represented by counsel yet, which means I can keep dealing with her directly. That's a good thing. Keeps costs down," she said.

He hesitated. "Keeping costs down is really important, but don't you think, in light of the past, talking to her lawyer might save you some grief? Might even save us some money?"

"Usually, in a heated dispute, a lawyer-to-lawyer negotiation helps. But I guarantee you that if Marion does hire someone, it'll be a Rottweiler. A rabid one, and that'll cost both parties plenty."

"Speaking of Rottweilers reminds me about her telling us to dig up our pets and move 'em. Can you think of anything more indecent? I sure as heck can't. You gotta' do something, Ms. Bergen. That'd break Hilda's heart."

"We'll find a way," she said and hoped very much she could.

2

Will Coigne closed the door to his pickup and headed inside. His temporary digs, the large tack room on the horse farm his uncle left to him two years earlier, was tucked beneath a stand of tall maples. Through them, he spied the farmhouse, now the home of his wife and daughter. When he and Norma split up, he said he'd follow wherever she decided to go, even agreeing to leave their horse farm. Well, it was the least he could do—Laney needed them both. In the end, Norma decided to stay put for Laney's sake. It was their daughter's senior year in high school, and she'd worked hard for the past couple of years to make friends and succeed in class. The other unexpected mercy from Norma was to withhold from Laney the truth about their break-up, his one-night stand with Misty Bubb. As she put it, "A daughter needs to respect her father, even if his wife doesn't."

He wouldn't complain. He was close to them, which was where he wanted to be, until he could convince Norma to give him another chance. At first, he'd been so shocked and ashamed of his infidelity he hadn't given any thought to reconciliation. But the sad truth was while he might be able to live without Norma, it made breathing very hard. And it wasn't just her physical beauty, which she tried to keep under wraps, literally. With her beside him, or in front, more likely, she lit up everything in his life. She had to come back to him, but it would be in her own time and on her own terms.

He knocked the mud and manure off his boots, fully aware it didn't really make much difference if there was dirt on the floor, but old habits die hard. He wasn't a slob. He tried to keep his surroundings, which included his person, in good shape. Norma would have called him a neat freak. God knows she'd called him everything else.

While he spent most of his time muddy and sweaty tending horses and the hundred-acre farm, he still showered and washed his full head of black hair every night and donned clean clothes the next morning. There was no real need except his pride.

His living space was about twenty by twenty-five feet with walls made of knotty pine. His kitchen consisted of a corner with a microwave, minifridge, small stove, and a table with three chairs. His bedroom, the corner opposite the kitchen, held a single bed he'd picked up at Goodwill. The bed was so short it had likely been the bottom of some kid's homemade bunkbed. He was grateful for the two high windows that looked out on the maples and farmhouse. Most of the tack supplies had been moved to the barn or just left where they were in the tack room.

He missed having someone to unwind with to discuss the triumphs and headaches of the day, who you ran into, and what was happening in town. At least he still had Laney. He loved when she stopped by in the evening, but then he had to endure watching her leave.

His phone rang, and he didn't recognize the number. Probably spam, but the caller really had the wrong number this time. Coigne got ready to unload. "*Who* is this?"

"Mr. Coigne? Will? It's Sheriff Law. Catching you at a bad time?"

"Sorry for the rough greeting, Sheriff. Not busy at all. I was just—what can I do for you?"

"I'd like to stop by in a few. Okay with you?"

Ten minutes later, Coigne led the sheriff to the safest seat in the room, a walnut captain's chair, part of the "kitchen set" of six that had been reduced over time by three. Coigne had gotten to know Sheriff Law over the last couple of years. He and Norma had put young Dell Spenser's killer behind bars, and Coigne admired the man. People easily mistook the sheriff's easy-going manner for a low IQ, and that was a serious mistake.

Coigne remained standing.

"It's about the Spensers, as a matter of fact." Law removed his hat and held it on his lap. "I was just talking to Geoff Spenser, and he tells me his nephew's moving back this way from up north in Frederick. Finn Spenser. I guess you could say he's a relative of mine too, by marriage." Sheriff Law paused and looked around the room as if searching for clues as to how to move forward.

He cleared his throat and placed the karate chopping side of his hand in the dent on the top of his hat. He moved his hand back and forth like he was slicing a loaf of bread.

Coigne had observed this harmless habit often and smiled as he watched the "slicing" now.

"I can see you're ready for this old fool to get to the point. I'm getting there, but it involves a favor."

Coigne gave him a tired smile, held up a finger, left for the "kitchen," and returned with two cold beers. He took a seat on the bed and leaned back against the wall. "I think we'll both feel a lot better if you just lay it out for me." They took long pulls on their beers and put them aside.

"Finns bought that farm for sale—big white house with columns—right down the road from your farm here."

"Mine and Norma's."

"Yes, sir. You see, Finn's a good-looking man, and his father, who died when Finn was still quite young, left the boy well off. Very well off, indeed. Well, he's hardly a boy. Nearer forty than thirty." Law sliced more bread. "With the good looks and the money, you'd think he'd be all set, but he has a way of stirring up trouble. Nothing too serious yet, but ...." The sheriff shrugged. "If he just slowed down. He's not a bad sort. Well, I don't know if he is or not. I do know he causes trouble. I guess what I'm saying is my life would be a lot easier if I knew when trouble was brewing. I like to head things off at the pass before there's trouble, and that's the long and short of it."

Coigne leaned forward to speak.

"I don't need him getting into trouble again and stirring up Geoff Spenser," the sheriff went on. "Last time—well, that's for another day."

Coigne didn't want to spy on his new neighbor. But he liked the sheriff and didn't want to give the guy a hard no. "So why isn't Geoff looking after his own nephew? And what kind of trouble did this Finn get into, if I'm not being too nosy?"

"I guess I underestimated this old county. If you didn't hear about it first thing when you and Norma moved here, my fellow residents have kept their mouths shut for once. For a while, everyone was talking about Finn taking an underage gal across state lines, which was, thank God, foiled at the last minute but not without a lot of Sturm and whadyacallit."

Coigne chuckled in spite of himself. "Drang. Sturm und Drang."

"That's the phrase."

As it happened, that very phrase described Norma perfectly, but Coigne was trying not to think of his wife. He took a long, final swig and placed his bottle on the floor. "You've just given me a boatload of worry, Sheriff."

"Call me Bud. If I'm making you worry, I'm doing it as a friend, not as the sheriff."

"Okay, Bud. I've got a seventeen-year-old daughter, as you know, and the last thing I want is to have Laney anywhere near a scum ball pedophile who kidnaps girls."

"How is little Laney? Should be graduating about now?"

"Yes, she is. And you may recall her steady guy is another Spenser, *Owen* Spenser. I imagine he'd be unhappy about this cousin Finn hanging around too."

"Now you see, this is just what I thought would happen. You'd jump to the conclusion Finn was the offending party. Now, I gotta say, I wasn't involved in the investigation, owing to the fact, as I said, he's a relative. But when all the shouting and crying was over, it turns out the gal admitted she had tricked Finn into picking her up, overnight bag in hand, and driving her toward the Virginia line. Convinced him she was being abused at home when all along she had some fella in Virginia waiting on her. At least that's how her story went, and no one could shake her out of it. But the point is, if you had an eye out for any problems at his place, him being so close, you'd be helping your own family interests. Besides, I'd never foist on you someone who might hurt Laney."

Maybe not, but he was foisting just the same. Coigne itched for a second beer. "You've convinced me Finn Spenser is a gullible fool, but if he's so innocent, why doesn't Geoff Spenser look out for his own nephew?"

"Excellent question. Here's the answer. He can't stand the guy and won't have anything to do with him."

"Well, after what happened and with the word all over town, I guess I can understand it, even if the girl lied."

"Nope. The trouble between the two men started before that." The sheriff slumped back in his chair and swept his hand over his bald head. "I've never understood the root cause, as they say, and I'm not sure old Geoff understands the animosity he feels. I guess Geoff isn't sure Finn is as innocent as he likes to make out. Like maybe there's some evil attached to him."

"That's a shame," Coigne said, "and it surprises me too. I don't know Geoff Spenser well, but I've had a chance to spend time with his wife, Evelyn, and there's no one as accepting of people despite her being loaded with—you know—worldly sophistication. She and Norma are like this." He held up two crossed fingers.

The sheriff nodded and got up. "I'm so glad you're able to help here, Will."

"But—"

"You're the one fella I knew could handle something this sensitive and important, seeing as Finn's going to be so close, and you were a state trooper up north before you decided to be a horse farmer. How's that going, by the way? I'll get you Finn's phone number; let you introduce yourself. Now I'll leave you to your evening. Let myself out."

Coigne went and got that second beer.

3

Laney tunneled through her closet for the right outfit, something that would electrify Owen Spenser. Unsuccessful in the closet, she shifted to her dresser. The backing for its mirror was a section of old picket fence, painted yellow, which matched her double bed's headboard. She and Coigne had taken the fencing from a long section in the barn left there by his uncle. They worked on their project the first few months after moving in. She guessed Coigne wanted to keep her from getting lonely. He was nice like that, which made her glad he was her dad.

She hadn't seen Owen in forever and wanted to look irresistible—or at least hot. She was fine with her long, straight blond hair and had been spared a skin problem, but anyone looking at her figure would say she'd barely made it into her teens. She'd read everything on how to dress like you had big boobs, but it all made her feel fake and ridiculous.

And her face. The best that could be said was she looked well-rested. Owen would sometimes compliment her on her "patrician nose." Patrician? Where'd he get that? And he'd go on about her light hazel eyes, the color of his favorite marble as a kid. Dumb, but it made her feel good. That time he pointed out she didn't look like either parent she'd had to tell him she was adopted. But that was early on, back when she worried he might think less of her because of it. He wasn't like that.

If only Norma had let her go to Bermuda with the Spensers, but no, she had the rest of senior year to get through. Owen had already finished and was taking a gap year because of his sister Dell's death and everything.

What worried her was, for all she knew, Owen had found someone else in Bermuda, although his texts were reassuring. And they had Facetimed often, but a lot could be hidden on a small screen. She checked the time. She'd know the truth in just ten minutes. She closed the bottom drawer of the dresser—no luck.

Never one for much makeup, she decided this day called for mascara. Who knew what sophistication he'd been exposed to on a moonlit beach? The blue top she now pulled out from under her bed would never pass muster with Norma—too much exposed back. She put it on.

Norma. What the heck had happened between Norma and Coigne? How could they break up a couple of years after they'd adopted her and gotten married? Coigne said the responsibility for the breakup was his, but Laney suspected the idea was Norma's. He was always steady, and Norma was always so...so *Norma*. There were times now when she hated her and had to remind herself Norma had saved her life, literally, and given her a home when the rest of her bio family had checked out.

Owen had been the one to convince Laney to return home after she ran away for a whole two days. *Big deal.* She'd been so furious with Norma the day Coigne moved out It all made no sense. Both of them were her parents. Theirs was the only stable home she'd ever known, except for a few years with Gran. How could Norma just upend her life? And in her *senior year*?

True, she saw Coigne almost as much as ever because he lived in the tack room—God, the tack room!—and still managed the horse farm. But it wasn't the same as having him around whenever she felt shaky. She suspected Owen knew what was behind her parents' split, the way he urged her to go back home that time and not blame Coigne or Norma. Coigne didn't want her to blame Norma either. What was up with that?

She needed a positive outlook. Worry lines—not cool. Owen would arrive in—she looked out her window. *He's here!*

Laney ran down the stairs, shoved open the back door, and ran into Owen's arms. They mauled each other with tender kisses and whispered extravagant promises. Then a strained shyness descended over them, and they stood in the driveway saying nothing. They'd always been able to chatter for hours on any subject, but now she couldn't even come up with, "How was Bermuda?" As so often happened in a pinch, advice from Norma rescued her: "Whenever things are awkward with a boy, make something to eat." Of course, should she really be taking advice from Norma after everything?

Laney led Owen to the kitchen and taught him how to make a brownie-in-a-mug. Side by side in the breakfast nook, they dolloped vanilla ice cream on top of the brownie and piled M&Ms and gummy worms on top of that, spilling half the toppings onto the tablecloth. The construction and eating of their brownies bought time, but still, they seemed to have nothing to say. Was he trying to find a way to let her go? She looked him over. He was as heart-squeezing as ever with his steel gray eyes, curly brown hair atop a six-two bod, and a suntan *in May*, for God's sake. But of all his physical qualities, it was his voice—gruff and gravelly but kind at the same time—that made her feel like she might just have to die. Now that the mugs were empty, she needed more hugging and groping. Why didn't he make a move?

"What was it like in Bermuda?" *So lame.* "Your photos were incredible at that golf course. Port Royal? The sea looked like dark blue stained glass."

Owen scooped at the bottom of his near-empty cup, his spoon clinking against its side. "Would have been great, but the wind was so high it was impossible to get off a good shot—not that I'm known for good shots."

The conversation dead-ended. When Owen finally gave up on his brownie, he picked up both their cups, took them to the sink, and ran them under the tap. It was something Laney had always liked about him—or maybe it was his mother she should thank. Evelyn Spenser had raised her son to be self-sufficient despite their being loaded.

When he finished, he turned to look at her, his head tilted toward his shoulder. "You look worried. What are you thinking about?"

She had to get over this feeling of impending doom. Maybe a different venue—more worldly wisdom from Norma. "I'm thinking we'd be more comfortable on the couch in the living room. Let's go."

She took some comfort in the fact he sat close to her. She turned toward him, hoping to see the lopsided smile she'd come to adore, but it wasn't there. "Come to think of it, you look worried too." She folded her lips into her mouth and then realized she must look lipless and released them.

"You go first," he said. "You can start by telling me why you're doing that funny thing with your hands."

She looked down at her hands. *God. I look like I'm playing chord progressions on the piano.* She stuffed them under her thighs and decided to be direct with him before she made a complete fool of herself. "I guess I'm wondering if things are the same between us?"

"The same? After all we went through with my sister's death and the murder trial? I don't want it to be the same. But—" He stopped talking for a second. "I couldn't have gotten through it without you, Laney."

What did that mean? Was that another way of saying you served your purpose, now kiss off?

"Must be pretty different around here for you, with your parents split. You know you can count on me, Laney. You know, when you need someone to talk to."

That's it. He's blowing me off, and he feels guilty because of my parents. It's that old "we'll-always-be-friends" bullshit. She felt like her skull was cracking open and wanted to scream at him, "How dare you come home just to break my heart?" But she was no screamer. She didn't break china. Her early years had taught her how pointless it was to throw a tantrum in an "empty" room. This was familiar territory.

"It's getting late." She stood up. "I've got to feed the horses, and you should probably get back to your parents."

Owen looked surprised but got up too. "Should I call you later or something?"

She couldn't look at him. Her mind clung to a hazy image of the two of them, their bodies soldered together. All the touching and exploring and now what? *It's over. Shake it off, loser.*

"You know, Laney, you look kind of cute with that chocolate in the corner of your mouth, but I'd better help you out there." He moved closer, bent down, wrapped her in his arms, and gave her a very thorough kiss.

Much better.

4

Finn Spenser leaped out of his Denali and opened the gate to Hawthorne Farm. Behind him thrummed the engine of a moving van the size of an aircraft carrier. Its driver rolled down his window and spat what looked like black tar into the road. "She won't make it. No one told us there'd be this sharp turn from a narrow road. And your driveway's too steep. She won't make it," the van driver said.

A complainer in every crowd. Finn had never driven an eighteen-wheeler and had no idea whether she'd make it or not. But since he needed his furniture delivered, getting the truck up the hill was essential. He signaled to the driver to go on and make the turn, and he'd guide her in.

As it turned out, the van suffered no real damage, and the mailbox, trash hut, and a section of the neighbor's split rail fence, all crushed, could probably be replaced. It was just money. And his new home was all he could have asked for— antebellum white brick with a wide front veranda, tall white columns, and long wings on either side extending way back. He had as many barns and silos, pens, pastures, and paddocks as there were trees on the place, and there were plenty over his two-hundred-acre spread.

Finn spent the next three days unpacking boxes and contacting tradesmen. Reaching out to Aunt Evelyn and his cousin Owen was high on his to-do list too, but he wasn't certain how they'd greet him. Sure, moving back to the county would drive Uncle Geoff crazy. But this was Finn's home ground too. And Evelyn and the boy were the closest family he had left. He'd heard about Dell's death but had known better than to come around for the funeral and rile Uncle Geoff. Maybe he should have at least called. Evelyn had always had a soft spot for him and stood up for him whenever he got into trouble. It was something he respected her for. Too bad she married a cold bastard like Uncle Geoff.

As for Owen, poor kid, losing his sister like that. It was a shame.

Finn finally located an old coffeemaker in a box in the master bathroom—*figures*—got it set up on a kitchen counter and made himself a cup. Why they'd put granite counters in an old place like this, he didn't know. Ruined the ambience. Then he sat down on a leather ottoman the movers had left out in the hallway and considered his future. Ideally, he wanted to fix the place up, raise animals—he was thinking about a dairy farm to secure his rightful place in the county. But every time he tried to make it happen, secure the things everyone else took for granted, someone or something tripped him up. It was like someone was always lying in wait, ready to sabotage him. He'd narrowly escaped a bad romantic situation, so now his new interest, someone worth keeping around, was trying to ditch him.

His phone rang.

"What the—"

He'd put in a landline as the reception in a state completely contained within a mountain range, the Appalachians, wasn't the best. But who knew his number? He picked up.

"My name's Will Coigne. We own the farm next door. Thought I'd come by on Saturday morning and say hello. That work for you?"

Finn fiddled with the receiver cord. He needed to meet people, find some shortcuts to getting this dairy farm thing going, and what better chance than right now, with this neighbor? But he wasn't set up yet. The place was a mess. Guy would think he's a loser. "I'm sort of busy."

"I won't stay long. Saturday's a big day for riding instruction at my place. Be there at ten."

5

"Not bad." Misty stood before her full-length bedroom mirror. Dressed in her black lace bra and skinny jeans, her fists on hips and her booted feet wide apart like Wonder Woman, she twisted around and admired the rear view. And why shouldn't she feel good this morning? The world was full of opportunity and prospects. She turned to face the mirror again and brushed through her thick, black waves. For closing in on forty, she looked damn good. Tall and slender, her olive skin remained smooth as a girl's, her dark, almond-shaped eyes clear, and her lips full and shapely. She moved closer to the mirror. So, her nose wasn't perfect. What had the kids in high school said? Her nose was so big it could substitute for a president on Mount Rushmore? Cheap shot. But who's the one laughing now?

Misty finished dressing and congratulated herself once more on still fitting into a size six when, based on her observations at her last high school reunion, her classmates had long given up the struggle. But why even think about them? She was the one who'd left home and broken away from that crowd of losers—even changed her name after her father got caught in a cheap swindle. She'd loved the guy, but if you're headed to jail, at least get caught doing something big. She was the one who'd gotten an education, started her own veterinary practice, and now had developed expansion plans for a doggy spa—Barks, Bubbles, and Beauty. She had everything to live for, and if anyone stood in her way, they'd be sorry. Putting herself first had always been her practice, one that had never let her down.

And how about you, Norma Bergen? Your husband didn't seem to mind the nose. Sexy Will Coigne. All right, so it was only that one time. He was soft in the head for confessing. Heard she'd kicked him out because of it. Norma really was a fool. He wasn't as rich as some, but that farm of his would be worth a bundle to a developer. Rumor had it he was pining for his wife, but why? Misty thought she and Norma had a lot in common. Strong as buffaloes, smart, no-nonsense, and good looks. And from what Misty could tell, Norma wasn't goody-two-shoes either. She'd bend the rules. But Misty would win him back because she'd not only bend 'em, she'd break 'em. And, yes, she wanted to win him back.

She chose a black, clingy, button-down blouse—none of this fishwife fashion for her—and finished dressing. Saturday was always a busy day, and she left for the animal clinic early. Though she limited clinic hours from eight to noon, her business interests took up the rest of the day, especially now that the doggy spa project was back on its feet.

Thinking about the doggy spa reminded her she'd heard Finn Spenser was back in town. She could just picture him—like an actor in an old cowboy rerun, fresh off the trail from rustling cattle, shoulders broad as a prizewinning bull's horns, face rough as scraped burnt toast—an old-fashioned hunk. Word had it he'd moved into the old Hawthorne Farm, and what an impressive piece of property. Well, why not? The guy was loaded. As a neighbor and the only nearby vet, it was only right she pay her respects one of these days. He'd be so happy to see her again— hardly. She'd heard through staff gossip something about plans for a dairy farm. Finn? No way. Good thing her passion was for working with large animals.

6

Coigne had no interest in spying on a neighbor or whatever it was Sheriff Law had in mind for him. But he could at least welcome a new neighbor to Shepherdstown and determine for himself whether Law's concerns were legitimate or not.

Initially, Finn Spenser seemed nervous as hell, sticking out the wrong hand for a shake and making a mess of the coffee-making process, but soon enough, the younger man must have decided to relax. What was quickly becoming clear to Coigne was that the poor sod knew diddlysquat about the sprawling farm he'd just purchased.

They sat on the veranda overlooking a vast field extending toward the same purple ridge Coigne's farm kept an eye on. It was brisk enough that morning to need a jacket, but the sun shone brightly, and there was no wind. They drank the coffee, dark roast, while they talked.

"Any idea about what you'll do with your land?" he asked. "Farmers around here are always looking for hay, and it's a damn good property tax break."

"I'm not sure." Finn chuckled as if a little embarrassed. "I had an idea about a dairy farm—sounds kinda cool. But to tell the truth, I don't know that much about it. I used to live near farms but never on one. I've always dreamed about owning a place like this."

Coigne took another sip. "So far as I can tell, plenty of folks around here started the same way. They moved here from New York or D.C., leaving jobs that had nothing to do with farming. Most of them make a go of it. I'm still trying to figure out if my horse farm will succeed. Up until two years ago, I was a state trooper in Massachusetts, so I'm only a step or two ahead of you."

Finn looked uneasy when Coigne mentioned his prior job, or maybe Coigne imagined it. After all, uneasy was the reaction many people had toward the state trooper title before getting to know him.

"Tell you what." Coigne placed his mug on the wrought iron side table. "I'll introduce you to Hilda Fingerhut. She and her husband, Jerry, have about a hundred head. Funny old bird, but she knows what she's doing."

"Great."

Finn's gratitude seemed half-hearted. Maybe he worried Hilda wouldn't take him seriously. "Don't worry, Finn. Hilda will turn you into another grandson."

After some sports talk, they wandered back through the house to the kitchen, where Finn placed their mugs in the sink.

A light blue Mercedes purred into the driveway, which curved around to the rear of the mansion. Finn walked over to the back door with Coigne, curious, close behind.

Coigne recognized the car and its driver at once. Evelyn Spenser was talking on her cell phone while the passenger, his wife Norma, recognizable anywhere in her frumpy coat and hat, got out and was now peering inside the window of his truck.

Finn turned to Coigne. "I think that's my aunt in the driver's seat, but hell if I know who the tall lady is with her nose in your truck."

Coigne patted him on the back and said, "Let's join them, shall we?"

Finn pushed open the door and threw his hands up in the air. "Aunt Evelyn! How'd you know I was here?"

"That's a good question, Finn." She put her phone away. "My only nephew fails to mention he's moving to a huge farm a stone's throw away from me." She came over and gave him a hug.

"Greetings, Evelyn. Hope you had a nice time in Bermuda." Coigne blinked. It hadn't been a pleasure trip, stupid. She'd gone there to grieve. "Hey there, Norma." He gave her a half wave, feeling worse by the moment.

"You know each other?" Finn scratched his head.

"Yes, we—"

"What brings you here, Coigne?" Norma said, her back against his truck door. She sounded annoyed.

"Norma, I'd like you to meet our—your—new next-door neighbor, Finn Spenser," he said.

She nodded at Finn and gave him a tight smile, which he returned. To Coigne, she said nothing further.

"I'm so glad you've decided to join us here, Finn." Evelyn threw her arms around him again, but she hung on tight this time.

Finn looked like maybe her kindness had choked him up. When he regained some composure, he said, "I'm so sorry about, you know."

"Your house!" Evelyn interrupted and clasped his hands in hers. "I've always admired Hawthorne Farm from the road, hoping someone would move in and give it the attention it deserves. I'm so glad it's yours."

Coigne and Norma stood side by side against his truck, neither moving a muscle, until Norma said under her breath, "I thought we agreed you'd leave the truck for me Saturday mornings. Am I wrong about that?"

He had agreed to that, but he'd forgotten. "I'm sorry. I was just about to leave. I'll put it in the garage for you."

She looked away, like she was fed up, but must have noticed the surprised look on Finn's face. "Oh, don't mind us, Finn. Like

Coigne says, we're neighbors, and I made Evelyn bring me over to meet you and see this palace."

Coigne knew he should leave, but it was rare he was able to get this close to Norma. Together, there was always a slim chance of a breakthrough. Finn invited the women into the house to look around while Coigne hung to the back.

"Don't mind the mess. I'll have you back when the place is fixed up," Finn said. "That's in about ten years."

They all laughed and stood around in the kitchen while Finn prepared a plate of Swiss cheese, Triscuits, and red grapes, and though it wasn't yet noon, he pulled a bottle of chardonnay out of the fridge and prepared a tray with glasses. He and Coigne carried the food and drinks into the living room and placed it on a dusty glass coffee table.

"This house is amazing, Finn," Evelyn said, her arms outstretched to embrace the ballroom-sized space. "I thought of you as more of a condo kind of guy at this point in your life. The house and farm will take a lot of effort if you plan to work it yourself. I hope you'll have help."

"Is this what they call Gothic Revival?" Norma chimed in, lips dotted with wheat bits.

Finn sputtered. Didn't have a clue.

"You're right, Norma." Evelyn looked around and made appreciative noises about the original oak flooring and crown molding. "This house was owned by a trust, I think," she went on. "How did you ever get ahold of it?"

Sounding on firmer ground, Finn said, "The beneficiaries couldn't afford the upkeep."

Coigne wished he could join the conversation, but he'd been struck mute by the bizarreness of the situation. He was a few feet from the woman he loved, desperately wanted her back, and suffered painful frostbite every time she glanced his way. He'd have to make an effort. "So Evelyn—how's Owen doing?"

Evelyn didn't answer at first. She stared into her wine, holding onto the glass stem and turning it one way, then the other. Coigne figured she was thinking of Dell and how, from now on, no one would say how are Dell and Owen or how are the kids. They'd just say how is Owen, which would be a constant reminder of Dell's absence.

But when Evelyn looked up, she was grinning, her blue eyes sparkling with mischief. "He's found plenty of consolation in the arms of his girlfriend, Laney Coigne-Bergen. He's probably at the horse farm right now. I'm sure you'll meet her, Finn darling."

"Wait. Now I'm really confused. Norma's daughter works on Coigne's farm?" Finn asked.

Norma cut in, "Oh, let's not beat around the bush, wherever the hell *that* expression came from." On the word "that" Norma flung her arm out to the side, spilling wine on the floor. Coigne jumped up and handed her his napkin. She grumbled thanks, wiped up the mess, and continued what she was saying. "Coigne and I are separated, and Laney's our daughter."

Evelyn quickly steered the conversation back to the history of the property.

Worried he had annoyed Norma with his subservience, and at the same time worried he needed to stand up to her more often, Coigne got ready to go.

"Finn, I'll get back to you with Hilda Fingerhut's contact information. Give me a day or so."

He shook his head as he exited, never more relieved to leave a place and never more regretful at having to go.

7

As she got in, Norma slammed the door to Evelyn's Mercedes harder than she'd intended. "So, if I ever wanted to plot revenge against Misty Bubb for seducing Coigne, I've found my secret weapon. I'd convince Finn Spenser to seduce her, swindle her out of her money, and then dump her. Does Finn fit the bill, or what? Mr. Sexy. He could probably go professional. You know, like *American Gigolo*."

"That's an awful thing to say." Evelyn grinned.

"So why are you smiling? And he's certainly got the dough. That house!"

Evelyn started the car rolling down her nephew's long drive.

"A revenge plan is just a fantasy, but, on the other hand—" Norma let "the other hand" hang there awhile. "If he had the incentive, he could probably make her life a misery, one would hope."

Still, Evelyn said nothing.

"Finn obviously adores you. He'd do anything for you."

Evelyn grabbed her sunglasses from the top of the console and positioned them on her nose. "That's exactly right. He would do anything for me, regardless of the cost to himself. And he *is* a relative."

"There's that."

"And besides, as you say, it's a fantasy. Those never work out."

"I know. I know. Now don't forget to drop me on the block behind my office. My car sure better be there. I forgot to feed the meter, but I don't think I need to on the weekend." The distance between Finn's farm in Shepherdstown and Norma's office in Charles Town was about eleven miles. Even if she should have fed the meter, she'd still make it back in time.

Norma took a quick look at her ringing cell phone and frowned. "Crap. What client calls on a Saturday? No dice. Not now."

"I'm sorry you've got to work on Saturday." Evelyn turned to her friend and made a face. "If it's any consolation, I've promised myself I'd clear out some of Dell's things this afternoon. Not looking forward to it."

"I'm so sorry." Norma didn't want to think of how she'd feel if she lost Laney and had to go through her things. She gave Evelyn a moment.

"So Evelyn, what exactly would be the cost to Finn? You said something about regardless of the cost to himself.'"

"To Finn? Loss of integrity, for one. Most people don't throw themselves into a game of deception without coming away feeling they've done wrong."

Though they'd only just met, Norma had a feeling Finn wouldn't fuss over matters of integrity. Just something about him. Maybe the fact he'd acquired wealth through no apparent effort of his own. But now Norma wondered if Evelyn thought *she* was lacking in integrity.

She let silence fill the car as she gazed out the window.

Norma knew her friend was right. Finn had the money and the looks, but even she'd feel uncomfortable feeding an innocent man into the maw of a monster like Misty Bubb.

They finally reached the tree-lined street off Washington, where tiny white buds sprouted from branches bronzed by sudden light rain. Some of the homes on the block were over two hundred years old, and a handful were even quite grand, with turrets, balconies, and dormers.

When the Mercedes pulled in next to the curb, Norma hopped out and turned to wave goodbye but then hesitated. She made a circle with her finger, and Evelyn obliged by rolling down the window. Norma bent over. "It would have been a public service to deal with that big rat once and for all, but I agree my revenge plan for Misty was not a good one. I thank you for squelching my inner demon."

Back in her office, Norma greeted Jess, who'd agreed to help her out that weekend in return for future time off. With all the disappointments Norma had amassed during the last twelve months, Jess wasn't one of them. In her late twenties, with spikey black hair at the moment, an off-center smile, a deep voice, and a small frame, she was organized and punctual. Too bright for her position as a legal assistant, she apparently wasn't ready to advance yet. Norma liked her for all the aforementioned reasons, including the fact Jess showed a slight preference for her over Drew Fox or The Fox, as he was affectionately known in the suite. This preference came in handy when Norma was pressed for help, and it wasn't her day to have Jess.

Jess pulled a file out of her side drawer. She nodded toward Norma's office, rolled her eyes, and whispered, "A visitor. Insisted on waiting in your office."

"No surprise. There's no comfortable place to sit out here."

"That's intentional," Jess said.

"Who is it?"

Jess handed her the file.

"Fingerhut? He's back again? Wonder what he wants," Norma said.

"Wrong party. It's Ms. Chatte, the woman who's taken offense. Get it? Taken a fence? Did you know her first name's Marion, and she's a librarian? Why would anyone choose a profession that rhymed with her name?"

"Ask Shirley Jones."

"Shirley Jones? Should I get her file?"

Norma closed her eyes in despair and flipped through the Fingerhut file, not caring too much if she kept Marion waiting. She was actually thinking about Shirley Jones and how it was a shame young people missed out on the old Broadway shows like *The Music Man*. As a kid, she'd never attended one in New York City, but her seventh-grade teacher had introduced her to the music of Rodgers and Hammerstein, Gershwin, and Kern. The kind woman had said whistling those show tunes would help you cope "if you were ever low or in a jam," which, as Norma thought about it, was how she'd spent much of seventh grade.

Before she headed down the short hallway to her office, she looked back at Jess. "Give me a buzz in five minutes to remind me I need to 'jump on that important conference call.'"

"Got it."

It had been more than six months since she'd seen Marion, and the woman had not changed much. She was attractive despite a slight case of proptosis, but Norma felt certain it bugged the hell out of her. She always dressed in pinks and lavenders and wore scarves wrapped at the neck like a *Parisienne*.

Norma found her seated stiffly with a cup of coffee in hand. She forced a smile. "Marion. To what do I owe this intrusion, and on a Saturday? Come to apologize for your ill-advised, incendiary letter about the Fingerhuts' fence?"

"Hardly. But anyway, I've not come about anyone's fence. And I know what day it is, but this couldn't wait."

Norma removed her coat and arranged it on the back of her chair and sat down. "As for the Fingerhuts' fence, you've made your point, but it's an unconvincing one. You're going to have to do better than a bald assertion of documentary evidence to prove your case. Back to the drawing board." She slapped her desk for emphasis.

"For God's sake, Norma. You're impossible."

"Only with people who insult my intelligence and integrity. Otherwise, I'm a lamb."

"Look, this isn't easy. I probably shouldn't have come."

She stopped talking, and Norma thought she might get up and leave. One could always hope.

"The thing is..." She bit her lip like she might cry. "I need your help."

Was the woman mad? Asking for Norma's help, of all people? This had to be a trick of some sort. But Marion's shaky, hesitant manner and her pinched expression convinced Norma to take the woman at face value for now.

She folded her hands on the table. "I can't represent you and Jerry Fingerhut, Marion. Your interests are adverse. I'm so sorry." She tried to look rueful.

Marion gripped the arms of her chair. "This has nothing to do with property rights."

Jess buzzed Norma about her "important conference call."

Distracted, Norma said, "Thanks, Jess. Tell them I'll call back tomorrow."

Before Norma had even replaced the receiver, Marion continued. "It's not your legal help I need. It's my son, Kaleb. I haven't heard from him in days. Don't say, 'What do you expect of a young man?' He's not like that. We're very close."

Maybe Norma could find someone to help Marion, but she'd have to know a few facts first. "Tell me about it." Norma pulled a legal pad from her desk drawer.

At first, Marion didn't face Norma. She seemed to seek some place to start her tale outside the window. Did she think her son might pass by? "Like I say, we're close. He's twenty-eight. Only just finished college, but he'd taken a few years off. Started his own business. Photography studio. We talk all the time. Needs my advice. Father isn't in the picture."

Norma scribbled notes and wished she could ask Marion if her old flame, the history teacher, could be helpful in finding Kaleb, but her sixth sense told her that was no question for someone hoping to get home by dinnertime.

Marion continued talking in telegram-speak. She sounded vulnerable, almost to a breaking point. "I've called Kale a million times. Talked to his friends." She closed her eyes, her lashes doing a poor job of damming her tears. "He's just vanished."

No doubt now. This was no act. "Have you talked with the police? Sheriff Law?" It was that kind of county. You had a serious problem, you started with the sheriff.

"Of course. So far, nothing." Marion got out of her chair and turned away. With her body hunched over, she made no sound, but her shoulders shook.

Norma took pity and brought her a tissue. "Look, believe it or not, I know what you're going through." She shared with her how several years before, when Norma still lived on Cape Cod, Laney had been kidnapped by thugs. Norma thought she'd lose her mind trying to find her. She'd worried they'd kill her—and they almost had, a fact she left out of this version of the story. "I'm just not sure why you think I can help you, much as I feel your distress."

Marion spun around; her cheeks smudged in black mascara. "You may be the world's most abrasive, aggravating person, Norma Bergen, but you're also the most tenacious and resourceful, abrasive, aggravating person."

Norma wasn't sure what to say or do.

"I need you, Norma."

Well, that settled the matter. It was the simplicity and desperation of Marion's appeal that pushed Norma over the line. "Look. There's nothing I can do for you before I clear it with the Fingerhuts. I'll need written consent from both of you. This isn't legal representation you're asking for, but I wouldn't want there to be a misunderstanding with them. Besides, I think one of two things is going to happen. Either Kaleb will walk through your door this evening, or you'll realize you need the help of law enforcement. But let's take one thing at a time."

The two spoke another fifteen minutes while Norma got more details down on paper. When Marion raised the issue of a fee, Norma turned it down. It'd feel like demanding money before starting the Heimlich maneuver on someone.

Marion left her with a photo of Kaleb Chatte. Nice-looking boy, shaggy head of black hair with odd cowlicks at the crown, blue eyes, and mischief written all over him. His T-shirt was maroon with the number 1215 in white across the chest. Strange sort of mug shot. Marion kept referring to him as Kale, which brought to Norma's mind someone with a cabbage head.

Next, she typed up notes for tracking down Kaleb Chatte. Although Sheriff Law had not been able to help Marion yet, Norma hoped he'd discuss with her the ground he'd already covered. If nothing else, it would save her time. Before she could reach him by phone, Jess popped in.

"I'm heading out now. You in on Monday? Your calendar looks clear." Jess pulled one ear bud out.

"I should be. Do you have a second? I'd like to run something by you."

Jess pulled out her other bud and sat down.

Norma still didn't know her assistant well, but her confidence in her own judgment about people had stood her in good stead, with the monumental exception of Will Coigne. Discussing her clients with Jess seemed like a safe bet. She'd been mulling over her visit with Finn earlier in the day and her meeting with Marion about Kaleb just now. She was inclined to put both men in the same frame, though Finn was much older. Of course, she based it on one visit with Finn and a secondhand visit with

Kaleb, but both men seemed unmoored, Kaleb's new photo studio notwithstanding.

"Do you know a guy named Finn Spenser?" Norma asked.

"Oh, my God. Finn Spenser. I remember my mother talking about him. She'd had him as a student in high school. She died a few years ago, but she taught trig and pre-calc and one class of algebra. It was algebra for dummies. He was cute but always getting into trouble. Mom felt awful for him, but then again, what a loser. She had to flunk him in algebra too."

Norma thanked Evelyn mentally for nixing the plan to use Finn in her Misty revenge fantasy and then did a quick time check. She needed to get home and see how the Laney/Owen reunion week was progressing, hoping it hadn't gone too far. She wondered if Coigne had covered the whole birth control issue with their daughter, seeing as he'd jumped in on the sex-before-marriage discussion with Laney without Norma—or maybe it was Laney who'd initiated the discussion with him. Either way, Norma had been left out of the loop. She grabbed her jacket and briefcase, which bore a striking resemblance to a saddlebag—two bags held together by a broad strap of leather. "Oh, and one more thing." She lifted the photo of Kaleb off her desk and showed it to Jess. "Long shot. You recognize this face?"

Jess took a look, and her own face lit up. "Where'd you get this? Of course, I do. I'm engaged to its owner." She stuck out her hand, and a single tiny diamond twinkled from a young, slender finger.

Norma put her briefcase back down. "So how is it that you didn't recognize your future mother-in-law when she walked in?"

"Huh?" Jess looked at Norma as though waiting for a punchline.

"The woman who just left is Marion Chatte. This is a picture of her son, Kaleb. He's missing, and she wants me to find him." She jabbed her thumb at the photo on the word "him."

Jess sat down in the chair Marion had just vacated. "I don't get it. I guess I got hung up on the Marion-the-Librarian thing and didn't connect her last name with Kaleb's. It's true, I haven't met his family yet. He makes excuses. I just figured he was embarrassed about something. You know, like maybe his dad's in jail. I've never pressed. But what do you mean, missing? I just heard from him a couple of days ago. He's away right now for work—a couple of weeks, he said. What the hell's his mother talking about?"

Norma was surprised by this aggressive tone from her assistant but not bothered by it. She sometimes wished Laney were a bit more aggressive with people, especially those who didn't treat her with respect. "Listen, Jess. I think his mom is honestly worried. Do you have any idea where he is? Could you just call and have him contact her?" Norma feared the solution wouldn't be so easy.

Jess tapped her foot nervously, like maybe she feared it too. "He's a photographer. Freelance. You should see his stuff. And no, I don't know where he is since he moves around. I'll call him." She reached into her pocket and tapped his number on her phone.

They listened to her phone ring until it reached an automatic message from ChatteSnap Studio. "He's not picking up. I'll leave a message. And that studio is fictitious, to—you know—make him sound established."

Norma recalled Marion saying her son had a photography studio. So, the guy lied to one of them.

Jess picked up the photo and swallowed. "I gave him the T-shirt he's wearing here. Took this photo and sent it to him. I'm surprised his mom had it and didn't ask him about it."

"Why's that?"

"See those numbers at the top, twelve-fifteen?"

"December 15. The day you met? No? Wedding date?"

"Yup." She handed back the photo.

Norma figured Jess's boyfriend was conning her, but that was a specter she wouldn't raise before she knew more.

"Keep trying to reach him, Jess, and when you do, tell him to call his mother. We'll get this sorted out, okay?"

"Oh, sure. You realize this is going to put a wee strain on the relationship, right?"

8

Misty aimed her red Maserati Quattroporte into a tight, shaded corner of the Hawthorne Farm driveway. She'd worked longer than expected on Saturday, so a short break early in the week wouldn't cause too much of a problem. Following her time-tested strategy of surprise, she neglected to call first and parked at the back of the house. Catching Finn off-balance would give her an advantage.

When she'd overheard the clinic techs gossiping about the "new guy" who'd just moved into Hawthorne Farm, she'd been on the phone with a veterinary cardiologist reviewing sonogram results. Even so, she couldn't block out all the gushing over Finn's good looks and his single status. That he was single was neither here nor there—those techs didn't stand a chance with Finn.

Misty gave a moment's thought to the seduction of married men versus single men. Of course, she never cared what their status was—they were all the same when it came to prioritizing their own lust and the satisfaction thereof. She'd spot a married man at a conference or party, and he'd try to ignore her or even act disdainful of her blatant flirting, making frequent references to his wife, perhaps to remind himself he had one. Only one of them had ever parted company with her before taking a nice big bite of the apple, and that was Geoff Spenser.

"Hello. May I help you?" a voice called out.

It was Finn. Misty faced the rear of the house and away from him. Now she slowly turned around.

"Misty!" Finn took a moment, then crossed over from the thick woods that separated his farm and Coigne's to her side of the driveway. Misty and Finn had parted on bad terms. No wonder he was shocked to see her. "New car. Nice," he said, inarticulate as ever. He lifted his cowboy hat in greeting. His gesture gave Misty a dazzling impression of a sun king with his crown of blond hair tossing in the breeze. Good looking didn't cover it. How did she forget that massive chest and shoulders? She stammered her way through a huffy greeting by the end of which she was certain she'd blushed.

Two more people emerged through the woods' opening— Hilda Fingerhut and Will Coigne.

Hilda was the only person Misty referred to, mentally at least, with that four-letter gutter word beginning with "C." Hilda thought she knew more about veterinarian medicine than Misty, a formally trained doctor with years of experience in the field. Hilda had even tried to discredit her to area farmers. *Why would anyone take Hilda's advice, that old pudding face?*

And then, of course, there was Will, whom everyone called *Coigne* for some reason. How to describe that dark-eyed stallion? The sweat seeping through his T-shirt, likely from their walk through the woods, just made him all the more desirable. He was Finn's equal in many ways, except he also had a brain—and a conscience, more's the pity. The poor man thought he could go on resisting her long enough to repair his marriage, evidently. But all that was for another day.

Misty took a deep breath and prepared a slightly revised program for the afternoon.

She'd have to steer carefully. She'd intended to bully Finn for backing out of their business deal, to say nothing of their romance, as a warning of what he was in for, but the presence of Hilda and Will made that impossible.

"Well, well, well," she called out cheerfully. "Hilda, Will, and Finn Spenser, our new member of the landed gentry." She reached out to hug him, which he welcomed as if she had onion breath. "I see you're already in very capable hands." She winked at Coigne. Why not remind Coigne of her own capable hands? She addressed the group. "I stopped by to welcome my old buddy to Shepherdstown and offer my assistance, as he's always been willing to stand by me."

Finn ignored her dig, and Coigne merely smiled, like maybe he knew something was not quite right but wasn't going to touch it. Misty chattered on, expressing her readiness to provide her services. Her grasp on Finn's hand was quite firm. With her other hand, she rubbed his arm, a gesture she'd refined over the years to convey innocent friendliness with an openness to more mature pleasures.

"Not one of your clinic days, Dr. Bubb?" Hilda asked. "Good, give those poor animals a chance."

"Do call me Misty, Hilda." She'd always felt Bubb, her surname, was inconsistent with her overall message. "And aren't you a little out of your range here? Shepherdstown? I thought you country folks kept to yourselves." Finn's farm, next to Coigne's, was located outside Shepherdstown, a tree-lined, historic college town nestled in the lower Shenandoah Valley and overlooking the Potomac River. It was populated by professors and D.C. retirees, among others. Hilda's farm was located amidst other farms about nine miles southwest of Shepherdstown and six miles northwest of the county seat. It overlooked Opequon Creek. Misty's home, in a new development on the outskirts of Shepherdstown, sat between their locations.

"Guess you found out I was here, but did you know I was starting up a dairy farm?" Finn asked, ending an awkward pause. "My cows are supposed to arrive later on this summer."

"Great for me. More business," Misty said, chuckling with self-delight.

"If it weren't for Will and Hilda here and the good advice they've given me these last couple of days, the dairy farm would still be just a dream."

"It's still a dream, Finn, but we're gonna help you." Hilda angled herself between Misty and Finn until Misty was forced to catch herself before falling backward. The group milled about, waiting for something to happen.

"We were just heading in for a cold drink," Finn said. "You want to join us, Misty?"

"Why not? Party time!"

If Misty knew nothing else, she knew how to read a man's temperature—tepidly interested, boiling mad, warmly aroused, and so on. Will Coigne seemed coolly amused. Why? Maybe she was imagining things. He was probably feigning indifference because others were around. She still had a grip on him.

Finn sent everyone to the library, promising cold beer and chips. The library's walls were Chinese red. The bookshelves, off-white, were empty, with no evidence of book boxes waiting to be unpacked.

Misty sat in the center of a loveseat covered in a gray fabric with a soft nap. Hilda stood before the fireplace, the back of her dusty, baggy pants against the brass screen with a tree of life design. Coigne took a seat in a plaid armchair that wove in the gray of the loveseat and the red of the walls. Each seating area included a table with a brass lamp and a couple of expensive coasters. Misty was surprised at Finn's sense of style. Of course, he'd always come to her place before, so how would she have known about his style?

"Should have guessed you'd be around sooner or later, Dr. Bubb." Hilda leaned hard on the word *doctor*. "So who've you been misleadin' lately?"

"Now, Hilda," Misty said, bright-eyed. Two could play this game. "I think you must be feeling the heat. You're sounding a little tired. May I get you some water?"

From thereon, Hilda addressed her comments to Will. "I'm worried about Finn's property. Not sure it's ready for a hundred head. Not sure he is, either. I'll tell him so to his face."

Coigne tilted his head. "What's your main concern?"

"He's got to do something about the fence and fast. I'm not in favor of electric fence. It's state of the art and a helluva lot cheaper to maintain, but I say stick with wood. But don't get me started on fences. We're working with your wife—er, uh, Norma—to take care of that. And then the water source. Not much of one here. Lack of water's a worry if you're countin' on it for your animals."

The bell-like tinkling of glassware and beer bottles announced Finn's arrival and cut short Hilda's fireside chat. She sat down and grabbed a bottle, popped the top, and ignored the glasses.

"Do sit here, Finn." Misty slid to the end of the loveseat to give him room. Finn looked around, perhaps for better options, but finally sat down beside her.

Hilda wagged her head and resumed her dairy oration.

Misty studied Hilda as she rambled on. She could probably trip Hilda up by asking her views on the treatment of trichomoniasis and bovine spongiform encephalopathy, but why bother? Of course, she wouldn't want to underestimate Hilda. The woman had the respect of the county's farmers—for now, anyway. Misty decided to stick to her other strengths during this visit. No way Hilda could compete in the sex and mayhem departments.

"Let's leave the herd for the moment, Hilda. Finn, how's your uncle, old Geoff?" Though she'd been unable to seduce old Geoff the preceding year, it was low risk to bring up his name now. Her failed effort was hardly the kind of thing stuffy Geoff would have shared with others in the community. Besides, she knew the mere mention of Geoff Spenser's name would irritate Finn, and that was worth the slight risk.

"Evelyn says he's fine." Finn didn't elaborate.

"Evelyn has been here to see the property and welcome Finn. She's a good friend to have here in the county," Coigne said.

"Don't I know it," Finn said.

"I'm sure Geoff will come around—for a visit, I mean," Misty said. A plan began to form in her mind. It was devious, destructive, and potentially deeply satisfying. She'd had many years to hone her skills at blackmail, and she'd draw on them now. She'd help Finn part from a healthy share of his wealth. He deserved it. Yes, she'd swell her bank account and settle some scores.

Once they'd finished their drinks, Hilda suggested she, Coigne, and Finn take a closer look at the fence in the fields south of the house, and Misty invited herself to join them. Along the way, the inspection plan was stalled because the gate that should have allowed quick and easy passage from one field to another was tied shut with a frayed clothesline. It appeared to have been tied in sailors' knots years before, but they finally got through.

All the while, Misty paid scant attention to Hilda's lecture and focused exclusively on her new scheme, wishing she were alone with Finn so she could lay the foundation for it. That wish was granted when the fence tour ended, thank God, and Coigne left the farm. Hilda tried to outstay Misty but finally had to go home herself. Finn looked exasperated by the sequence of departures. To Misty, it was very satisfying indeed.

"Is there something more I can do for you, Misty?"

"Yes, there is. I suggest we step back inside, and I'll give you the details over some more of that cold beer."

9

Owen never thought of the fourteen-year age difference between his cousin Finn and himself. Finn had always seemed like an older brother. Maybe he seemed youthful because he was always getting into trouble or because he liked to hang around his much younger cousins—Dell and himself. Whatever the reason, Owen hated how his father was rude to Finn, or at least kept him away. It had been years since he'd been invited to the house. Finn's parents had split up, and then his dad died in his private plane. From what Owen heard, Finn's mother hung with her side of the family and wasn't around anymore.

Finn was cool—you might even say dangerous sometimes, the way he acted before thinking. But wasn't that what sometimes led to high adventure? Like the time he decided he preferred the leather jacket in a second-hand shop in Winchester and wore it out of the store. It's not like he couldn't pay for it, so it didn't really seem like theft, or not at the time. Back then, it seemed cool and brave, but now he understood the consequences for that saleslady and the potential ones for Finn. Owen needed to look after him.

Whatever, he still cared about Finn and thought he'd gotten a bad deal from the adults in his life. It was for that reason, having overheard his parents "discussing" the fact Finn was back in town, he decided to invite Finn for a run along the C&O Canal.

They'd meet at Lock 38, like they used to, and run for about an hour at a modest pace.

"Good, because it's been a while since I put anything on my feet made of rubber," Finn said when Owen called him. "I could use some unwinding after the day I've had, but that's another story. After the week I've had, I should say. I moved in just a *week* ago. Can't wait to see you, bro. I'll be along around four."

It didn't surprise Owen that Finn was late. No sweat. It gave him a chance to enjoy the view, especially now the sun was out, and the wind had died down. He sat on a bench overlooking the Potomac. In this location, there were no rapids, and at that moment, the water was virtually still. He wished he'd been around when the locks along the almost couple of hundred miles of canal were operational. Each lock lifted the boats a good eight feet so they could navigate the 600-foot elevation between Georgetown and Cumberland, as his dad had explained it.

By four-thirty, and after several unanswered texts, Owen was ready to give up on Finn. Then he spotted his cousin clad in jeans and sandals. So much for the run. Shit.

"Sorry, kid. Got held up. Let's walk. How you been?" He gave Owen a sideways hug, then grabbed him in a headlock and knuckled his head. They set out along the towpath, its canopy of white sycamore limbs showing promise of shade to come, his cousin outlining his plans for his farm. Finn pointed to a Shepherdstown landmark across the river: the 75-foot Rumsey Monument perched atop a forty-square-foot plinth. "That guy got a raw deal," Finn said. "Everybody learns about Robert Fulton and the steamboat in school, but he was like ten years old when James Rumsey was floating his steamboat along the Potomac."

Owen thought he remembered a history teacher saying lots of guys worked with steam back then; at least Rumsey got a park out of the deal. He glanced up at his cousin. "Did you know George Washington came to see Rumsey and hired him to do some work?"

"Yes, well, that's something anyway. Somebody's always getting the shaft."

Owen didn't want to talk with Finn about Dell's death and was glad his cousin hadn't brought it up. No one could bring her back, and Owen needed to move on—or try, anyway. "Whatever came of your plans for a doggy spa? You were all about it a while back."

"Don't go there, bro. That's old news. Got new irons in the fire. Besides, it's not like the dairy farm won't keep me up to my ass in work." Finn bent over and grabbed a long stick, which he broke into pieces as they walked along.

"Why a dairy farm, if you don't mind me asking? Why not horses, like my girlfriend's dad, Will Coigne? Horses are, you know, well, you can ride them, for one thing."

"Cows, right? You either milk them or eat them." They ambled along. "So, your girlfriend's Coigne's daughter? I knew he had a daughter but never put it together with you. He and his estranged—and strange if you don't mind me saying—strange wife are my neighbors. He's nice. She's a harpy."

"Guess she's got reason to be. Norma's her name. She's okay."

"What do you mean, reason to be? That sounds interesting."

Owen explained he'd overheard his parents talking about how Will Coigne "got involved" with Misty Bubb. "Laney doesn't know about that, but anyway, it's over now. Just one of those stupid mistakes that have big consequences they're always warning us about."

"Misty Bubb, huh? Gal gets around." A couple who were speed-walking passed on their left. "So, cows. My farm was originally a dairy farm. It's still got some of the foundations of the old buildings they used, like where they took care of the milking. It just seemed right to see if I could bring it back to life."

Owen wondered why prior owners let it go but figured that was a question Finn had asked before he bought the place. And if he hadn't, Owen didn't want to mention it now.

Finn stopped walking. "What is this?" He grabbed the back of his shirt irritably and pulled. "Damn. New shirt. I've got a tag sticking into my back. Hurts like hell. Can you yank it?"

"Sure." Owen had more trouble than expected, but as the cousins continued to twist and struggle, two scantily clad young women passed, one of them calling out, "Hey, Owen. Glad you're back."

Owen waved.

"Thanks, man," Finn said, rubbing his neck. "Who was that?"

"No idea."

Another twenty minutes and the two turned back. "You hungry?" Finn asked. Without waiting for an answer, he suggested they head up to the Riverside Inn, a stone's throw from the towpath. "I hear they've got their own brewpub now. Really something, they say."

The Inn's chalet facade loomed majestically over the river and was a highlight for Shepherdstown visitors and the town's upper crust.

"If you want to know about Norma, I'll fill you in on the time she discovered a dead body at the Inn," Owen said.

"A body? Okay, man, you surprised me with that one."

10

Coigne had returned to his farm to find Maladora's foal wandering around loose in the side yard. *Damnit!* Little Boy had knocked through a section of the paddock fence where the post had rotted. Coigne was tired, but delaying the repair was out of the question. He got Little Boy settled with Maladora, hooked the wagon to his tractor, and drove his post hole digger, pry bar, and a new post from the barn over to the paddock. He set to work. First, he pried all the nails out of the three fence boards, then removed the rotted post, replaced it with a new one, and finally nailed the fence boards to the new post. If he'd only known before leaving the Cape how unrelenting the maintenance part of horse farming was, he probably wouldn't have dragged the family to West Virginia on a gamble. The whole asinine business with Misty would never have occurred. But he couldn't go there. It happened. He had to let it alone. Lost in these thoughts, he closed his eyes and fell back against the repaired post, his body spent. He didn't even stir when Norma's Prius arrived.

"You still here? We agreed you'd be finished for the day by six." Norma opened the back door to her car and hauled out two reusable grocery bags full to overflowing.

Coigne blinked several times, surprised he'd fallen asleep standing. "I'm just heading to the tack room." It had become his habit to listen closely to every word his wife addressed to him to detect any softening of her feelings toward him. A conversation between them with anything other than raised voices gave him hope. Her greeting this evening was the usual one if he was late finishing up, but at least she sounded more weary than angry. He'd count that a positive development. Maybe she'd engage in conversation.

"I spent half the afternoon with Hilda Fingerhut and Finn Spenser, the new guy over at Hawthorne Farm," he said. "She's going to help get him started with his dairy farm. You doing okay?"

"Of course. And you forget," Norma said. "This is Small Town, USA, where everyone knows everyone's business. Hilda filled me in at Food Lion on your afternoon, including the fact your girlfriend Misty was there, a fact you omitted from your evening update."

"You know Misty's not my girlfriend, and I don't mention her because, frankly, I wish she didn't exist."

"Whatever. Hilda said Misty had something up her sleeve— tried to wrap herself around Finn's neck like a boa constrictor."

Better him than me. "The thing about Hilda is, she may come across as, well, unsophisticated, but she's perceptive, as much about a certain vet as she is about her own cows."

"No surprise. Same species. So, what's the deal with Finn?"

"I think Misty and Finn have history."

Norma started to giggle, and then her giggle bubbled into a full outburst of unstoppable laughter. He had no idea why. He just laughed along with her.

He knew better than to offer to help her with the grocery bags, which was why he was so surprised when, after her laughter subsided, she said, "There are some bottles of wine and water jugs in the backseat if you care to bring them down to the house."

She didn't need to ask twice. Coigne followed her down to the back door of the main house and waited for her to signal where she wanted the drinks, then placed them on the kitchen table.

"Finn's a good-looking man, but I imagine it's his money that's the real attraction," Norma said.

They were having a conversation about Misty without all hell breaking loose. Even laughing about her, like she wasn't, and never had been, a threat. What goes on here? Whatever the cause, the last few minutes were a sharp improvement over previous acts of passive aggression, like tossing out his mail, saying she'd mistaken it for junk mail. Might the ice be melting?

Laney pushed through the back door at full speed and nearly knocked Coigne over. "Whoops! Sorry, Coigne. I need to go— Coigne? Wow! You here? The two of you in the same room? This is odd. Maybe even exciting."

"Enjoy it while you can, honey," Norma said. "He's just leaving."

"I'll follow you out, Coigne. I need a ride to Owen's for dinner. He's helping me with calculus since you two know nothing." Under her breath, she added, "About anything. Smiley face." She gave them a big smile of her own.

"Give me ten minutes to get my tools put away—if your mom says it's okay." He glanced at Laney. "Meet you at the truck."

Usually careful with his tools, Coigne tossed them into the tractor cart along with the rotted wood he'd removed and drove the tractor to its station in the large garage. His mind was focused on Finn Spenser. The man seemed to be just as Sheriff Law had portrayed him. Perhaps clueless was too strong a word, but certainly spoiled. Seemed friendly enough, though. But there were moments when he had seemed like he might explode if Misty needled him anymore. And what was that about when she said he always stood by her? It sounded like he'd done anything but. Come to think of it, he really didn't give a damn about Finn or Misty and returned to rosier thoughts about home, Norma, and a glimmer of hope for a second chance.

He texted Laney to come on, shot a wad of trash from the garage floor into the trash can, sunk it, and whistled his way to his truck.

11

Norma caught herself in time. She'd almost slipped back into the common patter of husband and wife, finding amusement together at the expense of a mutually disliked third party. Slipping into anything with Coigne would be a mistake, one she could ill afford to make again. What was that saying—once trust is breached, only a fool rushes in.

Of course, that meant dinner-for-one for the time being, now that Owen Spenser had returned from Bermuda. She paired some Ritz crackers with Gouda cheese, heated them up in the microwave, slathered on the mustard, and flipped on the news. But her heart and mind couldn't face suffering on a large scale that night. She needed to focus on the remarkable response of her assistant Jess when shown the photo of Marion Chatte's son. How could Jess be engaged to him? She'd never said anything about it. Then again, Norma didn't exactly invite confidence sharing.

Norma flipped off the TV and returned her half-eaten plate of crackers to the kitchen, where the landline was ringing off the counter.

"Evelyn here. Sorry to call at dinnertime. The kids are out getting pizza. Would you mind coming by for half an hour? Geoff and I need to talk to you. It's about Owen. Well, really, it's about Finn and Owen. We've got a slight problem on our hands, and I thought, or Geoff and I both thought, maybe you could help."

Seemed like suddenly everybody needed her to solve their family problems. Ironic, really, when she had so many of her own. But this was Evelyn. Of course, she'd go. "See you in ten."

Like a number of new homes in the Eastern Panhandle, the emphasis at the Spensers' "Italian villa" model was on size rather than suitability and taste. You'd find similar architectural wonders overlooking the Aegean Sea; only this one overlooked a golf course in West Virginia.

All things considered; any trace of Evelyn's Appalachian origins had been obliterated by the Dartmouth-scholar-turned-Big-Pharma-executive she married. But again, who was she to judge someone else's interior design—or marriage, for that matter?

As for the purpose of her visit, Norma hadn't a clue. What common interest would unite Finn Spenser and his young cousin, and why would Evelyn and Geoff be concerned? From the furious look on Geoff's face when she arrived, Norma knew she would soon find out.

"That damn fool. I knew no good would come of his return to the county. I told Bud Law there'd be trouble. Now, here we go again. By God, I feel like giving up and heading back to Bermuda."

"Oh, darling, please, calm down." Evelyn handed him a gin and tonic, which surprised Norma. She'd seen Geoff at a handful of evening social events but never with a cocktail in hand. Evelyn led Norma to the kitchen to get a Mountain Dew and then to Geoff's study, a nautical nightmare along the lines of *Flipper* meets Magritte. They each sat around the table at the room's center, which was made of teakwood pried off someone's boat, presumably, and bordered with nautical instruments in mother of pearl inlay. The wall facing Norma was an aquarium filled with several live, two-foot blowfish.

It had been a long day, and her to-do list for the morning filled two legal-size pages. She meant to keep the meeting short and turned now to the couple. "Tell me exactly what's happened, minus editorials."

"Let me explain it to her, Evelyn," Geoff said. "Then you can fill in the details. You see, unbeknownst to us, Owen got in touch with my nephew, Finn Spenser. Apparently, you've already had the…pleasure. Well, they've met up. This is something I strictly forbade Finn to do when we last spoke, the damn—"

"*Minus* the editorials," Norma said.

"Yes, well, it's just that he's up to something. We don't know what, but if Finn's involved, it will be big, bad, and public. I never should have—"

"I hope you've got some details," Norma said, turning to Evelyn.

Evelyn recrossed her Stuart Weitzmans and smoothed her long, black wool skirt. Norma knew of no woman over twenty who got away with wearing those thin pleats. Even at seven on a Tuesday evening, Evelyn looked ready to address the United Nations. She cleared her throat, ready to begin, but again, Geoff cut her off.

Norma gave Geoff a dirty look.

"What concerns me," he said, ignoring both women, "is that, in the past, whenever Finn's been around, something awful has happened, something I had to deal with once my brother died, and even before that, which just goes to show the nut doesn't fall—"

"What are we talking about here, Geoff? Graffiti at Rumsey Park? Armed robbery?"

"Oh, no. It's nothing like that," Evelyn said. "You've met him yourself. I'm afraid Geoff has a tendency to fly off like this because of some bad decisions Finn made when he was younger: some DUIs, drugs, that sort of thing. I'm sure his couple of years away have made a difference. He certainly seemed—"

"Bad decisions when he was younger? Bah! He was a grown man, Evelyn. And there were a couple of things more serious than that. Why didn't my brother put him in the Armed Forces while he could, for God's sake?"

Norma'd never seen Geoff so worked up. He was usually Shepherdstown's own elder statesman—tall, trim, silver-haired, stiff-lipped. Now he acted like someone had swiped his new putter.

"How did you know the two of them met?" Norma asked.

"Owen told us, of course," Geoff snapped.

"Good. You must know I have complete confidence in Owen's judgment. If I didn't, he wouldn't be seeing Laney. So, I think you can rest assured he won't be influenced negatively by his cousin, even if Finn is still making bad decisions."

"Exactly what I told him, Norma."

Geoff sighed heavily. Silence descended over the table. Geoff walked over to his blowfish. He stood ramrod straight, hands behind his back, feet shoulder-width apart.

Norma expected him to make faces at the fish. Hard not to. But, instead, he studied them.

"Believe it or not, they calm me down," he said, his face closing in on the one closest to the glass wall. "I'm sorry for the temper, ladies." He rejoined them at the table. "Everybody has their Achilles heel, and Finn is mine."

"No worries, darling. I think Norma's seen it all. But here's the reason we've asked you here, Norm. Geoff and I reached a sort of compromise, if you'll agree, of course. We figure since Laney and Owen are together so often and—"

"I can't spy on them if that's what you're going to ask me. If I know nothing else about teens, it's that spying is o-u-t."

"Of course not. We'd never ask you to spy, Norma. It's just that if, when you're keeping your eye on the ball and ear close to the ground," Geoff said, groping for as many trite phrases as he could get his hands on, "you happen to sense something doesn't smell right, something involving Finn, you'll sound the alarm. That's all."

Norma looked at Evelyn, whose eyes studied the grain of the teakwood. This little scheme was such a bad one. Norma knew it, and Evelyn obviously knew it as well. At least they hadn't played the Dell card, making her feel guilty for not having suffered the loss they had. She hoped Evelyn would have the guts to tell her husband to forget all about their scheme. She waited.

"What with Dell's death, we just can't take any more hurt, Norma. It's that simple," Geoff said. Evelyn took his hand.

The day had been a strange one. Norma drove home through town, all quiet now. She'd promised the Spensers nothing, but they were counting on her anyway. As she descended German Street, the main drag, she glimpsed pink-tinged blowfish clouds clearing the mountains' vaporous surface and ascending into heaven. She definitely needed a good night's sleep.

12

Norma rose at five the next morning and prioritized her agenda as she drove to work. The sun shone brightly, and, despite the fact that late May could still drop a cold snap on the county, she left her barn coat at home. She waved at her neighbor, Judd Spud, né Judd Lamb, who kept chickens on land Coigne lent him for that purpose. Neighbors considered Judd so dumb they nicknamed him Dumber-Than-A-Spud-Judd. Coigne thought the nickname unkind, so in light of his sensitivity, Norma referred to him as Judd Spud.

With skin that looked like a walnut shell and teeth so black it looked like he hadn't any, Judd Spud posed no threat to any NFL heartthrob. Still, Norma admired him for the way even a thunderstorm or blizzard or even a night's revelry at the local tavern couldn't keep him from his early morning chore of feeding his chickens.

She'd have a busy day tracking down Jess's boyfriend and Marion's son, Kaleb Chatte, to say nothing of her mounting backlog of billable work. The Fox was probably waiting for her at that very moment to help him with a criminal matter. He was defending a security guard accused of ripping off elderly patients at the local healthcare clinic. She had experience in medical malpractice matters owing to her insurance defense work. Those cases had given her a feel for the clinic layout, schedules, and personnel, about which The Fox claimed ignorance.

"Put that law journal away, and let's get busy. It's already seven, and I've got a lot to do," Norma told The Fox as she entered the reception area. She put her saddlebag down on Jess's desk and gave the upstart, as she thought of him, the once over. He was a GW law grad, which was impressive, and he was eager. About five-ten, his biceps bulged beneath his tight, gray suit jacket. His hair flopped in a sandy-colored mass across his forehead, and his smile, when he was with Norma, anyway, was always tentative, as if gauging her mood. She'd noticed some minor friction between The Fox and Jess but chalked it up to hormones.

Coffee and bag in hand, Norma led the way to his office. They worked an hour or so until Jess arrived and stuck her head in.

"Thanks for saving me some coffee," Jess said to The Fox.

"My fault, Jess. I've been guzzling this morning. Had a latish night." Norma lowered her voice and faced Jess. "Any word from you know who?"

The Fox turned their way.

"Nothing yet." Without another word, her assistant booted up and got to work.

Norma and The Fox strategized and made calls in his office until eleven when Norma returned to hers to check her email. Jess caught her in transit and told her Coigne had been trying to reach her. "Don't you keep your phone with you?"

"Of course."

"Well, turn it on sometime."

Norma grumbled but holstered her nasty comeback. She knew what was gnawing at Jess—her missing fiancé.

An hour passed before she remembered Coigne's call. If it had been something concerning Laney, he would have told Jess. That was their deal. It occurred to her it would've been useful to bat around with Coigne the subject of Jess's missing fiancé. Say what she would, Coigne's was a keen mind in an investigation. She could confer with The Fox about it, but that might aggravate

Jess. Her best bet was Sheriff Law. She grabbed her phone just as Coigne's name popped up on her screen. She took his call.

"Where've you been?" Coigne was breathing hard.

Normally, she'd answer that question with "none of your business," but something in Coigne's voice, a hint of hysteria, made her hesitate. "I was in conference. What's up? Where are you?" Sounds of large engines, radio static, and loud voices began to register.

"Can you break away and meet me here? I'm down by the Opequon. Marion Chatte's cottage. I was on my way to Hilda's and—"

"I know where Marion's cottage is. But *you* sound like you're lost. What's the matter with you?" The phone seemed to go dead, which roused her anxiety. Then his voice returned.

"There's been a bad fire. I was the first one here and found a—body. I know—I know, an ex-cop should be used to finding bodies but—"

"You called nine-one-one, right?"

"Yes, a deputy showed up, and Sheriff Law was already down this way, so he showed up too. We've got the police, firetrucks, ambulances, hazmat suits, gawkers. It's madness—the airport at Kabul."

"I'll be right down." She thought she ought to say more. He sounded upset. "Now buck up. You know this drill."

As she drove, she thought back to their prelapsarian period. Coigne had invited Norma to an afternoon of rowing down the lazy, narrow Opequon. He'd had to sell it to her first. "Imagine you're a princess floating beneath the shade of weeping willows." In fact, they rowed through farm waste and fallen timber, but she made the best of it. Coigne had tried so hard to please. He'd filled a basket with chilled wine, bread, and soft cheeses, and filled the time with recondite explanations of flora and fauna. All went well until the shooting started—bank-to-bank target practice common among creekside residents. Norma, quite understandably, as Coigne later assured her, sprang up in terror and capsized the boat. They both survived none the worse for wear, and one lucky copperhead feasted on their Boursin. The afternoon made for a funny story at gatherings, but it should have served instead as a warning that no good comes from the Opequon.

Now that she'd arrived at the cottage, she understood why Coigne was so rattled over the phone. The scene looked grim. Even the sun cinematically slipped behind a cloud as she approached the cordon of yellow tape. A nasty stench of burnt plastic filled the air, and much of the cottage was charred, but the worst of it was in the kitchen.

She knew from her insurance defense work that the investigators would try to find the fire's origin to determine if the cause was arson. If the fire had a single source, it was likely to spread sideways, creating a "V" shape pointing back to its origin. How anyone would discern an outline in the clumps of sodden debris left by gushing firehoses, she didn't know.

The roof over the small kitchen addition had caved in, crushing appliances and leaving only the doors and window frames, one wall, and the tall brick chimney intact. Horrified yet fascinated, she got as close as she could to the crime tape. Scattered pots and pans poked through a mixture of drenched insulation and drywall. She recalled reading about the "alligatoring" char pattern on walls and spotted them by the stove. She noted ax gashes in the one standing wall and, always, that awful smell.

She looked around for Coigne but didn't see him. She did see a familiar face, though.

"Hilda Fingerhut!" Norma spotted her client across the road from the cottage, seated on a narrow bench, her back against the side of an old, wooden, one-car garage, now grayed and rotted and leaning at a precarious angle. Norma crossed the road to Hilda, but the stench of smoke and char was still overpowering.

Hilda was more Coigne's friend than hers, but that didn't make Norma any less willing to comfort the old farmer in her present condition, haggard and, for once, speechless. But the shock to Norma's system was the fellow seated next to her, Finn Spenser, the new guy in town. He was slumped over, a blanket around his shoulders. Norma barely recognized his face beneath all the dirt, sweat, and soot. What the hell were they doing there? And where was Coigne?

Norma sat down beside Hilda and put her arm around her bony shoulders. "Can you tell me what happened?" Before Hilda could answer, Sheriff Law waved to Norma from across the way in the cottage area, signaling he'd be with her in a minute. Or maybe he was asking her to stay with Hilda. She couldn't tell. He said something to a man dressed in a hazmat suit, probably Law's investigator. Norma knew that because they'd found a body, Law and his team would take control of the scene to safeguard whatever evidence could be salvaged.

Norma reached for Hilda's hand while she studied what once was a cozy, attractive cottage, one she'd visited just months before when she'd made groundless accusations of murder, and Marion Chatte had run her off the place. "Can you tell me what happened here, Hilda? You're shivering. Where's your blanket?"

Hilda blinked and shook her head as if trying to wake up. She hunched lower into her oversized coat. "I don't know what happened. Only got here myself—well, I guess it was some time ago. Saw the smoke and found Finn over by the creek holding the body, her body."

"Surely it was an accident." Who would harm a librarian?

Hilda pointed toward a shed on the Chatte property. White markers surrounded two red gasoline cans.

Norma gave voice to the unthinkable. "Arson? Who would want to harm Marion?"

"No."

Hilda turned to Finn. "What did you say, Finn? No, what?"

"No." Finn muttered something else, but his lips barely parted, so his words were hard to make out.

"Why do you say no, Finn?" Norma asked. "You don't think someone intended to hurt Marion? Unless she used those containers herself—"

"The body isn't Marion's."

Hilda placed her claw-like hand on his arm. "But, sonny, I saw her. Well, I saw her dark hair...Oh. I see what you're saying."

"Well, who is it then?" Norma asked.

Finn heaved himself up and stumbled away, but as he left, he said loud and clear, "Misty Bubb."

"Are you sure?" But Norma didn't get an answer, or she answered for herself. Finn knew Misty, according to what Hilda and Coigne had told her, so he'd certainly have recognized her. But what was she doing at Marion's house, and had she been there with Finn?

Hilda explained how she'd smelled smoke, come running, and found Finn holding Misty's body out in the yard but was unable to enlighten Norma further.

"Your teeth are chattering, Hilda. You need to get home. Have you called Jerry?"

"I couldn't reach him. You know—crap service. Anyway, Sheriff Law—"

"You're probably in shock. Where's the ambulance anyway?"

"Come and gone," she said.

Norma was able to reach Jerry Fingerhut on her first try. He said he'd be there in five minutes, so she sat with Hilda until he arrived.

She knew how frequently the cause of a fire remains unknown even after a full investigation. Here, of course, the gas containers provided an obvious clue in the direction of arson. Rather too obvious, she'd have thought. Finn's memory of the color of flame and smoke would be important in confirming gasoline as the cause. Or did Coigne arrive first?

Once Jerry gathered up Hilda, Norma had no further reason to stay put and decided to look for Coigne. She crossed the road where Sheriff Law's jeep was parked and slowed as she heard voices on the other side. She recognized the voice of one of Law's deputies debriefing the sheriff. It never hurt to know more than the other guy thought she knew, so she stayed quiet and listened. When the conversation between Law and his deputy died down, she made her presence known.

Chief Deputy Baker looked to be in his sixties, like Sheriff Law, with florid skin and tight gray curls, and he had a sofa cushion for a chest, also like the sheriff. After the introductions, Sheriff Law sent his deputy to find Coigne, but Norma spotted him first. He was headed their way. He wasn't as crazed-looking as Finn and Hilda but not on top of his game either. His head hung while he trudged along, but once he saw her, his face brightened, and he picked up his pace.

"They finish rubber hosing you, did they?" she asked.

Coigne threw his arm around her shoulders, and she let it stay there. "Thanks for coming. For a moment there, I wasn't sure I'd feel up to driving home."

"No problem." She'd been kidding about the rubber hose, of course, but what had Law's deputies or the other responders been doing with him all this time? Asking him questions, but couldn't it wait until he got a shower and pulled himself together?

While she pondered, she also remembered something she'd seen as she'd studied the cottage moments before. It was something vaguely familiar that her brain was only registering now. It lay in the living room just beyond the kitchen and had one of those white markers by it. It was shiny, about four inches in length. Looked just like Coigne's. Why hadn't the investigator picked it up yet? He had all the evidence bags. She wished she'd gotten closer to it. It worried her in light of what she'd overheard. She'd ask Coigne about it later.

"Is Marion aware she no longer has a home?" she asked Sheriff Law.

He swatted a bit of ash off his sleeve. "Marion doesn't know. We're trying to find her. Even the press hasn't turned up yet."

Norma tried to take stock. Why was Misty at Marion Chatte's house? Did they know each other? And what was Finn doing there too? She didn't even want to think about the four-hundred-and-fifty-dollar pocketknife she'd given Coigne as a wedding present. He must have rushed into the fire and dropped it when he lifted Misty and took her outside. But Hilda had said Finn was holding Misty over by the creek as if maybe he'd put her there.

And why was Coigne so shaken? Did she have to remind him Misty meant nothing to him?

13

Back in the car, Norma called Jess, explained without going into detail she'd been held up, and asked her to tell anyone who called she might not get back to them until the next day.

"Hold on, then. The Fox picked up a call while I was out on an errand. It was Marion Chatte. I've told him a million times not to pick up when—"

"Holy shit! Put him through."

"Whatever."

The Fox summarized for her. Marion was following her own lead on Kaleb's whereabouts, a lead given to her by a friend of Kaleb's who phoned and refused to give her name. "But Marion said the gal had a French accent—"

"Did you just say 'the gal'?"

"Uh, no, you misunderstood. I said 'pal.' According to this pal of Kaleb's, he's in a show, an exhibition at Union Station in D.C., and wouldn't be back for a few days, and she was not to worry. This pal said she was with a law firm—Mrs. Chatte figured she gave her that information to sound legitimate. The law firm's name she gave was something like Blow and Ask Him, and Mrs. Chatte knew that wasn't right, but the woman got off the call. Mrs. Chatte also said the call showed it was from 'Caller Unknown.' The long and short of it is Mrs. Chatte drove to Union Station to look there for her son. And she asked you to call her when you had a chance."

"Listen, Foxy, I have to use you as my assistant on this matter rather than Jess, but there are good reasons. Can you call Mrs. Chatte and ask her to call Sheriff Law right away? Let her know it's not about Kaleb—at least not that I'm aware of. It's her home. It's burned down, but let Sheriff Law tell her that. I've got some other things to attend to. Can you do that?"

"Course."

At least that call took Kaleb Chatte off her list of people to worry about—Marion had found her son. She was able to give full attention to the conversation she'd overheard between Chief Deputy Baker and Sheriff Law at the fire. She tried to recall every word:

"Just tell me what happened from the time the call came in, Deputy."

"The call came from Mr. Coy—"

"Pronounced *coin*, like the penny," Law said.

"The call came in from Mr. Coigne. I was first on the scene, parking, and from the road, I saw Mr. Spenser, Mr. Finn Spenser, and the deceased at first, and Mr. Spenser's lifting the deceased from where she was, which was a few feet away from the cottage in the grass. Then Mr. Coigne, who was on the phone, came running over from the shed over there. He told Mr. Spenser to leave her where she was, not to touch anything, but Mr. Spenser didn't listen and grabbed her anyway and took her by the creek while the old woman—"

"Ms. Fingerhut."

"Right. Ms. Fingerhut showed up out of nowhere and was standing over Mr. Spenser and the deceased, and she asked him to let go of the deceased because Mr. Coigne said she's dead. But Mr. Spenser didn't do that. He said she wasn't dead. By then, I was able to get everyone's attention and move the three of them over to the bench where you found them, and, fortunately, the medics had just shown up and come over to the deceased. Then

Mr. Spenser came after me to tell me he needed to speak to me in confidence. He said that before she died, the deceased said 'Coigne.' Just like that, the deceased said, 'Coigne.'"

"So, to be clear, Mr. Spenser is saying the deceased, Misty Bubb, spoke to him when Mr. Coigne and Ms. Fingerhut were saying she was already dead?"

"That's right. Yes, sir."

"And you say Ms. Fingerhut appeared out of nowhere. Now, we know she's not a ghost, so tell me what you really mean?"

"Sorry, sir. She came over to Mr. Spenser from the direction of the woods. She later told me her farm is over there, through the woods, and she'd been following the smell of smoke."

"Okay, so it sounds like she was basing her assessment of the deceased's condition on what she'd heard Mr. Coigne say about her and not on her own observation. Is that what you'd say, Deputy?"

"Yes, sir."

"Where was Mr. Coigne located when Mr. Spenser told you what the deceased said to him privately."

"He was helping Ms. Fingerhut on the bench—you know, buttoning her coat and rubbing her shoulders. She didn't look so good, and he was trying to help her get comfortable, I guess."

"Thanks, Deputy. Anything else you want to add?"

"No, sir."

"Then that's all. And thank you for your thorough report."

"Yes, Sheriff."

Norma would have to wait until she got home to ask Coigne what he made of Finn's odd behavior, moving the body a second time, then lying about Misty being alive and saying Coigne's name. Coigne could have been mistaken about her being dead, of course. He was no doctor. But his priority was to get Misty out of the smoke and try to resuscitate her, and if she was dead, from that point on, he wouldn't want anyone touching her. Her body was evidence.

Norma thought back to the scene. She hadn't seen Misty's body, but she'd had as much opportunity as anyone there, other than Chief Deputy Baker, to study the kitchen where the body had been found and the living room just beyond it. Norma also figured she had a cooler head for making observations than Finn or Coigne, not having absorbed the shock of coming upon a dead body. Finally, Marion's cottage was a place she'd visited on prior occasions. She might note if something seemed out of place, such as Coigne's knife. She was sure it was his.

Of course, he'd be able to explain why it was lying on the floor of the living room. It could have fallen out of his pocket when he lifted Misty's body outside. But if she'd been lying in the kitchen when he found her, and he took her out the back door, which was the closest one to the kitchen, how did his knife get to the living room floor and under that table?"

She put that conundrum aside until she could talk to Coigne at home and turned her thoughts to Laney. What would she make of Misty's death? Her daughter was still unaware of the role Misty had played in breaking up her parents' marriage, but even if she'd known, Laney was someone who would still be horrified, if not traumatized, to learn someone she'd known had died so tragically. Not many kids Laney's age had lost their entire family to criminal violence. The kid was still fragile.

Norma arrived in the driveway and noted Coigne's truck in the garage. The garage door was open, but she didn't imagine he was going out anywhere soon. Either Laney was still at school, or Owen had ferried her off somewhere. Good.

Norma needed more quiet time before she and Coigne talked. What concerned her was that she was the one who'd confided to Sheriff Law about a year before about the possibility Coigne was in Misty's thrall. And Law, in turn, had given her enough clues for her to figure out Misty was an Olympian gold digger and homewrecker. In that brief conversation, she'd given the sheriff a potential motive for Coigne to have killed Misty. Depending on the time of death, it could be Norma's motive too, but her concern at the moment was for Coigne.

Wait a minute. What was she thinking? Who would ever think Coigne had any role in Misty's death? She was being foolish.

Norma opened her car door and headed into her house for the bathroom medicine cabinet.

She'd given herself a headache.

14

Sheriff Law received Chief Deputy Baker's written report, which included the signed statement of Mr. Finn Spenser. He propped his feet on his desk, leaned back, and flipped to the Spenser statement.

It was about 10:10 a.m. I was driving by what I now know to be the home of Marion Chatte. I was on my way over to visit Hilda Fingerhut, who's been helpful to me in getting my dairy farm up and running. She invited me to come see her set-up. She has a dairy farm, too, only she's been at it a long time. I don't know why she invited Coigne to come. He came in his own truck.

I saw smoke blowing out of a small cottage. I didn't see anybody else around—I didn't see Coigne or anybody at that point—so I figured I better go take a look. I know I should have called nine-one-one right away, but, you know, sometimes you just don't think.

In the driveway, I saw Coigne's truck, which I recognized because his farm is next to mine. I also saw a red Maserati. Turns out it belonged to a Dr. Misty Bubb, a vet, but I didn't really put two and two together right then.

I got close enough to see the cottage was pretty far gone, and then I saw Mr. Coigne doing something to someone lying on the ground. I don't know. It might have been CPR probably. Then he saw me and said she was dead, but you know, how can you be sure?

I got her over by the creek, away from all that smoke. I tried CPR myself. That's when I knew she wasn't dead because she said something. Most of it I didn't understand, but she said Coigne's name. Now don't take that the wrong way. He'd just pulled her out of a fire—at least, I assume that's what happened, and maybe she was thinking I was Coigne. I don't know. But she said very distinctly, "Coigne." Then there was Hilda Fingerhut, telling me to come away because Coigne said she was dead. So that's when the police arrived and the paramedics, and I was told to go sit down across the road.

Law dropped his feet to the floor, opened his drawer, and pulled out a bottle of Jack Daniels and a glass. He hesitated, started to put them back, then shrugged, poured two fingers, and put the bottle back. He thought about what he'd read so far.

It didn't appear Finn recognized the woman he'd carried to the creek, and Law wanted to follow up on that. Seemed to Law he'd heard Finn and Misty Bubb were an item some time back, but he knew better than to rely on the grapevine. It probably was only natural Finn thought he was carrying the owner of the house in his arms, whom he said he'd never met.

Then Chief Deputy Baker had asked Finn an inspired question, whether he knew Kaleb Chatte, who also lived at that address. In the summary, his deputy said Finn didn't answer at first but finally said, "The name sounds familiar."

"Yeah, you know him," Law said to himself. He settled back in his chair, suddenly quite tired as he thought how long it took in the Mountain State to get DNA results. Six months—if it was urgent. He wasn't sure that time lag would matter much, seeing as how both Mr. Coigne and Mr. Spenser contaminated the cottage, the gasoline cans, possibly the shed, rooms in the cottage, the victim's clothes, and whatever else they could get their hands on.

15

Chief Deputy Baker had told Finn to go back home, put on some coffee, think about what'd happened over the last few hours, and see if he could come up with anything else that might help them get a clearer picture of what went on at Marion Chatte's house. In the meantime, they'd follow up on some of the helpful details he'd already provided.

Finn was just doing his duty, being a model citizen. When he got home, he did the opposite of what he'd been instructed. He wanted to put his mind as far away from the morning's drama as he could. He hopped into the shower and let it run as hot as he could stand it. He watched the filthy water pool at the drain. He could use a drink, but the thought of being alone with his thoughts discouraged him. He called his cousin and asked him over. He put on one of his new Armani shirts and rolled up the sleeves, relieved he still had enough tan to work with the white linen.

Some guys had set up his billiards table, so he told Owen about the morning's misadventure, minus some details, over a game with Coltrane playing in the background.

"That's awful, Finn. God. And we were just talking about Misty the other day."

Finn thought quickly. What had they said? What had *he* said? Then he remembered.

"That business about Misty and Coigne. I sure hope he doesn't get into trouble because of it."

"What do you mean?" Owen looked puzzled.

Did Finn have to spell it out for him? "You know, you told me Coigne was boinking the vet. I'd hate to think Coigne had—you know."

"You're crazy, man. Coigne's a good guy." Owen played his shot and blew it.

"Sorry, man. Lost your edge. You've got to concentrate." He'd keep the pressure on. "How's Laney doing? She's not going to be worried, is she? I mean, about her dad and Misty? It's all bound to come out if there's a—"

"Look, Finn. You've got to knock it off about what I told you. That was in strict confidence, and besides, it has nothing to do with what happened to Dr. Bubb."

"Okay. Settle down, kid. I'm just getting the lay of the land." *The lay* of the land. Good one.

This could work out well. Finn didn't need the cops on top of him, and this angle with Coigne and Misty was bound to distract them. Anything for a little peace. "Feel like some lunch?"

Owen slammed his cue ball down on the table. "May as well. I'm playing like my mother."

"Don't take it so hard, kid. Stick with me, and I'll make you a pool shark."

16

The back door slammed, and Coigne jumped up from the desk in the living room. Norma was home. They greeted each other politely. "I got my mail off your desk." He held it up to show her. "Hope you don't mind. Figured since I was here." He felt awkward, maybe even a little embarrassed by how he'd had to call to ask her to be with him at the fire, like he was some ninny instead of a retired, decorated Massachusetts State Trooper. "Laney's going to be home soon. We should both let her know what happened. It will be on the news and—"

Without a word, Norma sat down on the sofa, a tired red plaid monster Coigne's uncle had left behind. If he'd had any impression of a thaw the other day, Norma's expression told another story. Was she thinking what he was thinking, that rather than getting Misty out of their lives, she'd be with them now for some time to come?

The back door slammed, and it sounded like a backpack slid across the kitchen table. Then the refrigerator opened and stayed open longer than necessary unless you were cleaning it out, and Coigne was sure that wasn't happening. "Close the fridge, Laney, and come on in. Norma and I need to talk to you."

Laney sauntered in, a cold slice of pizza in hand. She looked a little surprised, probably because they didn't usually sit around during the workday, but otherwise, she looked carefree.

Coigne hated he would have to change that.

"Sometime early this morning, a woman was pulled from a burning cottage over on the Opequon," Norma said, never one to shy away from unpleasant tasks. "The woman died. It was Dr. Bubb."

"Who's Dr. Bubb?" Laney said, her mouth full, sitting Indian-style next to Norma.

Norma glanced at Coigne, but he gave her nothing back. She'd grabbed the wheel; she could drive the bus. "It's Dr. Misty Bubb, the vet who took care of Beauty."

"God, Norma. That's horrible. Was it like a kitchen fire or something? Didn't she have smoke alarms? Poor Misty."

Norma explained that the cottage didn't belong to Misty. It belonged to someone else, a person who, by chance, Norma was assisting with a matter. "Sheriff Law doesn't yet know the cause of the fire or why Dr. Bubb was even there."

Coigne said nothing and let Laney ask all her questions. "So how come you know all this? Sounds like you've talked to Sheriff Law."

Coigne sat down in an armchair next to her. "By coincidence, I was on my way to Hilda Fingerhut's farm. I saw the smoke and did what I could to resuscitate Misty, but I was too late. Fortunately, Sheriff Law was in the neighborhood. Norma and I wanted you to know about it in case it's on the news."

Laney had many questions about why Misty was there and why Norma, Finn, and Hilda Fingerhut were there, all of which seemed quite normal for her to ask. What surprised Coigne, in a good way, was that she seemed sorry about the news but not traumatized by it.

"I need to call Owen. You said Finn Spenser was there. Owen will want to know. Is there anything else you can tell me?"

"Maybe that's a good idea to call him," Norma said. "I'll give Evelyn a call too. She'll be glad to hear her nephew tried to render help." She looked over at Coigne, and he nodded.

"Is there anything else I should know?" Laney asked. "You're acting like there's more to the story."

Norma leaned over and grabbed Laney's knee and squeezed. "Nothing more, sweetheart. I just hate having to give you bad news about someone you knew. That's all. Now go give that Owen a call."

The way Laney bounded up the stairs assured Coigne his daughter had taken Misty's death in stride.

Coigne wished he never had to hear Misty's name again, even to learn of her death. The name itself kindled awful thoughts for him. He couldn't say he rejoiced at the news of her death, but he was honest enough to acknowledge he felt no sorrow. Norma had been kinder than he'd expected, coming to the fire when he called and not rebuffing him in front of the sheriff. But he figured Misty's death had made them lose precious ground on the road back to marital bliss. Their separation and the cause of it was bound to come out in public, and that's something that would bother anyone, but especially someone with Norma's pride.

"Let me see your knife, will you? The one I gave you," she said.

Coigne recognized the tone. And he wished like hell he'd mentioned he'd misplaced it. Now she had his carelessness, on top of everything, to begrudge him.

"Funny you should ask. I haven't seen it in a while. I'm really sorry, Norma. How did you know it was missing?"

"Where did you last have it?"

Coigne scratched his head. "My pocket. I take it with me everywhere. You know that."

"How long has it been missing?"

Coigne's lips bunched to one side, a habit of his when he was confused. "What's this about?"

"I'm no prosecutor, but you may be talking to one soon. I don't have the knife in hand, but I saw it at Marion Chatte's house. You'll be glad to know it looked to be in good shape," she said, full of sarcasm. She walked him through what she'd overheard about his movement of Misty's body, how he'd lifted her from the kitchen floor and presumably taken her out the kitchen door and tried to resuscitate her, and how Finn had carried her farther away toward the creek. "Did you go anywhere else in the house? Think."

Coigne felt a touch of anxiety. "I called out to see if anyone else was in the cottage, dashed up the stairs, and called some more, but then I had to get out. The smoke was overpowering."

"The living room? Did you go in there to look?"

"Sure. Well, no. I ran past its doorway. Didn't need to go in— it didn't have a door. There's not much to the house—I would have seen if anyone was in there. You found my knife in the living room? How'd that happen?"

Norma's eyes never left his. "Did Finn go into the house?"

Coigne gave the matter thought. "After I left Misty in the grass, I focused on phoning nine-one-one and explaining the situation. I didn't see Finn until later. I never saw him in the house, but that doesn't mean he wasn't there."

"You were by the shed, where those gasoline cans were."

"That's right. When I finished the call, Finn was moving the body, and I guess he was doing CPR. He could use a refresher course. You're sure the knife's mine?"

"I won't swear it's yours, but before I bought one that expensive, I became an expert on really good knives. It was no piece of tin, and it looked just like yours. Of course, I was nowhere close enough to see the three stars. But someone will be. Look, obviously someone else picked it up. Could have been Misty, Finn, even Marion Chatte. And she's got a son, Kaleb. He might have picked it up somewhere. When did you last have it? Think, Coigne."

He knew how unlikely it was the knife Norma saw was the one she'd given him, but whenever Misty Bubb was involved, or even whenever her name came up, he felt a sense of overwhelming doom. He thought of the three stars Norma had had inscribed on the knife, one for each member of their new family. Again he tried hard to think where he'd last seen his knife. "I got nothin.'"

"You never mentioned that you couldn't find it."

"Do you blame me? The knife was a precious gift from you, and I was careless enough to misplace it."

"Simmer down, Coigne. The question now is whether to go ahead and let Law know about the knife, how I saw it there when I came to pick you up, et cetera, or keep quiet and hope like hell it isn't your knife I saw in Marion's living room. Give it some thought."

When she stood, Coigne grasped her hand. "Do you realize this is the second conversation in a row where we haven't torn one another's face off? I call that progress."

"Call it what you want—Just let me get some office work done before *Christmas.*"

17

Laney sat side by side with Owen at the McDonald's in the Food Lion shopping center. "We don't have to hang out with him. I'm just saying Finn's a cool guy. That's all." She'd been dying to tell Owen about the fire over on the Opequon. He might not know about it and how his cousin had been there along with Coigne. She'd only finally caught up with him at dinnertime. Somehow the conversation had turned awkward. She tried to lighten the mood, cheer him up. "May I?" She leaned over to dip her French fry into his tiny paper cup of ketchup and, with her available hand, squeezed his thigh.

He smiled. "I think he's cool, too. But when you get to know him, you see another side to him. He's complex. I mean, you've met him how many times?"

She looked around the room, wondering how to make the one time she'd met Finn Spenser seem like more than just one time. She noticed her history teacher had just walked in with a small boy in hand and her husband, presumably, who carried a younger one. Her teacher looked so different out of the classroom with her kids—her long hair loose, wearing jeans instead of one of her three pantsuits. She looked less knowledgeable. Laney pretended not to see her for now.

"Finn's been around to talk to Coigne and Hilda Fingerhut about farming," Laney said. "She was there at the fire, too, by the way."

"I know. Finn told me. What I'm trying to say is sometimes he doesn't tell the whole truth about things. He spins things."

Having just spun something herself, the extent of her acquaintance with Finn, she hoped Owen wasn't quibbling over something that minor. But it seemed like he had something more on his mind, something in particular about Finn that was troubling him. "Give me an example of what you mean." She stayed quiet, hoping he'd feel okay telling her something disturbing about his own cousin.

"Misty Bubb. And this whole thing about the fire. You know it could be arson."

"As in, someone set the fire on purpose? Who told you that?"

"Just an impression I had, but I guess you could ask your folks. But what I'm trying to say is, if it was arson, then the vet's death is murder, so, you know, that's a fuckin' big deal."

"Of course." She wanted more ketchup but didn't want to interrupt the flow. She ate her fry plain.

"I get the impression whenever her name comes up these days, Finn acts like he doesn't know her well, just knows her by reputation, you know? But when he used to live here, he talked about her a lot. About some business they were going to go in on together. Now, it's like it never happened. I was pretty young then. Maybe I've got it wrong. You want some more?" He gave her his ketchup and his barely-touched fries.

"Hey, Laney. Nice to see you." Her teacher guided her young son toward the bathroom. Laney introduced her to Owen.

"I remember you, Owen." She suddenly became serious. "How've you been?"

Her tone revealed she was really asking how he'd been since Dell died. That happened a lot when they were out together, and she needed to be mature about it. It was selfish, but she wanted him not to have to think about it so much. She wanted him to think about her.

They finished up, and Owen got her home early. School night. And, besides, Owen seemed distracted, and she'd run out of cheer-up tricks, at least tricks appropriate for McDonald's.

18

As a student of Civil War history and an Appalachian Trail hiking enthusiast, Norma was well aware there was almost no place to park in downtown Harpers Ferry, about twelve miles southeast of Shepherdstown and the farm. She kept her annual Harpers Ferry National Park Pass in her wallet, which allowed her to park free and enjoy the ride on the clean shuttle bus through dense woods and winding roads into the lower town. This time she'd regrettably had to forgo her usual picnic on a perch where the Shenandoah and Potomac Rivers converged. After yesterday's fire, such a dramatic explosion of natural forces would have reassured her that something more worthy than mankind had some impact on the world.

A phone call to The Fox the evening before had brought Norma up to speed on Marion Chatte's status. She had not found her son, and there was no show or exhibit at Union Station—

or at least not one for photography. Norma phoned Marion the following morning and learned firsthand how the woman felt when the fire chief insinuated she might have started the fire herself, accidentally or otherwise, before she left for Washington. Once that was out of her system, Marion provided Norma with information that was marginally more useful.

"I can worry about important papers and baby pictures later. What I'm concerned about right now is Kaleb. Can you tell me anything, Norma? Sheriff Law gave me nothing. I tell you, he's not taking Kaleb's disappearance seriously. I'm counting on you."

Norma wished she hadn't agreed to help Marion find her son. She'd spend lots of unpaid time chasing a grown man who was probably only trying to get away from his controlling mother, and she was sure to disappoint Marion Chatte, who'd never let her hear the end of it. But she had agreed.

"I'm sorry, Marion, but I've not made much progress (*much?*) because of the fire and everything, but I'm pursuing a lead right now and will contact you as soon as I have something solid. I don't want to waste any more time by going into detail now, so let me get at it. You focus on finding a place to stay. You have relatives in the area?"

"I'm okay. The provost has a two-bedroom garage he's converted into an Airbnb. But please, Norma, let me know the moment you hear anything. Something awful has happened. I've had this feeling all along, and now the fire confirms it."

Norma didn't see the connection, but rather than argue, she made soothing noises and said goodbye.

Kaleb may not have had a bricks and mortar studio called ChatteSnap, but he did have a website at that address, which showcased at least a hundred of his works. She was surprised at the sensitive portraits and scenes probing social matters like race, sexual orientation, and homelessness. The site included no contact information or studio address. The lead Norma alluded to in her call with Marion had to do with the mysterious law firm, Blow and Ask Him. She now had a choice to make. She could either spend time researching a law firm by that nonsensical yet suggestive name or visit the firm in Harpers Ferry called Blough (pronounced like *cow*) and Assim. From there, how hard would it be to find "the pal" with the French accent, as The Fox had referred to her?

The shuttlebus placed her among a street full of historically restored shops, which displayed clothing and kitchenware that satisfied the needs of households in the nineteenth century. She compared her own attire of drawstring flax pants and a T-shirt featuring Rin Tin Tin with clothing displayed in the Dry Goods Store window. Her body almost began to melt at the thought of wearing long sleeves in several layers of clothing in the riverside humidity.

The Blough and Assim address led her on a vertical hike up High Street to a three-story, whitewashed stone building, its attic dormers facing the street and its tiered balconies in the back overlooking the Potomac. From the third floor, the morning sunrise and the majestic view of Maryland and Loudon Heights would serve a photographer quite well. On instinct alone, rather than march directly into the first-floor offices of Blough and Assim, she opted for the back staircase and prayed the stairway door was unlocked.

Norma bounded up three flights of forest green, carpeted stairs to reach a long, wide hallway. Upon examination, there was only one door with signage, and well, now, what do you know? The sign read ChatteSnap Studios. The glass door was locked, and another sign, hanging on thick string at the center, read Closed. Norma peered in at a reception area, the walls bearing large, framed photos of faces in a mood and texture more like something painted by Andrew Wyeth than something photographed—so bleak, muted, lonely, and beautiful. No wonder Jess was crazy about him. He had such ability. And too bad for her. Throughout their concentrated, though seemingly fruitful, courtship, he'd failed to mention the imaginary studio actually existed. The Closed sign gave no indication of studio hours or when its owner might return to open its doors. She resorted to Plan B for Blough and Assim.

She returned to the first floor and buzzed into the law firm after identifying herself as "Norma Bergen of The Law Offices of

Norma Bergen & Associates." The receptionist, Ms. LaBomba, according to her nameplate, sat at her black, horseshoe-shaped desk and finished a phone call Norma's arrival had interrupted. High points for Ms. LaBomba, who'd greeted her new arrival with a smile and welcoming wave at the same time.

LaBomba did not seem like the name of someone who would have a French accent, but based on the phone call Norma had just overheard, Ms. LaBomba had a real one. She appeared to be in her mid-forties, though her skin, a delicious shade of caramel, was smooth. She dressed simply and accessorized with modest gold hoop earrings. From what Norma could see, she also took good care of her figure. What was it about women like Ms. LaBomba? They could make a black, short-sleeved knit top look sexy, sophisticated, and professional all at once. She wore her dark, wavy hair short and outlined her best facial features, which was all of them, in well-applied make-up. There was still one more thing about her that attracted Norma's notice. Her photograph hung in the studio reception area on the third floor.

"Good morning. I'm looking for my client, Kaleb Chatte," Norma said, "but his studio seems to be closed."

"Bon! Tout le monde cherche Monsieur Chatte, but he is not here. You are his attorney, perhaps? It is important that you find heem? Would you please forgive me?" She answered another call, which gave Norma time to examine the law office. It sure had hers beat—the recessed lighting, brass accents, and plush seating areas with magazines that looked current. But then, Blough and Assim had been around for a while, whereas Norma was starting from scratch in West Virginia. Paying the malpractice premium was this month's financial goal for Norma Bergen & Associates.

"I am so sorry. Mr. Chatte has been away for some time. He is often away, but this has been a long stretch even for heem."

Norma decided to circle around a bit before getting personal. "Does he have any employees who might know where he is?"

"Non, he works alone. Have you tried his phone or email? It ees possible he's checking them. I can give you his number if you like, but then, as his lawyer, you must have it already?"

The way Ms. LaBomba raised one eyebrow, Norma suspected her pose as Kaleb's lawyer wasn't working.

"I do have his contact information, thank you." Norma gave her head a little shake. "Such a mystery. Even his fiancée can't find him."

Well, well, well. Never has bronze skin turned so pale, nor dark eyes so suspicious, after such a short little sentence. It was clear Ms. LaBomba was shocked by the news of a fiancée, yet she didn't question Norma about it. What's up with that?

Norma pulled a chair from the nearby seating area and dragged it closer to Ms. LaBomba's desk. "I noticed when I checked at the studio upstairs that among the photographs is one of you. It's lovely. You must be friends with Mr. Chatte?" Norma propped her elbow on the desk, ready for a leisurely siege.

The receptionist's response was to sort the paperclips from rubber bands and sticky notes from pink message slips, all with great care. "Don't make something out of that. He takes everyone's picture." She rapidly opened one desk drawer after another, although Norma could have told her she wouldn't find Kaleb in there. "I am so sorry I can't help you. And I'm afraid I'm quite—"

The telephone buzzed. With an exaggerated sad face, she dismissed Norma.

Norma bought some thinking time by opening her saddlebag and fussing with its contents. And then a sudden brain puff hit. It was probably nothing she could work with, but she hoped the puff would transform into a complete action plan before, in keeping with professional decorum, she had to get up and go.

She'd gathered Ms. LaBomba was close to young Kaleb—he'd taken a lovely photo of her, erasing a gray strand here and there, and the receptionist had been surprised and nettled by the news that Kaleb had a fiancée. Of course, how would Ms. LaBomba know about Jess, who only showed up in Kaleb's other life? Putting all this together, the photo and the surprise and irritation, Norma had a hunch based on her experience with men who fixated on mother figures and older women who fixated on young men. If, for some reason, Kaleb needed to go underground, *to whom* would he turn?

19

Norma left the Law Offices of Blough and Assim, grabbed a cheeseburger at the foot of the hill, and ran a quick search for LaBomba's address on the There-u-r app. Conveniently, she lived within walking distance of where Norma sat at that moment, scrubbing ketchup off Rin Tin Tin's outer coat.

She left a generous tip and sallied forth, climbing the hill once more. She walked several blocks over toward the old Storer College, a massive, clifftop, red brick building that admitted and educated freed slaves following the Civil War and played a central role in fostering the twentieth-century Civil Rights Movement. As impressive to Norma, the anti-Jim Crow movement had headquartered there. The neighborhood was not of the first order. Many of the small farmhouse-style houses on small lots looked beaten down by years of apathy and empty pockets, the yards filled with nothing but auto and tractor parts, cans and bottles, and fast-food containers.

Ms. LaBomba's home was a different matter. It was an Arts and Crafts red brick, two-story home with a wide and welcoming front porch. As she approached, Norma spotted a couple of interesting stained-glass windows on the second floor and imagined a clever photographer might have fun with those at different times of the day.

On that wide and welcoming porch, a young man gently rocked on a cushioned glider, book in hand. Norma recognized

Marion Chatte's son instantly. Admittedly, his hair color and style were not at all like that in the picture Marion had given her, but was it all that likely someone other than Kaleb Chatte wore a T-shirt emblazoned with the numbers twelve-fifteen? Norma answered her own question with an emphatic *No!* tempered by uncertainty as to how to approach her sitting duck or even whether to approach him. Now that she had him, she didn't want to frighten him off.

She slowed her pace and, in order to move closer without alarming the man, assumed the look of a hapless tourist consulting the map she'd earlier picked up on the shuttle bus. It occurred to her how easy it had been to locate Kaleb, which made her wonder why Marion and the sheriff had found it so difficult. Maybe she underestimated her own powers of observation and her ability to see patterns and meaning where others simply absorbed information and let it rot there on the vine.

Now that she stood at the foot of his front steps, the porch swinger looked up, and Norma waved her map at him. "Hello there. Are you, by any chance, Kaleb Chatte?" The young man hesitated just long enough for any doubt she had about his identity to disappear, along with the young man himself, who scampered through the front door.

The right thing to do at that moment was to call his mother and let her know her son was alive and well and had found himself a new mama, Ms. LaBomba. But Marion was most likely dealing with the catastrophic loss of her home or perhaps answering tough questions from the police about why Misty Bubb died at Marion's home. Better to grab this tiger by the toe while the toe was in hand.

Norma scooted up the front steps and rang the doorbell, an ivory button attached to an art nouveau brass base. When no one answered, she tried the door and, to her surprise, it was unlocked. She pushed forward and called out, "Game's up, Kaleb. How about some conversation so we can at least put—"

Hard, cold steel pressed against her left temple. She could feel and perhaps even hear her vein throb against the pistol's barrel.

"Back up. Don't stop to think; just back up and keep going," he said.

How could she have been so stupid? She opened her mouth to speak, but her tongue was a balled-up wool sock. A beam of red light shot her in the eye. He pulled the trigger, and she was dead. It's true what they say. Never felt a thing. But the beam moved, or she did, and she realized it was not a bullet, but sunlight shot through a pane of red stained glass from the stairwell. She'd never been so frightened in her life. Kaleb must have felt the same. The tremor from his hands traveled from the pistol grip, through the cylinder, down the barrel, vibrated against her skull, then pulsated into her brain.

"I'm just going. I'm leaving," she said, slowly backing out. "I just came to tell you there's been a fire at your mother's home." She continued backpedaling.

"Wait. Stop. This is a trick. Who are you, and who sent you?" This time he moved closer. Sweat, caught by the red light in the stained glass, spotted his forehead with flecks of blood.

"My name is Norma Bergen. I'm a lawyer, and your mother hired me to find you. If you'll let me reach into my—"

He pressed the gun harder against her temple.

The longer they were at a stalemate, the more chance he had to pull the trigger. "I can show you my card. There's one in my pants pocket. Your side."

Never shifting his gaze from her, he found the card and read it. But he still didn't lower the gun.

"I don't think you want to kill me, Kaleb. You want to know about your mom and your house. So would you put the gun away, please?"

Kaleb sagged against the wall. His gun arm dropped as well. "Let's go to the kitchen," he said, his voice faint. "I could use a beer."

He followed her through the living room and into the kitchen. She regained enough mental clarity to note fresh polish on the oak floors, dimly lit period lamps, the claret-colored armchair she longed to faint on, and a captain's desk, complete with map rack. But she was still rattled. Her mouth had gone dry, and her pulse beat so hard, she could almost hear it.

The kitchen was tiny, but there was room for a round table that seated four, so long as only two people sat at one time. Kaleb flung the pistol into a straw basket of unfolded laundry and opened the small fridge.

He must have read her surprise at the cavalier disposal of a firearm. "It's not loaded. I'm not even sure it's real. Mimi keeps it to scare tourists away."

Norma's body remained in a locked position.

"The house is famous for its preservation of an original Sears and Roebuck kit house. People come around all the time taking photos, getting too nosy. She's annoyed by it, but I understand their interest. You want one of these?" He reached for a beer.

It was a lot of information to take in—the gun that wasn't loaded, the famous house, Kaleb's sympathy for nosy tourists. But none of it was information she could process yet. "Sure, I'll have a beer."

Kaleb went through the motions, even offering a glass, and sat down across from her. She continued to notice things. It was helping her calm down. The table was covered in a green checkered cotton tablecloth, one of those light touches that contributed to the overall comfortable atmosphere of the place—or would have, had she not stopped breathing three minutes earlier.

"So, what are you doing here, Kaleb? I met Mimi if that's Ms. LaBomba of Blough and Assim. I don't imagine she's your girlfriend, not that I'm saying she'd be too old for you. I'm not fussy in that way. It's just that your fiancée happens to be my law clerk." And why shouldn't she give Jess a promotion? Look at the guy she's had to put up with. "And I am fussy about my law clerk being deceived."

At first, Kaleb squirmed during Norma's breezy commentary. But after a long draw on his beer, he shucked any hint of embarrassment. "None of what you're thinking is what it seems, but I thought you were going to tell me about my mother. The house burned down? I don't believe you. We've lived there forever."

"Like that means it couldn't burn? You obviously aren't using your phone for the latest news." Norma pulled out her phone. "Check it out." She scrolled to an article on the fire, which quoted a local man as saying the source of the conflagration was "God's wrath." Kaleb read the story, his face blank, and Norma shared other highlights with him, including the identity of the "unidentified body" found among the ashes.

A spasm twitched at the corner of Kaleb's mouth, and again Norma had an overpowering sense of his frailty. "Is my mom okay? They don't mention her in the article. You're sure the body they found isn't my mom?"

"They are sure it isn't your mom, although their natural assumption at first was that your mother had died in the fire. How sad it would have been had that been true—her dying, worried sick about you."

Kaleb stood abruptly, causing the table to bang down hard on the floor. "You don't know what you're talking about. I'm only here because of my mother." His face burned with anger and hurt. He jerked his head back to flip his hair off his forehead. It landed in the form of an ocean wave about to crest. "Why doesn't anybody get that?"

Now they were getting somewhere. Norma needed to go slowly, not scare him, and let him tell the story. Whatever was going on, he'd kept it hidden for a number of days, and he had no reason to trust her, notwithstanding her brand-new business card, which she would've liked to get back. "I'll make us some coffee. Probably help us keep our fannies on the chairs," she said.

Bustling around the kitchen, opening and closing the drawers in search of coffee supplies, making note of all she saw, she remembered the photo of him in her pocket, how mischievous he'd looked about those dark blue eyes. At the moment, the charm was absent. Every so often, he'd slip on that tough look he'd worn when he held the gun. But he couldn't keep it up. "Why don't you tell me about it, Kaleb? I'm pretty good at straightening out problems."

He nodded in the direction of the gun on the pile of laundry as if to say, "How good at it were you a moment ago?"

"Don't let my waltzing into the gun fool you. I know what I'm doing." She worked on the coffee while he argued with her about whether she did or did not know what she was doing. She set the cups of coffee down on the table and said, "Begin."

He leaned back with his eyes closed and hands clasped behind his head. "I'm in a situation where I may have led a person on more than I should have. It might have had something to do with wanting this person to help me get established with my own studio, generate publicity for my shows." He opened his eyes and looked at her. "You saw the place, I assume. It's worth doing just about anything for, wouldn't you agree? Oh, wait. Being so capable, you wouldn't have had this kind of experience, I guess."

Norma helped him along. "So, your lover delivered the goods, your studio over on High Street, and you are no longer willing to deliver yours. If it's as bad as all that, let the person take the studio back."

"I tried. No good."

She stirred her coffee, wondering if that was the truth.

"Whatever. The thing is, this person made threats. This time the threat was against my mother. You're *sure* it wasn't my mother in that fire?"

"I'm sure." Norma was bewildered. Kaleb couldn't be talking about Jess. She couldn't afford to set him up in the studio. And why would he be wearing the shirt with their wedding date on it if he was running from her? And why was he hiding from his mother if she was in danger? She could only hope he'd tell her in his own good time.

"You sure haven't hidden in a great place. If I found you, and I don't even know you, isn't it just a matter of time before your pursuer does?" she asked.

"What, you think I have dozens of places to go stay for weeks, maybe for months? I was lucky Mimi was so generous."

"Okay. Let's back up. You've been hiding out for a long time, but what does that have to do with Jess? Why doesn't she even know about your studio? Your actual studio."

She needed only to see his face to know she'd hit the jackpot of all deceptions.

"It's beyond belief complicated."

"Try me."

Norma checked the time, worried his story might take the rest of her life. Her client had asked her to find her son, that's all. This meddling and poking around in Kaleb's love life was for Jess's sake, not Marion's. Was this any of her business? She said nothing and let him finish his beer while his coffee grew cold.

Even with air conditioning blowing, the house felt still and stale. Kaleb got up and grabbed an open bag of sour cream and onion chips from the counter, and threw them on the table. When he finished his beer, he threw the bottle in the trash under the sink.

Ever hear of recycling? Norma propped her fist under her chin. His predicament had given her a headache only a week on a couch in the dark would alleviate. She raised her head warily. "But you guys are supposed to be getting married. Didn't she ever once wonder where you live?"

"She never got the chance."

"Ah. You moved in with her after the first date. I don't even want to know what story you told your mother when you stopped coming home. She obviously doesn't know about Jess and the impending nuptials."

The boy had the gall to look at Norma like she was mad. Like she should have known no guy in his right mind these days tells his mother he's getting married. Like that was an eighties craze or something.

"Look, buddy boy. You know I can't keep the truth from Jess. I work with her, and besides, I can't be a party to such deception. Do you tell her, or do I? I'm assuming you have real feelings toward her. Or is that a charade too?"

"Of course I do. I'd never do anything to hurt her."

She let that declaration blow across the sands of Bullcrap Desert.

"I regret what's happened. And you're right. I've got to tell Jess the truth. But I can't do it now. I can't tell anyone where I am."

"But why can't you tell your mother all this? She's worried to death about you."

He stared down into his cold cup of coffee. "Because if she doesn't know, and the person can see she doesn't know, maybe she'll be left alone."

"Or maybe just the opposite."

20

Laney kept her eye on the back door. Still no sign of Norma. She grabbed her phone and furiously tapped Norma's number for the fifth time in the last hour. Where the hell was she? Why was this happening? Why couldn't this family have one full year without something awful happening? A sound on the back steps, no louder than a raindrop, made her toss her phone on the kitchen table and lunge at the open doorway. "Why the hell didn't you pick up? Coigne's been taken by the police. We've got to do something!"

"Slow down, Laney." Norma's hair had blown into her face, and her arms were full. She set down her laptop, saddlebag, and bottle of Mountain Dew. "I can't take in what you're saying, but I can tell you're upset." She stuck her hair back under her hat. "Now tell me."

"We've got to get down to the sheriff's office." Laney grabbed Norma's arm.

"I think it has something to do with that fire."

"Okay. Okay."

"What's happening? Why are you holding your heart like that?"

Norma dropped her hand and took a deep breath. "I'm okay. You just shocked me. You can tell me more in the car. Just get your jacket."

They speed-walked out to the car, Laney in the lead. "He told me to let you know where he was going. He wanted to ask you to represent him or, if you couldn't, find a lawyer who would. Why wouldn't you help him? I'll never forgive you—"

"Stop, Laney. There may be logical reasons why we'd need someone else to be his lawyer. You've got to calm down and not rush to conclusions, or you'll make us both sick." She caught up to Laney and turned her around. "Look at me. Of course, I'll help him. Why would you think I wouldn't?"

"And why would you ask me that question after everything you've put Coigne through these last months?"

She wished she hadn't said that. She didn't have the full picture of Norma and Coigne's split, and the way she kept blaming her mom for all of it might not be fair. But it was too much for Norma to ask her to be fair-minded right now. She ought to be able to see how confused Laney was about their relationship and just fix everything. She always used to be able to fix everything.

Once inside the car, Norma broke the silence. "Those personal things between Coigne and me don't matter when one of us is in real trouble. I mean—not that Coigne's in real trouble. I just mean in a situation like this. Coigne was first on the scene, and they need more details. I'm not even sure he's had a chance to give them a formal statement yet about finding Misty in the fire by the Opequon."

Laney weighed the possibilities. "You think they're going to arrest him, don't you?"

"Are you listening to me at all? Why would they?" Norma's hands tightened on the wheel, which did nothing to soothe Laney's nerves.

"Slow down," Laney said.

They'd come to a red light. Norma's eyes looked like they were pinned open. She put on the turn signal and waited. To Laney, it sounded like a hammer pounding the hell out of a nail. "Norma. It's green."

They rode in silence. While Laney had waited for Norma to arrive home, an awful thought germinated into a detailed nightmare. Now, if she didn't voice it, her head would explode. "You didn't have anything to do with getting Coigne into trouble, did you? I know you and Sheriff Law are friends. Did you say something bad about Coigne?"

"No. Absolutely not. You've got to let me drive without all the hounding, or we won't get there in one piece, and how will that help?"

"Then why do you sound so guilty?"

"Stop, Laney! You're driving us both nuts." Then she smacked her forehead like she'd forgotten something.

"What? Tell me."

"It's nothing." She looked down at the gas gauge. "I just wish I had thought to get more gas."

"It's not that far. You were thinking of something else. What was it?"

"Nothing. Like I say, they probably just want his help. He has valuable know-how, having been a state trooper who investigated serious crimes."

"It didn't sound like that. They talked to him like he was a criminal."

"What gave you that impression?"

"It was crazy-scary. We were talking out on the screen porch. I think Coigne was worried you'd be unhappy to find him in the house again, so he got ready to go. That's when we saw their headlights. Then a couple of those officers—"

"Deputies."

"Whatever. We could hear the chatter from the radio when they got out. We weren't worried about anything."

"Who was it? The sheriff?"

"No, it was someone I didn't know—Chief Deputy Baker. He had a woman deputy with him, but I didn't see her name tag.

You've seen her. She's been in parades. The one with the receding chin you don't notice once she smiles."

"I know who you mean." They were close to the sheriff's office, and Norma slowed down. "It's not easy to find the turnoff out here in Sheepland. What happened then?"

"That chief deputy smiled at me—made nice, you know. Then he said something in a low voice to Coigne. Then he put back on his smile and said out loud to Coigne, 'We'll wait for you here.' You know, like he was being all trusty, letting Coigne use the bathroom by himself." Laney had to admit she was feeling a little calmer now that she could talk with someone.

"I'm glad he was being trusty, as you put it. It's never smart for law enforcement to show their untrusty side. Just gets well-meaning citizens riled up."

"Coigne never gets riled up. That's you, Norma."

"Go on." They'd reached the turnoff. The sheriff's office was lit up like a ten-pump gas station at two a.m.

"Coigne asked Chief Deputy Baker if he could call you. He said sure, and in a lower voice that I could still hear, he said, 'You're *not* under arrest.' But you know the way he said it, it was like, 'You're not under arrest *yet.*' But you didn't pick up, Norma. You didn't answer your phone when he called. Was that on purpose?"

"I'd never deliberately avoid Coigne's call."

"I don't believe you."

"I never would. It could've been about you."

They entered the one-story brick building, and, unlike interiors of police stations in old movies or TV, there wasn't much other than a sign that said "Sheriff's Department" to let you know what the building was for. She'd accompanied the police and her bio-mother down to the station plenty of times as a kid, but she'd never visited a sheriff's office. Now, she smelled fresh paint on the yellow cinderblock walls. In the waiting area, which had no chairs to sit on while you waited, a large display case with shelves full of medals, framed citations, and awards covered an entire wall. Hung above the doorway were photographs of stern-faced sheriffs of yesterday. A large wall of glass separated the waiting area from the administrative staff seating area, nameplates visible on their desks. The one thing Laney appreciated—the place was spotless, with no spit or food wrappers on the floor.

A door opened slowly, and Laney held her breath. Sheriff Law and Chief Deputy Baker emerged, but it was the third man that counted. "Coigne! Are you coming home now?" Laney lunged at him and held on, her head fast against his chest.

He folded his arms around her and waved at Norma. He looked tired but untroubled. "Aha! My escorts. I hope we didn't keep you waiting?"

"So, Sheriff," Norma said. "Do I need to file a lawsuit for police brutality, or are you going to tell me why you dragged a law-abiding citizen from his home?"

With Norma, Laney could never be sure if she was kidding or not.

"No dragging needed if he'd just answered his phone," Sheriff Law said.

"My bad," Coigne said. "I turned it off when everybody on the Community Center board started texting with their personal views on a proposed scheduling change. About drove me crazy, and I forgot to turn it back on."

"Figures," Norma said. Then the door opened, and she took a step back. "My, my. Finn Spenser. Are they questioning everyone out our way?"

21

The reception area grew crowded. Norma stepped aside for a young man and woman who looked like siblings—both skinny with long, oily blond hair and impressive scowls. The man asked for—demanded, in fact—a concealed weapons application. Sheriff Law's receptionist, Sheila, slid open a small window and handed it to him.

The setting sun put half of Finn's face in shadow and left the other half ablaze. Norma didn't know what made her wary of Finn, aside from Geoff Spenser's angst-extravaganza the other night. Maybe she should give him a break.

As if reading her mind, Finn said, "I apologize if I was weird at the fire the other day. I wasn't at my best." He smiled.

"None of us were. Least of all, Misty," Norma answered.

Across the room, Laney broke from Coigne. "Finn! What are you doing here?" She bounded over to him like Lassie. At least she wasn't fretting anymore.

Norma turned her attention to Coigne. When he entered the room moments ago, he'd cracked a joke or two, probably to let Laney know he was fine, but now that she had a chance to observe him closely, she could see he was exhausted. And yet, damn that man. With those deep-set eyes and five o'clock shadow, he looked great. Maybe she could get Kaleb to photograph him. She shook her head. That was a messed-up thought. She had no need to rhapsodize about a man she intended to divorce. She did, however, need to size up Sheriff Law's intentions toward Coigne. Were they as benign as his humble, countrified persona tried to suggest?

She walked over to Coigne. "Are they through with you?"

He nodded. "Let's go. I'll fill you in at home."

They looked over at Laney. Finn had a hold on her shoulder. Laney never took her eyes off his. And why wouldn't she be enthralled? He was gorgeous and older. Finn glanced at Norma and let Laney go.

Coigne said in a hearty voice, "C'mon, Laney. You've had enough thrills for one evening."

"Sure, but maybe we should wait for Finn. He might need our help."

"I'm sure Finn can take care of himself," Norma said. "You and Coigne go on, and I'll be there after I have a word with Sheriff Law. Finn or one of Law's fine deputies will give me a lift home."

"Are you coming soon?"

With that question, Laney reminded Norma she wasn't completely over her panicky afternoon. At least her facial tic hadn't reappeared, the telltale sign Laney was about to spiral down into depression, something she'd fought, off and on, for years. Norma reached over and tapped the tip of her nose— "Don't *worry*"—as though she were still that same frightened urchin dumped by her bio-mother on her grandmother's stoop ten years earlier.

As if on cue, Sheriff Law broke away from Sheila. "Finn Spenser? Come on back now, son."

"May I have a quick word with you first?" Norma nodded toward Finn. "Give you a chance to rest up before you work over your next law-abiding citizen helping you with your inquiries. Coigne tells me you're removing their fingernails now."

"Sure. I can take a minute with you. Give me a chance to limber up." He exercised his fingers and winked at Finn as he led her back to his office.

She took her usual seat in front of his desk and stifled a laugh at the small bowl of Jolly Ranchers he always kept in the corner. She'd rather reach into his desk drawer for what he always kept *there*, but she couldn't afford to let her mind cloud any more than it had. In the car with Laney, she'd suddenly remembered her worry, that by talking with the sheriff several months ago about Misty and Coigne's affair, Law might view that as the lead-up to a motive for murder. She wasn't sure she should be trying to clear that matter up now; Law had probably forgotten all about that talk. Better feel him out first.

"Last year, you and I sat right here, and I told you some personal things, which I now wish I'd kept to myself."

"Hm." Law reached into his drawer and pulled out the scotch. "I don't suppose we're talking about Misty Bubb and your suspicions about her interfering in your marriage?"

"Yes, I am." She did an imperfect job hiding her astonishment at his perfect memory. "I need to make sure you're not drawing any conclusions about Coigne or me in this investigation based on anything I said back then."

He handed her a glass.

"No, thanks. None for me." She motioned his pouring hand away, and he put the bottle back in the drawer after pouring himself a glass.

She told him she was mistaken about her suspicions and, in fact, any little blip in their marital bliss Sheriff Law may have heard about was completely unfounded.

"You sound like a lady who protests too much." He tossed back his drink and set down his glass, folded his arms, and leaned way back in his chair. "Just why *do* you think I asked Mr. Coigne down to the station?"

"I assumed it had something to do with Misty's murder. I mean, what else around here takes priority? It's not like we get a fire-and-murder doubleheader every day."

"Mr. Coigne has been helping me out with something. I'd assigned him to be a sort of Big Brother to Finn, you might say. So, I was just checking in. But I'm sure he'll tell you all about it."

Norma thought for a minute. "Somehow, that benign explanation doesn't jibe with today's *Schutzstaffel* ambush back at our farm."

He chuckled. "I don't know Schutzstaffel from apple strudel, but the word sounds like it describes just how someone Laney's age would view the unexpected arrival of law enforcement needing her father's help."

"I'll accept your explanation with reservations, but I've got one more question for you, and then I'll leave you to your other business." Norma slipped off a shoe that had caused a blister earlier in the day. "So, are you familiar with a young man named Kaleb Chatte?" She knew the answer since Marion Chatte had filed a missing person's report, but Norma wanted to see how seriously he'd taken the report.

"I am familiar with Kaleb. Why do you ask?" He glanced up at the wall clock.

"I'm not going to keep you much longer, Sheriff. I'm wondering if he's *known* to the police, or do you have any other intelligence on him beyond what his mother told you?"

"I take it she's hired you to find him?"

The way he emphasized "you" made him sound annoyed. She couldn't imagine why. It's not as though his department needed a missing persons case on top of an arson-murder case. She didn't feel she could disclose her arrangement with Marion until she'd at least let her client know she'd found her son. And as for what Norma intended to say when Marion asked for Kaleb's whereabouts, she wasn't sure of that either. "You should talk to Marion, Sheriff. I'm just looking for background now."

Law shifted his eyes toward the window. He looked pensive, as though trying to decipher some very small writing just outside. He rose, rounded the desk, and took a seat against the wall, causing Norma to have to twist his way.

"I'm going to tell you something. I'm not sure why I'm telling a mere civilian these facts, but you've generally shown yourself to be helpful to my office. Oh, I don't know about this."

"Let's have it." She flipped her hands back and forth like a ground crew member guiding a plane with batons. "Nice and easy. Come to Mama."

"All right. It's just confounding the way things in this county tend to intersect. Some might call it a coincidence. I call it spooky."

A knock at the door made for an annoying cliffhanger. Sheriff Law told Sheila he'd be out in a jiff, and she withdrew.

"Our murder victim, and yes, it's now time to call Misty a murder victim, wound up at the home of a missing person we, and perhaps you, are looking for—Kaleb Chatte. How does that strike you?"

She shrugged. The thought had already struck her and she wasn't going to share her reaction to it with the sheriff.

He grew thoughtful again, but Norma withstood the pressure to fill in the silence. Let him do his own homework. She couldn't rat out a client—or a client's son.

Law rose, making clear it was time the meeting ended.

Just as well. Norma had more to mull than he could possibly know. She picked up her saddlebag.

"Ms. Bergen—was there something you needed to tell me?"

"Such as?"

He gave her a lopsided smile.

Coigne's knife. Is he asking me about the knife?

"Well? Anything to tell me?"

She looked straight at the sheriff. "Not a thing."

Norma wasn't an expert at many things outside the legal profession, but when it came to lying, she could have authored a whole chapter in Ripley's *Believe It or Not*. Some would even argue lying was *not* outside the legal profession.

"You're absolutely sure now?" he asked. "There's nothing on your mind?"

"I've got an idea," she said, eyes wide. "Let's play *Jeopardy!*— you give me the answer, and I'll try to come up with the question. How's that?"

She and Law had a history of word game playing whenever one of them, because of their conflicting roles, couldn't easily provide the other with a straight answer. This was just such an occasion.

"Fine. Have it your way." The sheriff held up an imaginary index card and read, "A four- or five-inch knife with three stars on the blade cover."

No point in lying now. Besides, she may be a liar when necessity required it, but she'd never cheat in a game. "Buzz! I've got the question: What is the item found at the Misty Bubb crime scene the other day?"

"Daily Double, Ms. Bergen."

"I suppose you talked with Coigne about the knife?"

"It strikes me you should be asking that question of Mr. Coigne rather than me."

She fired a finger pistol at him and left.

22

Coigne rounded up the few horses that remained in the upper paddock and got them settled in their stalls for the night. Figuring Norma would be awhile, he gave Blister, in grave need, a good brushing and then headed up to the "DadPad," as Laney called it.

For dinner, they decided on a shameful pleasure—leftover pizza topped with pepperoni, red peppers, and pineapple, sprinkled with extra shredded mozzarella. Laney washed a handful of cherry tomatoes in the old utility sink and, after searching his mini fridge, scraped up some limp lettuce leaves for a salad. Coigne, whistling away, placed the pizza slices in the microwave oven.

"I'm opening a window. Pizza and your dirty clothes pile don't mix," Laney said over the roar of the oven. "And, by the way, you and Norma are getting along lately. Should I prepare myself for something?"

Coigne eyed the pile in the corner and stuffed them in the dirty clothes bag from his Navy days. "You think we're getting along? I do, too, but what makes you say so?" He brushed crumbs off the table into one hand and emptied them into the sink.

"Since you moved out here, the only times you two have made eye-to-eye contact was never—that is, until a couple of days ago. Now you're even cooperating on things without making it a big deal." She handed him three mismatched plastic plates.

"Three plates?"

"I'm an optimist. Norma might just join us. But I can't wait, so let's eat now, and we'll save her some. But what I mean is, just a while ago, the way she said she'd meet up with you later to go over things that never could have happened, not even a week ago. She would've launched into one of her crushing closing arguments before you'd even announced the topic. So what's up?"

Sorting through his jumbled flatware gave Coigne a moment to consider what *was* up. Things had changed, and the change was noticeable, even to Laney. And when did things start to change? It would make sense if Misty's death had warmed up the atmosphere—the source of Norma's doubt and anger had been eliminated. But that couldn't be right. Whatever the source, Misty's death wouldn't have eliminated it. Norma had said, "If you could so casually break a promise once, why not twice or three times? And with anyone?" Besides, the warming trend started before Misty's death. He thought a moment and traced it back to three or four days ago when Norma had just returned from Food Lion. It could be they'd grown so far apart, they'd lost all sensitivity to the other's bludgeoning and were now able to get along like mere acquaintances. He hoped that wasn't the reason.

He checked the time left on the microwave. "Twenty seconds to paradise."

"Aren't you going to answer me? What's changed?"

"Sorry. I was puzzling through that question myself. It could be that all the things that caused the rift don't seem to matter anymore. Or—"

"You mean like Misty?" Laney's fists rested on her hips, still too slim for much purchase there. "Was Misty one of those things?"

She's known all along. Their desperate contortions to hide the sordid incident from her—and he was certain Norma hadn't said anything, not to protect him, of course, but to protect their daughter—had been pointless. Then again, maybe Laney was just guessing. "Why do you ask that? About Misty, I mean."

Laney threw a bag of paper napkins across the room at him, and he caught it. "Don't treat me like I'm stupid," she said. "I'm better off knowing what went on than imagining things. So just tell me. Why did Norma think you and Misty were having an affair? She's such a whack job sometimes."

Did she know, or was she fishing? Should he lie to her?

The timer dinged. Coigne opened the microwave. "We need to eat." He served up.

"Right. And you need to talk. You needed to talk a long time ago." Her flash of anger almost masked the pain in her eyes.

"Okay. You're right." Normally the aroma of lava-like mozzarella jabbed with chunks of citrus fruit brought on sustained, silent enjoyment. Now, Laney kept her eyes on him.

Try as he might, he couldn't look at her and talk, so he talked to his plate. "I won't try to diminish my guilt by saying it was a one-night stand and meant nothing at all, though that is the truth."

Silence.

"Wait. What?" Laney stared at him like he'd lost his mind. "What are you saying? You mean Norma was right?" She rocketed out of her seat so fast she upended her plate.

"Yes," he barely whispered.

"All this time, I thought Norma was paranoid, but it was true. How could you do this to me? You're married. You cheated on your wife! My mother. You cheated on *Norma!*"

She spat her words at him so fast there was no question of answering. The best he could offer was a willing target for her venom.

The distance between them, moments ago imperceptible, lengthened across continents with hypersonic speed. Laney was nowhere near finished pouring out her loathing. "I don't get it. You love Norma, don't you? I mean, you guys just got married.

If your commitment to her means nothing, what does it mean to me? How do you expect me ever to trust anyone? You're disgusting."

He'd thought he was doing the right thing, keeping his infidelity from her. *God Almighty.* "If I try to explain myself, it will just sound like excuses. I know there are none." He wanted that message to sink in. "How do I explain hurting the people who give my life meaning?"

"Spare me." Her eyes welled. She pressed a clean napkin against her eyes, then flung it down. "I hate you." She got up to leave and hurled herself at the door just as Norma opened it.

Norma grabbed Laney to keep her from tumbling backward. "What's happening? I heard yelling from the driveway. Coigne?"

He couldn't answer.

"Why didn't either one of you tell me Coigne was...fucking Misty? You both are sick." Laney's spittle hit Norma on the cheek.

Coigne couldn't bear to look at Norma. But he couldn't leave them to sort it out. If he did, he'd have to add cowardice to his growing list of flaws.

"I'm waiting for an answer, Norma. Does everyone in this town know what went on except me?" Laney's voice shook. "Owen knows, doesn't he? I feel like such an idiot for believing in you, believing you and Coigne were different than every other low life. There you go. You've done me a favor. You two make my birth parents look good."

A pretty low blow in light of her parents' abandonment of her in favor of their lives of drugs and crime. "Let's sit down at least," he said.

Norma took a seat at the table, a grim look on her face. She shook her head, and he could only imagine what she was thinking—*Once more, Coigne screws everything up, telling Laney about the affair without giving me a chance to be present.*

Norma reached for Laney's hand, but Laney recoiled and stuffed her hand in her armpit. "Listen, Laney, there are two things you need to know, and I'm going to tell them to you, and then I won't talk about this subject again. You can take the rest up with Coigne.

"First, if you thought either of us were anywhere near perfect or even goodish, you set yourself up. We've both got feet of clay and as pertains to Coigne's dealings with Misty Bubb, he's got feet of dung," she said, nodding in Coigne's direction.

"The second thing is, what Coigne did was not in any way a reflection of his feelings about you—or me. His character failed him disgracefully, and we have to suffer the consequences, but he's no better or worse than most other people."

"So why'd you kick him out?"

Fair question. Coigne waited for Norma's answer.

"And this really is the last thing I'll say." Norma picked up a piece of pizza, thought better of it, and let it drop. "It's a matter of what I can bear. I've got so much of my own insecurity and just plain sadness I could probably use a few rounds of electroconvulsive therapy. In other words, I can't afford the risk to myself of letting him come back. There. That's it. No more." She folded her arms across her chest.

She'd never spoken to Coigne of how much he'd hurt her. She'd only spoken of what a jackass he'd been. To hear her now, it almost sounded, not quite, but almost, like she still cared for him. Otherwise, how could it still hurt her so much? It must be a reflection on how pathetic his life had become or how he'd slipped into a world of fantasy to believe, at this awful moment, there could be hope for them.

The night ended the only way it could. Laney wailed on until she wore herself out. She left the DadPad, pushing away Norma's attempted hug, spewing wave upon wave of anatomical and scatological terms as she left.

Coigne and Norma agreed to wait until they had clearer heads to help Laney adjust to the big revelation. But Norma said there was something she needed to discuss that couldn't wait.

She resumed her seat at the table, brushing onto the floor bits of shredded mozzarella. "What are these, maggots?"

Coigne reached into the fridge for two beers and handed her one.

Norma put aside the beer. "This is no time for decompression. New subject. What did you say when Law asked you about the knife?"

"The knife?"

Norma hissed with disgust. "You remember, the one with the three little stars you're most surely suspected of dropping at the murder scene?"

"All right, all right. I'm not thinking clearly. Law never asked me about it, or not in so many words. The whole interview was strange." Coigne took a sip of his beer. "First, we talked about Finn and how I thought he was getting along, which seemed a weird topic in light of the police escort I'd had down to Law's office. Then he consulted me like a colleague, even shared confidential matters about the fire and death." He wiped some foam off his lip. "Said a knife was spotted at the crime scene. Might have been used to threaten someone. He expressed 'every confidence' its owner would identify him or herself. He didn't describe it, and I didn't ask him to. He moved on to other unrelated, inconsequential things. Did he ask you about it?"

Norma tapped her fingernails on the table. "It's interesting— his theory that the knife might have been used to threaten someone. I'm sure he never thought for a moment it was Misty's knife. She'd never keep a knife so big it'd make a bulge in her spandex. I'm serious. Besides, I essentially confirmed it was yours once he mentioned the three stars. He knew I'd seen it, I'm sure. To have lied would have made us both look worse."

Coigne stood up and stretched a moment. In the olden days, Norma would have reached over and played a few bars on his ribs.

Instead, she said, "We've got to figure out a plausible explanation for how your knife landed in Marion's living room. If it wasn't on you or Misty, it had to have been Finn who dropped it there."

"But how could he? I got there first. And when I went over by the shed and those gasoline cans, he was probably still doing CPR on Misty."

"But you're not sure."

"No, I'm not."

"Did you go inside the shed? He might have run inside at that point?"

"No, I never went in the shed."

They both were silent, staring at leftover pizza so hideous it looked like dried, bloody flesh, pepperoni, and pineapple.

"Did Sheriff Law happen to mention the postmortem?" Norma asked.

"No. Why? Are you wondering if Misty might have been stabbed?"

"It could have happened, but I didn't see blood on the knife. From that distance, I'm not sure I would have. I just don't know."

Coigne hoisted himself up. "Let's leave it for the night." He gave her a lopsided smile. "He hasn't arrested me yet."

23

"Are you Laney?" A young woman dressed in black with spiked hair, a FedEx envelope under her arm, and a smile that said S'up Bitch? leaned against the doorframe.

Laney was barely awake, though it was ten a.m. She still had on Owen's high school football jersey and her own red plaid pajama pants. "Are you maybe looking for Norma Bergen? I haven't seen her around, but I can call her office for you. Oh, wait, it's Saturday. She's on a run. She should be back soon."

"Norma runs? What the—? She wear her barn coat?"

"I guess you know Norma. Believe it or not, she has a sweatshirt for running."

"I should introduce myself. I'm Jess Harper. I work with your mom." Jess stuck out her hand, and they shook.

"Of course. Norma talks about you a lot."

"I just came from the office. Had some cleanup stuff to do, and FedEx dropped off a package. Thought Norma might be waiting for it."

"That's nice of you. Like I said, she'll be back soon. You want to come in?"

"For a minute. So this is the farm." She admired the entrance area, its walls made of logs and chinking. "Fantastic to have a fireplace in the front hall. It smells like someone's been burning logs made of real wood for a change."

Laney took Jess back to the kitchen and seated her in the breakfast nook. They'd found a booth at a diner going-out-of-business sale that slid right into the nook. The adjacent window gave a nice view of sloping woodland filled with daffodils. Laney felt shy in front of this cool person in her low-rise jeans and tight denim shirt that stopped above an eye-catching, emerald belly ring. "Are you a lawyer?"

"Hell, no. When I see what your mother and the other lawyer I work for have to put up with—some of their clients are total boobs—that's not for me."

Laney wasn't sure how to respond. "Can I get you some coffee or something? I was just going to heat up an oat bran muffin. I've got plenty."

"Whatever you got, I'm in."

Laney filled the coffee pot with water and fresh ground coffee, grabbed some butter and honey, and shoved a half dozen muffins into the oven.

Jess raised her voice over the microwave's hum. "Aside from seeing your photo on Norma's desk every day, I think I'd know you anywhere. Your mom talks about you a lot. She says things like she never can tell what's brightest—the sun, your smile, or your noggin."

"Oh, God. Do you retch?"

Jess shook her head. "Must be nice, having a mom that feels like that."

Laney looked at her suspiciously. "Did she put you up to this visit? Trying to make up for the other night?"

"What happened the other night?"

Laney considered saying more but decided against it. "Nothing." But she wished she had someone like Jess to talk to about the smash-up with Norma and Coigne. The young woman had a way of acting like nothing really bothered her, and she wouldn't judge. Laney served the muffins and sat down on the bench opposite Jess. Between chews and sips, they talked about their backgrounds, where they'd lived, and where they'd gone to school until a rattling at the back door cut them off.

"Hello? Anyone home?"

"Owen." Laney slid off the bench, jostled the table, and spilled some coffee. She met Owen at the door and whispered about her unexpected guest.

"I can come back," Owen whispered back.

"Hell, no," Jess called out. "Come around here and let me take a look."

Owen and Laney rounded the corner, both a little hesitant with a stranger so at home in the breakfast nook.

"Hey, Owen," Jess said, motioning him to join her.

"How'd you know my name?" he asked.

"Because Laney just called you that."

Laney laughed, then stopped when she saw Owen was blushing, but his embarrassment didn't last. In fact, he and Jess got along like old friends.

"You look familiar," Owen said after a prolonged, almost rude, going over. With Laney's encouragement, he'd helped himself to two muffins and now reached for the butter. "Were you ever a teacher around here or something?"

Jess and Owen went several rounds seeking possible connections when Laney said, "His last name is Spenser. Owen Spenser, son of Evelyn and Geoff Spenser."

Jess's eyes grew large. "Got it." She cocked her head to the side as if mulling over memories. "I babysat for you and Dell. My mom's a teacher, and she was always setting me up with gigs. Oh, God." She covered her mouth with her hand as if to put words back in her mouth. "I'm so sorry. I heard about Dell." No one said anything. Laney wanted to rescue Owen from the painful moment, but Jess took care of it. "It's been at least ten years since I took care of you two one summer. No wonder you turned out so well."

Owen laughed, and the tension disappeared. Laney was glad the two hit it off, sharing a past and everything, but she also felt jealous—of whom she wasn't sure. She didn't like the feeling and hoped it was some kind of byproduct of all she'd been through with her pathetic parents.

To block her own thoughts about the other night, she said, "I wish I knew where Norma is. On Saturdays, we usually all—I mean, we used to all hang—"

"Don't stress, Laney. I know about Norma and Coigne, the separation," Jess said. "Your mom doesn't talk about it, except she made this one big-ass proclamation back when we first met, like, you know: 'Coigne and I, we split, now shut the fuck up about it.' You know, subtly hinting I shouldn't pry."

Again, Laney laughed, only she didn't think it was so funny. Sure, Norma should guard her private life from the people at her office, but not from her own daughter. Laney was no outsider. At least she'd never felt like one before.

With only a few crumbs left, Jess pressed her finger against them and stuck her finger in her mouth. She gathered her dishes. "I better run. Just tell your mom I brought the FedEx." She opened her mouth to say something more but instead walked her dishes to the sink.

"Did you need something?" Owen asked.

"Aren't you nice, buddy boy? Hey, Laney, you want to trade boyfriends?"

The question was spoken in a lighthearted way, but Laney could've sworn she saw a shadow cross Jess's face.

"Please don't give her any ideas." Owen flung his arm around Laney's shoulder as they accompanied Jess to the front door, but when the moment came to say goodbye, Jess kept jabbering. Maybe she still hoped Norma would show up. Or maybe Laney was supposed to say something or do something, but she hadn't a clue what it was.

"Okay. Enough. Just let your mom know I stopped by and—oh, if you think of it, ask her to call me about this person she's looking for. There's something I need to tell her."

24

Finn had been reading up on shedding cows into a loading pen when his phone rang. He fumbled with it and took the call, but when his brain connected with the name on his screen, he wished he hadn't. His caller was freaking out.

"Keep it together, Owen. Whatever it is, we'll straighten it out. Look. I need to pick out a tractor at Farm Supply in Martinsburg. After that, I'm on my way to Winchester. I'll get back this evening. Then we can talk."

"It can't wait until this evening. We need to meet now. It has to do with something Laney told me about that fire and Misty. She'd been having dinner with her dad and mom, and then there was a big argument among the three of them, and she stormed out of there but overheard them say something that involves you and me."

Finn squeezed his phone to near-crushing point to avoid hurling it. "And you're sharing all this anxiety with Laney right now? No, don't say another word. Get your own ass down to Farm Supply, and we'll talk there. Now."

He should never have gotten back in touch with his family. Nothing but trouble. Does this damn phone do anything but ring? He threw his book down in frustration and answered the call. "I told you to meet me at Farm Supply—" Finn managed to hold back an expletive and listen. "Sorry, Ms. Bergen. I thought you were someone else."

"You may wish I were. I need to speak to you in person. Where are you?"

Bergen meant trouble. He knew it the moment she showed up at Marion Chatte's charred remains of a house. He'd heard about her reputation as a nosy bitch who hung out with Sheriff Law. All he needed now was for Bergen to hassle him.

"Speak up, Finn. I'm busy."

"I'm just headed out—some business that can't wait, but I'm happy to meet later this week. Catch some lunch, maybe? Of course, it all depends on not having a problem here. I tell you, this dairy farm business is a—"

"Spare me the hardships of a rich man's heir."

"Right. Ha. What I'm trying to say is I can't always be certain—"

Click.

Crazy broad. Couldn't have been that important. He made himself a sandwich and set out.

Finn parked his Denali on the corner of the paved lot farthest from the dealership entrance. No need to get his new baby rammed by a zero-turn.

He didn't have much experience with farm equipment, but he didn't want to get dicked around by a know-it-all salesman, either. Judging by the pasty face, jaunty gait, and bright orange cap of the man fast approaching, he'd be the salesman. Something about the way he beamed for no reason made him look like a simpleton. Finn relaxed a bit.

"Hey there! Mighty fine day, am I right, sir?" The man reached out his hand. He had a belly the size of a kettle drum and looked like he might burst with goodwill and candor. "Just call me Cecil."

Finn wasn't in the mood. He gave Cecil his best explanation of the various processes his new tractor would need to perform, as he didn't want to have to learn how to operate more than one machine. But even he knew he'd spent too much time explaining and not enough making sense. Cecil didn't seem to mind, though. The bumpkin used the time to worry the lunch meat lodged in his teeth with his tongue.

"Well, you got any tractor that can do all that?"

"Just follow me, sir. I know exactly what you need."

Finn hesitated. He didn't want to miss Owen. On the phone, his cousin sounded ready to blast into orbit and explode. On the other hand, he couldn't stand there watching Cecil pick his teeth forever. Owen would recognize the Denali and look for him inside.

They turned toward the showroom building. "As a matter of fact, I'll need to stop just a shake on the way to speak with a nice young man who's looking for a tractor too." He pushed open a massive door to the showroom, vast as an airplane hangar and split down the middle by mote-laden sunlight. On one side were tractor models, on the other were beige cubicles. Finn shrugged and fell in step behind Cecil.

The young man in the cubicle turned out to be Owen. Finn rolled his eyes and greeted him.

"Well, now. It seems I've brought two friends together. Good for me." Cecil sounded as though he'd just made a sale. He slapped Finn on the back and pointed toward one of the cubicles. "Now, sir, if you would just wait right—"

Poor fool. He thought he had two new customers instead of one. "We need to excuse ourselves for a moment, Cecil." Finn said.

"Oh. Of course, yes, sir. You come and find me..."

"Why the hell all the cloak and dagger? Why didn't you just tell Cecil you were waiting for me?"

"I wasn't sure you'd come. I don't know. But it doesn't matter. What I need to tell you is more important. It has to do with something Laney overheard when her parents were talking about the fire. Something about a knife."

"What knife? What are you talking about? Get over here."

Finn prodded Owen toward the back of the showroom, where a combine provided more privacy. "Now, tell me exactly what they said."

"I don't want what I'm telling you to come back and hurt Laney or her folks in any way. Are we agreed on that?"

"Why would I want to hurt them? Coigne's been helping me out. So what's it about? What knife?"

Owen searched his cousin's face. "All right. I've got your word?"

"Come on, Owen. We're not Boy Scouts. Spit it out, will ya?"

"Laney said Sheriff Law found a knife at Marion Chatte's house. Something about finding it in a place no one was supposed to be. But the description of the knife—it had three stars on it—sounded like the one you handed me to clip the tag off your shirt. We were walking the towpath? Did you have it on you at the fire?"

Finn needed to be careful how he answered. There might be pros and cons of admitting to having a knife that wound up at a crime scene, but he doubted it. "Where'd she say they found it?"

"Laney didn't say exactly. Maybe the living room? I can't remember. They think it's Coigne's knife, but it sounds exactly like—"

"Hold it, Owen. I don't even remember you clipping my shirt tag, much less what my knife looked like. I've got lots of pocketknives. Why are you so jacked up about this whole thing?"

"Because my fingerprints are on it. I had Laney describe Coigne's knife. Really expensive. Really heavy. The stars weren't some logo. The knife was customized—a star for each member of their new family. It was Norma's wedding present to Coigne. It sounds just like the one I cut that tag with, Finn."

"C'mon, Owen." He gave him a friendly shove. "You're out of your mind. If it's the same knife, which it isn't, it's going to have lots of prints on it, including mine. But the main thing is, to protect Coigne, you've got to shut up about the knife. You don't know any knife. You got it? You promise? Boy Scouts honor?"

Owen nodded and smiled sheepishly. "I guess I'm just being weird. Since Dell was murdered, everything seems, well, you know, suspicious."

Finn rubbed his cousin's head with his knuckles. "Let's go back and buy a tractor and give old Cecil a hard-on."

25

Norma owed Evelyn a call. She should have called her yesterday, but the "pizza party" with Laney and Coigne the night before had left her drained of energy and sense. Besides, she had reason enough to put off the call knowing it would draw her into something she'd already decided to stay out of—monitoring the activities of Laney and Owen to safeguard the latter from his cousin Finn's bad influence. She was also afraid that what she had to say would harm her relationship with Evelyn, her one good friend. If she were sure there was something more behind her concern than gut feeling, she wouldn't hesitate to make the call. But how could she be sure? She'd better call. Whenever she failed to act on a gut feeling, she almost always regretted it. In this case, such a regret could involve not just some trivial consequence but a dire one.

On the call, Evelyn wanted a bit of gossip about the arson-murder. "What is it about you, Norma? Involved in every murder this town has had."

"Yes, well, I'm glad there aren't that many."

"I won't be a hypocrite by mourning over a woman I despised," Evelyn said. "I've no doubt Misty brought her death on herself with one of her schemes."

Norma nodded. "Matter of time, surely, but since when did you get so cold? You're the one always telling me to have a heart."

"Misty played a dangerous game, seducing men to get at their money."

Norma struggled to remove her running shoe with her other foot and considered the heartbreak Misty had caused. She wasn't sure who'd had the worst of it. She'd lost her husband to a silly affair. But Evelyn was still grieving her daughter's death when Misty lied and told her she and Geoff Spenser had had an affair. One thing was certain—Norma wouldn't shed a tear over Misty's death.

"I've got to stop by the Marinoff Theater later on," Evelyn said. "I hope you've got tickets to the theater festival. The shows are fantastic this year. Well, they are every year, but this time—"

The Marinoff housed a 180-seat theater whose dramatic, copper-plated design attracted as much gazing and gaping as any other Appalachian wonder in the Eastern Panhandle. It shone like a beacon of culture in such a small eighteenth-century town. And to the surprise of many big-city visitors, the original plays performed there were outstanding.

"How you find time to promote your work with the arts and play in a bluegrass band and cultivate the most beautiful garden in the Mid-Atlantic, I don't know," Norma gushed, and she meant it.

"Meet me out front. There are tables and chairs, it's warm out today, and we can talk. I'll pick up the coffee."

Norma marveled at her friend's resilience. It was only a year ago she'd lost her daughter, and yet, if you didn't know Evelyn, you'd never guess she'd experienced anything other than the usual ups and downs of a sophisticated, wealthy woman approaching her sixties.

Her friend arrived in spotless white jeans, a soft blue and white blouse, huge sunglasses, and a beribboned straw hat. She completed her outfit with red sandals and a matching red canvas shoulder bag. Norma couldn't have put that outfit together with twenty pages of instructions.

"You look deeply perplexed," Evelyn said, handing Norma her coffee. "Cheers."

They gently knocked their take-out cups together. "Just curious what you wanted to talk to me about. I have something to tell you, too."

"All right. I'll get down to it. Geoff and I were talking, and we may have overreacted about Finn's influence over Owen. I hope you'll forget about our meeting the other night. You must have thought we were both crazy."

No, just Geoff. But, Norma had to admit, this was the last thing she expected to hear. "What allayed your concerns? Geoff was pretty excited the other night."

"I sensed something was bothering Owen yesterday and told Geoff I'd ask him whether it had anything to do with Finn." She stopped long enough to sip her coffee. "Geoff objected to any confrontation, but I told him it was time."

"Whoa, girl. When Geoff lays down the law, discussion time is usually over. Am I right?"

When Evelyn didn't respond, Norma worried she'd made her friend uncomfortable. So, what if Evelyn let her husband make all the rules and decisions? And after all, where had her own confrontational style landed her, nuptially speaking?

"Geoff can be authoritative, but these days, the *appearance* of wifely submission is rather more important to him than the fact of it."

"You go, Sistah. Your trip to Bermuda did you a world of good. But getting back to cases, how did Owen answer you? Was Finn causing him problems?"

Evelyn reached into her bag, took out a red-hot peppermint stick, and snapped it in two. "I asked him that direct question and prepared to be trounced. But he shocked me. Said he planned to stay away from him and didn't want to talk about it." She handed half a stick to Norma.

Norma pondered this new information as she sucked on the stick. Finn had landed in the middle of a crime scene. Did that have anything to do with Owen's sudden disaffection? Did Finn say something to him about it? "Have the two of them had any contact lately?" she asked. "Did he give you any hint of what caused the breach?"

Evelyn pulled a small plastic sandwich bag from her purse, placed her sticky wrapper inside it, and stuffed the bag into her purse. "Not that I could decipher. He also said something about Laney, but I wasn't able to get him to elaborate. Something about how she 'didn't get it' about Finn, and that seemed to bother him. But then he buttoned up. I wish I could tell you more."

"Now you've got me concerned." She remembered the zealous greeting Laney gave Finn the other evening at the sheriff's office. The moment had disturbed her. She couldn't have said why at the time, but she could now. If Owen was disenchanted with his older cousin, there must be a problem with him.

"I'm sorry. That's all I can tell you, Norma. But what did you want to tell me?"

She hated to cause Evelyn concern about her nephew, especially when her friend had just rid herself of it, at least as far as her son was concerned. How to proceed? Norma sought inspiration from the campus across the road. How discordant any talk of murder would sound against the masculine yelps and whistle blows from the soccer field of a striving university.

Norma took Evelyn through what she'd learned from Coigne. Coigne told her Hilda had asked Finn and Coigne to arrive at her place around ten-thirty. Hilda was going to show Finn her farm, and I guess they all knew, without saying it explicitly, that it would help Finn with his start-up if his next-door neighbor knew the same drill. That's why Coigne went along. But after setting the time, Hilda asked Coigne to come a half-hour early to go over some environmental protest they were planning with their local group. Coigne would have arrived on time had he not stopped when he saw the fire. But Finn was on the way to Hilda's way too early for a ten-thirty meeting, which is when he says he first spotted the fire. "So, I'm asking myself, why'd he arrive so early?"

Evelyn tilted her head one way and then the other, like a bird. "I agree it's a little odd, especially since Finn is always late to family events. But I can't think that this exceptional occurrence points in the direction of—"

"I hear you. It's nothing. I have no reason at all to think he was on the road early in order to kill Misty Bubb. Sounds ridiculous. There is one other thing, though. You'll still think I'm nuts, but here it is. I don't know how much of this made it to the press. You may have heard that Coigne pulled Misty out of the cottage and tried to resuscitate her, unsuccessfully. Then Finn moved her again, farther away from the cottage, and tried some more CPR; only Coigne said he wasn't good at it. I thought about that and how odd it was for Finn to move her, especially since Coigne told him not to because he'd be disturbing potential evidence without any cause to do so. Misty was dead—period. I asked Coigne to tell me what Finn was doing that looked so odd. He pressed very slowly with one hand on her heart, instead of two hands, steadily and rapidly. Why would he do that? I'd say if anything, it would have killed her if she hadn't already been dead."

A group of students burst through the glass doors of the theater entrance, grabbing and mussing one another's hair.

"What are you saying? You really think Finn had something to do with Misty's death? Based on what you've just told me? I've known Finn almost all his life, and he's a rascal, I'll grant you that. But murderer? No."

"I did say it was just a hunch, Evey."

"What you didn't say, and what the grapevine does say, is that Misty was alive when Finn picked her up, and she even had something to say—'Coigne.'"

And Norma thought she could guess where Evelyn heard that rumor—from the rascal himself.

26

Arriving at her office Monday afternoon, Norma wasn't sure what to think. Jess and The Fox were toasting one another with their coffee cups, and then Jess kissed his cheek. She called out to Norma, "And here I thought he was just an airtight puppy—I mean, an upright preppy!" Jess looked uncertain.

"I think you mean uptight preppy." Norma agreed he was uptight, but he was anything but a preppy, at least not in the traditional sense. He'd attended public schools and graduated from the local university before waltzing into GW Law on the strength of a 4.0-grade average, a phenomenal LSAT score, and two summers of impressive volunteer work for the public defender's office. And while he hadn't fought his way out of the Appalachian cliché played up in the news and bestsellers—abuse and neglect by his parents brought on by serial layoffs they cushioned with opioid addiction—he hadn't gotten much help from them either.

"Spit it out. What are you two celebrating?" She flung her bag on the floor and, spotting the near-empty champagne bottle by the wastebasket, poured herself the last of it.

Jess took a deep bow and looked toward The Fox. "You tell her, your highness."

"We won the Coughlin case." The Fox beamed bright as a searchlight.

"Goddam," she said. "That was a guaranteed loser. Even your gallant attempts to plea bargain were pointless. So, how many jurors you bribe?"

"Don't forget the judge," Jess said. Her eyes twinkled through all that Halloween zombie goop she wore.

After more ribbing, The Fox gave Norma a serious summary of his winning moves in the courtroom. His recitation was brief, though told in his halting, humble way. He left out the self-congratulatory tangents litigators were so ready to go off on. But The Fox deserved all the time to bore Norma he needed. His client was the type no jury would want to find innocent, even if they knew he was. Though Coughlin was easy on the eyes, he was a nasty man who'd wasted every chance providence had sent his way. And when he was charged with the armed robbery of the old antique shop in downtown Charles Town, owned by a bald gnome of a guy on the verge of retirement, even the clergy wanted to put him away. Yet, despite the fact all the evidence was stacked against him, and as off-putting as he was as a person, Coughlin had one ace in the hole: The Fox's belief in him. He'd given Coughlin what all the clever lads and lasses in the big firms wouldn't have. Norma was certain that's what had moved the jury.

Norma felt proud of The Fox and Jess. And she recognized the moment for what it was, a golden one, so rare in the last year or so. She'd like to savor it a while longer, but couldn't afford the time.

"Everyone, back to work. Jess—in my office. Bring *Gracie's Groceries* with you. Make it snappy."

Norma would have been more efficient working her case for Gracie's if Jess hadn't popped in every hour to see if she had a moment to talk. Norma knew what was on her mind—Kaleb Chatte, her missing lover. If she'd been the type, Norma would have felt guilty harboring knowledge of his whereabouts from both Jess and his mother, Marion. It had been four days since she'd found him in Ms. LaBomba's hidey-hole. Norma was also mindful of the fact Sheriff Law had asked her about him too. Well, she had been quite busy.

She argued back and forth with herself over whether she should give Kaleb up. She'd even dialed Marion's number a couple of times, breathed a deep sigh of relief when she couldn't reach her, and left her oblique messages. There was just something about Kaleb's air of desperation that had thus far kept her quiet. His belief his life was in danger was sincere, as best she could judge.

While celebrating The Fox's victory, Jess had had a reprieve from her Kaleb worries, but now her emotional weathervane pointed south. Even above the noise of phones, copiers, printers, and deliveries and a heavy door between them, Norma heard all the sounds of Jess's patience ebbing and her agitation mounting. If a file cabinet drawer slammed one more time, Norma would have to talk with her legitimately anxious assistant. And Jess delivered. Bang.

Jess rested her elbows on the arms of the chair opposite Norma, yet nothing about Jess suggested rest. Her spikes looked stiffened by electric current, which made her dark eyes look too large for her gamine face.

"To begin with, Jess, I can't tell you where I found Kaleb—"

"Holy crap. You found him?"

"—because there's the slightest chance, depending on how trustworthy Kaleb is, that his safety and that of his mother is at risk."

"I don't understand. I should be with him, not kept in the dark. Why didn't he at least get in touch before he went into hiding, that little fuck?"

Her assistant's face looked more troubled than angry, to the point of biting her fingernails. Norma wanted to relieve her concern somehow, but she had nothing but scrambled eggs to work with.

"He does seem to be leading a double life, kiddo. What I can tell you is that it didn't seem like he intended to mislead you, and he acted like he cared for you a great deal."

"Stop with the qualifiers, will you? You're talking like a lawyer, not a real human being, which makes me feel worse than if you said nothing at all." Jess started to say something else and then stopped, then started again and stopped.

"You won't know the answer unless you ask the question," Norma said.

"Damn it." Jess's lips compressed until they almost disappeared. "Can you tell me if that other life of his includes a wife and a kid or something?"

"No wife, no kids. Just a big fat problem of his own making. Editorially speaking, kiddo, your fiancé is, at best, immature."

"And a liar. I can see by the look on your face you can't believe a supercool woman like me would plight her troth to someone about whom she knows jack shit. Well, I can't explain it. I'd plight it again so long as..." Jess froze, then studied her fingernails.

"So long as what, Jess?" Norma asked softly.

She didn't answer, just shook her head, her spikes holding firm, and got up. She adjusted her pants legs, then moved around the room, picking up a paper clip here, a law journal there. She paused by the large window overlooking Washington Street. Finally, she sat back down. "I had the feeling his mother was against us getting married. He never said that specifically, just things like how she'd hate losing her 'little man.' He'd scoffed— you know, acted like he hated her calling him her *little man*, but I could tell he liked it. Something just the two of them shared. I worried he hated that she'd have to lose her little man too."

"At least you know that isn't the problem that keeps you apart." Or not the only problem. "You shouldn't assume he's even told her about the two of you."

This new hurt made its way to Jess's eyes, and the tears began to flow.

Norma loaded up her saddlebag with slip opinions, judicial rulings that were published prior to inclusion in a bound volume of decisions. She preferred to be able to fold, mangle, or shred her nighttime reading as opposed to reading it online. "Let's get the hell out of here and go find a bar."

27

This wasn't Norma's first cocktail at the Lincoln Casino and Racetrack, but this was the first she'd heard that Jess's uncle practically owned the place. As Jess put it, "My Uncle Bobby likes drinking, gambling, horses, and women. Here, he'd have them all. So, he bet some big shot out of his stock in the place. Now he's one of the owners."

Nine months back, when Norma started up her law practice, she'd had a hard time connecting with the best source of client referrals, other lawyers. Most often, male lawyers still managed the biggest clients. It was Coigne who suggested inviting other lawyers, male and female, to hang out with her once a quarter at the racetrack. Then, as now, she didn't know much about horse racing, and what she did know she'd learned from Dick Francis novels. But she suggested to a few folks at a bar meeting they join her at the racetrack, and the biggest winner could choose the charity they'd all donate their night's winnings to. The idea worked, and the referral spigot opened, a dribble at first and then a respectable flow.

Aside from the professional benefit, who wouldn't enjoy watching sleek, powerful thoroughbreds demon-driven toward a single line? But she'd also heard rumors about how certain horse owners treated their beautiful animals cruelly, pumping them with drugs and running them when they should have rested.

If morals couldn't persuade an owner to take good care of his golden goose, the high cost of maintenance should have. All that bothered her, and now that she knew about Jess's Uncle Bobby, she could try to do something about it. For now, she'd enjoy the strong drinks, tender steak, and free nibbles.

Norma and Jess sat side by side at the large glass window overlooking the track so they could watch the nighttime sprinters. They toasted one another and sat back. "Did you know I came by your house yesterday?" Jess said. "Did Laney tell you?"

Norma nodded. "You really made a hit with her. And with her boyfriend."

"Owen. Little Owen Spenser. What is he, six-three? I used to babysit him when he was less than half that size. Did she tell you that too?"

"I had no idea. She must have forgotten." She took a long sip of her stinger and set down her glass. The waiter had forgotten cocktail napkins, which annoyed her, and she wiped her hand on the tablecloth. "But what a coincidence, huh?"

Jess didn't answer. She looked lost in thought. What could you expect from someone whose devious boyfriend led a double life?

Increasing her volume, she said, "Now that you mention it, Laney did say you had something to tell me, but she didn't say what." She waited for Jess to respond, but again she didn't get her attention. "Hey!" she shouted.

Diners at the nearby tables looked their way.

"Sorry, Norma. Now I've completely forgotten whatever it was I was going to tell you," Jess said. "Isn't that crazy?"

Norma gave her young assistant a closer look. Something was on her mind. More about Kaleb? "No, Jess. I don't think it's crazy. I think it's a lie. Now spit it out."

The server brought a small dish of fried almonds to the table, which delayed Jess's response, but Norma wasn't willing to give her a chance to make up something. When the waiter cranked up his spiel on specials, Norma said, "Will you please just get us some napkins and leave us alone?"

Jess smiled. "This is what I like about you. You say things people want to say but know better than to say, including you. But you're right. I'm being mysterious. Let me ask you a question first. Has Laney ever mentioned anything strange about the goings-on at the Spenser house?"

Norma stirred her drink with her finger. No napkin, no stirrer either. "It's hard to answer that question. It would be strange if there were nothing strange going on in a home where the daughter was murdered eighteen months ago. So sure, there's plenty that's strange. But before you go any further"—she pointed her finger at Jess—"you need to know Evelyn Spenser is my

friend. If she bathes in a tub of ketchup or cuts her husband's underwear into paper dolls, I'm fine with that."

Jess took a sip, then pushed the glass aside. "I'm not saying this to gossip. I mean, what do I care? But your daughter has a— thing going with Owen so—"

"So?"

Jess pulled nervously on the cuffs of her black leather jacket like she was training them to reach her wrists. "Let me just say there's nothing so grotesque as a family man hitting on the babysitter. Seriously disgusting."

Norma had no idea how to respond. Geoff Spenser, a molester? But he'd even resisted the charms of Misty the Irresistible.

Jess tossed her head back and chuckled like all this was no big deal, but how could it not be?

The horses were lined up at the starting gate, but neither woman seemed interested.

"The worst part of it was it started out as the best summer of my life. I'd been a counselor for a month at this really neat camp near Deep Creek Lake. I'd never been anywhere so beautiful in my life. Then I was going to spend all of August sitting for the Spenser family and get paid a shitload of money for watching just two kids. It was going to pay for a semester at Blue Ridge. You know, the community college. And before you ask me did I report anything, I didn't."

"You tell your parents?"

Again with the fake laugh. "No. They had their own problems. Drugs."

Norma hadn't expected anything like this from Jess. She was so practical and competent. Not like someone who'd grown up on her own and had to deal with a groping older man. "When you say disgusting, what are we talking about here? Let's have it."

Jess looked toward the track, and Norma expected she was gathering her thoughts before laying out the whole story. Instead, she'd recovered interest in the race.

"I don't really want to get into it. I just thought you should know. If Laney hasn't had any problems, that's good. He probably knows better than to fuck with *your* daughter and his own son's girlfriend."

Norma listened to the chink of glassware in the background. She was surprised by how ordinary and even cheerful it sounded, despite the horror story she'd just heard. She could push Jess for details, like time and place and the extent of sexual activity, but dinner overlooking a racetrack might not be the best setting for her to relive a traumatic experience.

"I just thought you should know," Jess repeated. "Let's order."

28

Coigne leaned over the ground beef in the meats and poultry case at Food Lion. He had only a short list of items to purchase—coffee, milk, eggs, ground beef, and bread—but would stretch out his time selecting the meat in order to cool himself down from the humidity he endured on the short walk from the parking lot. Not even summer and the thermometer had hit ninety degrees. He hoped Norma wouldn't give him trouble about using their outdoor grill on the deck for some burgers. She wasn't a petty person, but relations had returned to their most strained level ever since the night of his big confession to Laney—what was it?—four days ago.

When he realized what he must look like, hanging over the meat case in his sweat-stained T-shirt, he righted himself, grabbed a 93% fat-free pound of beef, and headed to the coffee aisle.

It was nearly three p.m., and the store was surprisingly full. Still, a small boy pushing a grocery cart managed to get up enough speed to ram Coigne in the back of his legs.

"Holy shhhh!" It hurt like hell, and he wanted to yell at the kid, but something about him struck a chord.

The boy stood stricken, his eyes pooling with tears.

A haggard woman rushed over. "I'm so sorry. I should have watched him more closely." She bent over the boy and hugged him. "It's all right, sweetie. Say you're sorry."

The boy remained silent. Coigne could almost feel the pain of a sharp knife in his own throat, the pain he'd get as a kid when overcome with shame and fear.

"Don't worry," Coigne said. "It was an accident, right, buddy?" He tousled the boy's hair and hobbled toward the Folgers.

He wondered when or if Laney would ever speak to him again. Every time he started to travel down the road of self-pity, and it was often, along the lines of, "I've been through all of this with Norma, and now it's Laney's turn—oh, woe is me!" he snapped to attention, brushed the thoughts away as unworthy, and shifted into a more productive frame of mind. It was during just such a shift upward that he recognized a familiar face, one that usually meant security and friendship, but at this moment, the man's no-nonsense expression prompted uncertainty.

Chief Deputy Baker headed down the aisle, staring straight ahead. Another deputy Coigne didn't recognize followed. The second deputy looked apprehensive. The vibe told Coigne he wasn't going to like what Baker had to say. He could have projected a more imposing figure in response to their approach had he not been leading with a grocery cart. Baker held up a finger, and Coigne instinctively moved his cart to the right as the two men closed in.

"Hey there, Mr. Coigne." He cleared his throat. "William Coigne, you are under arrest for the murder of Melissa A. Bubb, also known as Misty Bubb. You have the right to remain silent. Anything you say can and will be used against you in a court of..."

What the hell was going on? Coigne looked around. Was this a gag? People started to congregate and mumble. Still in a fog, he felt a strain in his back as the second deputy cuffed him.

"You can leave the grocery cart right where it is. The manager will return the goods to the shelves for you."

All his state trooper training and experience failed to train Coigne for what it's like to be on the receiving end of an arrest. What the hell were they talking about? He'd tried to save Misty

Bubb. God Almighty. Was that just five days ago? His chest heaved. He tried to breathe normally but couldn't. His body was on fire. *Don't faint, for God's sake.* He knew better than to make a fuss and draw even more attention to himself. Breathe in—and out. Breathe in—and out. He got control of his breathing. *Probably just more questions, like the other night.* But he'd sure have words with Sheriff Law for this humiliating public arrest when Coigne would have been happy to stop by his office. Then he remembered what Chief Deputy Baker had just said.

He was under arrest for murder.

With Chief Deputy Baker on one side and the second deputy on the other, they moved awkwardly down the aisle and through the self-check-out area, causing more heads to swivel. Once they arrived outside and into the heat, Coigne's temper got the better of him. "Just what is this, Deputy?"

Chief Deputy Baker said nothing, just nodded in the direction of his Explorer. Coigne held his breath through the indignity of having to fold himself into the vehicle in reverse.

Coigne heard nothing over the static of the police radio, or was it the blood pounding at his temple? He might be going mad. How was he being arrested when he'd spent almost all his adult life bringing criminals to justice? Did the prosecutor think he had a case? On the basis of what evidence? Any forensics they found would show everything had happened just as he'd told them.

He tried to focus on the future. Once he got out of this mess, he'd be gracious in forgiving Sheriff Law for making such an absurd mistake, one that might cost the man his next election. Then he imagined Norma's face when he reached her. Could he bring any more shame on her than he already had? And Laney. He had to straighten out the error before the women in his life ever found out about it.

29

Coigne was processed and "detained" pending his arraignment by the magistrate. Assuming he was to be held for trial and the charge was murder one, the likelihood he'd be released on bail any time soon was slim to none. That much he knew.

Coigne sat at a table waiting for Chief Deputy Baker to return. He was "in the box." He knew if he couldn't get matters cleared up before he was brought up for arraignment, he'd wind up at the Eastern Regional Jail in Martinsburg, a place he'd never want to go even if only for a brief time, especially not as a retired member of law enforcement.

He knew all about these procedures, having been through similar ones in Massachusetts many times. Only this time, he wasn't the one hauling in the suspect. His humiliation didn't stem from the vision of Norma and Laney when they learned he'd been arrested for murder. It was from the certainty his father would learn of his arrest.

Coigne had spent his entire life distancing himself from that soulless killer, someone who hadn't a capful of empathy for another living being and for whom the only higher authority was money...lucre...*coin*, in fact. The last time they'd met, in a jail outside Boston when Coigne, Sr., awaited his own murder trial, he'd taunted Coigne. "Don't kid yourself, you self-righteous sonuvabitch. Cruelty's in your blood too. Hey, maybe one day we'll have adjoining cells. That suit you?"

There was a difference, of course. Coigne was innocent, and his father, emphatically, was not. The age, sex, or race of his father's victims or even their close personal relationship never mattered one whit to him. He was an equal rights killer—no one was off limits.

All this concern over his father was not to say it wouldn't crush him to have to explain his situation to Norma and Laney. Misty had been determined to break up his family. Now, with her death, she'd struck again.

Chief Deputy Baker sat down opposite him while his side-kick deputy got the recording equipment running and then hung back in a corner. Coigne knew he should insist on having counsel present, but he was certain he'd be able to clear up whatever mistaken notion led them to arrest him. He'd be home before Norma or Laney found out.

"Tell us about your knife," Baker began. "How did it find its way to the living room if, in your signed statement, you say you only entered the cottage to remove Misty Bubb from the *kitchen* and then reentered the house to look for anyone else caught inside the fire but did not enter the living room?"

Coigne continued to deny he'd gone into the living room but recognized he'd have been better off if he'd just lied and said he'd forgotten he also searched in there. But it wasn't the truth, and he knew he'd get tripped up on the lie at some later point.

The questioning only got worse. When he'd visited Sheriff Law the week before, he'd given him his written statement and his schedule of activities throughout the morning of Misty's death. He had no alibi because he'd been out in the field by himself.

"Even if you'd had one," Baker said, "Ms. Bubb hadn't been dead long at all when you pulled her from the fire. And that assumes Finn Spenser was lying about Misty still being alive when he tried to resuscitate her. So you knocked her out, started the fire so the cause of death was asphyxiation, then acted like you were trying to resuscitate her when Finn Spenser showed up, all in a matter of minutes. And no coroner's time of death would be precise to the minute unless somebody broke their watch during the killing. It's almost always a best guess."

Coigne hadn't seen the charge sheet yet, so he didn't know if they had something more to pin on him. Then he remembered Finn's assertion that Misty was still alive when he grabbed her, and he heard her final word on this earth, "Coigne." Even if all that was true and she was still alive, Misty could have said his name for many innocent reasons. But she hadn't been alive. He was sure of that.

"Let's move on," Baker said. "You had an intimate relationship with the deceased. Tell us about that."

What was Coigne to tell him—that it was a one-minute mistake that had destroyed everything he'd ever held dear, not the least of which were his integrity and his family? That he'd been tormented by guilt because of it? That he'd been clueless as to why he'd done it and still was even now? And that it was the worst sex he'd ever had? And Jesus-God, did the whole world know about the deed? Because if they did, they'd know it ended as soon as it began, almost a year ago. "There's nothing to say. It ended as soon as it started."

"But your phone and text records show us Ms. Bubb tried to reach you many times since you say the sexual relationship ended."

"Then they also show I almost never took her calls or answered her texts unless I was pleading with her to stop calling."

"Well, Mr. Coigne, I can see exactly how it was, and I pity you. Sounds like she's the kind of gal who could apply enough pressure to make any man crazy enough to—"

"That's not what I said, and you know it."

"So why do you think she wanted to meet with you that morning?"

"I was to meet with Finn Spenser and Hilda Fingerhut. I have no information on Misty Bubb's intentions whatsoever. You're asking me questions I don't have answers to. And I also doubt the phone records said that."

That would have been a good time for Coigne's counsel to jump up and say, "My client has been harassed enough, you don't have probable cause for his arrest, and next, you'll be hearing from Mr. Coigne and me in the form of a civil complaint against the whole lot of you for false arrest, false imprisonment, defamation, and anything else we can think of." But his one phone call had been to Norma, and he'd only reached her voicemail.

"You're kinda saying you never took the call, Mr. Coigne, yet we know you listened to her voicemail. It'd only take two or three seconds to hear what she wanted."

Shit. Could Chief Deputy Baker really know he listened to the voicemail, or was he bluffing? Yes, he'd listened to it for a second, but as soon as he'd heard Misty's voice, he'd deleted the message. At least, he thought he had. He'd been baffled she was again trying to make contact with him, and he'd never heard the message say anything about meeting up with her.

Coigne kept his hands and body still. He wanted to give no indication he was nervous. But inside, he felt like that boy in the grocery store who'd rammed him in the legs.

Chief Deputy Baker turned to his subordinate, who responded with a nod. They'd obviously performed this act before because after the nod, the subordinate left the room, and Baker informed the recorder he'd left.

"Now then, Mr. Coigne, you didn't recognize Misty's voice. Just between you and me, I know if I'd kept company with a lady, I'd recognize—"

"Well, I didn't." Coigne slammed his fist on the table. "And if I had, I would have repeated what I told her months ago, which was, 'Don't call me. It was all a terrible mistake.'"

"Would you care for some water, Mr. Coigne? I've just sent my deputy for some."

"No...thank you."

"Well, now. We've got this call that you say you deleted. We've got the deceased asking to meet you—"

"Not me. She must have intended to meet with someone else."

"So, you did know she wanted a meeting, just not with you?"

Coigne jumped out of his seat. "I knew no such thing." *Shit. Stay calm.*

Without a sudden move or a raised voice, Chief Deputy Baker stood too. "Have a seat, Mr. Coigne. I don't want to have to cuff you. I'm out of shape, and you're younger than I am. Those folks watching us behind the mirror will see me make a fool of myself." He turned and waved at the mirror.

Coigne sat down, and Chief Deputy Baker moved on again. "No reason to get excited, but we can't overlook the fact she went to the same place you did, and there she was killed. Who else would have shown up there other than someone she called? Right?"

"There are a dozen answers to your question, Chief Deputy Baker. But I won't suggest them and possibly get some innocent person in trouble. Do your own legwork."

Chief Deputy Baker shook his head as though considering Coigne's point. "I suppose you're right, my friend. But I want you to understand something. Here, we know all about Misty Bubb and the kinds of things she's been up to. She was trouble. We don't go hard on a man protecting himself and his family against such a person, especially someone who's one of us." He pointed to his badge.

"Then you're a disgrace to that badge."

The deputy re-entered with a pitcher of water and some plastic cups. Chief Deputy Baker recorded his reentry and flipped through the file in front of him.

Coigne tried to regain his composure and think through the answers he'd given. Baker had said no alibi could help Coigne because Misty hadn't been dead long at all when both men arrived and tried to resuscitate her. Baker was just blowing smoke. Sure, it would have taken just a few seconds to knock her out, but a lot longer to find gas cans and light a fire and wait around until she was asphyxiated. If he could time that interval and find someone who'd seen him up until he did, in fact, arrive, he'd be better off. But where does a guy who runs a horse farm spend every minute of every day? Is he at meetings with other people, flying on airplanes with other passengers, or inspecting the factory floor with his manager, all good opportunities to be seen by others? No. The only ones who could give him an alibi were the horses who'd watched him repair a fence. He couldn't remember if he'd used a chainsaw or some other tool that made a lot of noise, but if he had, someone driving by might have heard and seen him from the road. But he had to give Baker some reason to go look for that someone. He was sure they'd finished their neighborhood canvassing on the day of the fire.

Out loud he said, "What could possibly be my motive for harming Misty? She caused her damage a long time ago. Norma and I separated last summer. In fact, Norma and I have been closer lately than we've been for a long time. So where's the threat? Where's my motive?"

Elbows on the table, Chief Deputy Baker rubbed his hands together like he was just getting to the good part. "I wondered about that too, but that's it. You say you and the Mrs. were getting along together so well, better than you had been for so long. Now, like I said, we all know Misty. And two people in a marriage getting along better than they have in a long time may just as well paint a target on their own foreheads, as far as Misty was concerned. She'd never let that situation stand, and she didn't, did she?"

Coigne shook his head in frustration. He sat back and tried to see the big picture. He'd given Chief Deputy Baker motive and opportunity. But as Baker himself had said, there were plenty of people who had motive to bump off someone like Misty. The knife? Finding the knife in the living room only meant, worst-case scenario, Coigne had dashed through parts of the cottage he'd forgotten about. In any case, he hadn't seen his knife for weeks, and he hadn't been in that living room ever. Obviously, they had evidence she was with her killer in the living room, but what evidence other than his knife, he didn't know.

As for Misty supposedly saying his name when she was at death's door, the explanation he'd given Chief Deputy Baker made perfect sense—he'd just tried to resuscitate her. Of course, she'd say his name. And as for the phone call, he had no idea what she wanted. As for means, everyone in the county has gas cans for their tractors, and anyone could have grabbed gas cans out of that shed. They must have more than this on him, but he couldn't imagine what. All he knew was that he'd been a fool not to wait for counsel. Of all people who should have known to keep his yap shut, it was he.

30

On the way home from the casino and racetrack, Norma obsessed over the blow-up with Laney the other night. Why did Coigne jump the gun and blab about the Misty affair without Norma there to advise? Then there was Jess, who revealed that horror story about Geoff Spenser, Norma's best friend's husband. How could Norma help Jess if she didn't want to talk about the molestation? Her young assistant said she'd rather just forget about it. Well, she obviously hadn't forgotten about it, as she'd brought it up after more than a decade. And then poor Evelyn.

With her focus on these distractions, Norma drove far too fast up a short, steep hill. Her stomach flip-flopped as her car flew several feet in the air, just as a deer leaped in front of her airborne headlights. She whipped the steering wheel to the right, then back to the left, and barely missed its hind legs. As soon as she found a clearing, she pulled over and rested her head against the steering wheel and tried to slow the pounding of her heart.

What else could possibly happen? Norma finally pulled into her driveway.

And as for Coigne—always back to him. He'd broken her heart, but she may as well admit it, if only to herself—she probably still loved him. How simple life would be if they could just pick up where they'd left off. A bit of selective amnesia would serve her well. But such a fantasy was short-lived. She plucked her phone out of the center console and checked for messages. She was reluctant to return a call from a number she didn't recognize, but it could be from a client. In this case, a voicemail had been left. "What the hell is it now?" She listened to the call.

"Norma. I-I'm so sorry to tell you this."

She looked at the phone. "Coigne?"

"There's no way to brace you for it. I've been arrested for Misty's murder."

It was Coigne's voice, but she couldn't process the words.

"Oh, Coigne. Tell me you didn't."

Norma couldn't speak with Coigne the night of his arrest, but the next day, with The Fox's help, she was able to finally reach him by phone at the Eastern Regional Jail in Martinsburg.

"I was wrong. I thought, you know, the charge is so absurd," Coigne said. "I thought I could explain things then and there, and that would be the end of it. I spoke to Chief Deputy Baker without counsel, and I shouldn't have."

"Don't say another word. These phone calls are taped. I've asked The Fox to represent you until you find someone of your own choosing. I'll be there soon."

"I am truly sorry."

"Didn't I just say don't say another word?"

Norma sat across from her husband. They were "alone" in a room set aside for the accused and counsel, with an officer just outside the door. Norma had noticed the door was stained with splotches of blood, but nothing appalled her more than the stench of human waste. She'd heard about conditions at the facility, but the description paled in comparison to the reality. The room was empty but for a battered wooden table and two black aluminum folding chairs. A round ceiling light, the only light in the room, cast a jaundiced hue over their faces. Coigne gave her an idea of his conversation with Chief Deputy Baker.

"You call that a conversation? I call it a confession." She spoke softly, but her frustration was trumped only by her anger. "Don't sugarcoat. This is not the time to fudge how much you messed up, Coigne. Tell me exactly what else you said."

Norma wanted to console him, but she needed him to toughen up. For that reason, he'd only get her lawyer-to-client look. For the time being, there was no other relationship between them. The same went for her. She could only see Coigne as a defendant, one whose future was at stake and who'd screwed up royally.

"The Fox will explain all this later today when he's finished with his hearing, but you've got to understand—you'll get no discovery on what they have against you, nothing more than what's on your charging sheet, before your preliminary hearing, which is when they'll decide if there's probable cause to hold you over for trial. Then the prosecutor goes before the grand jury, which won't be called for months. You have no chance for bail until after the prelim, and you probably won't get it then. Now, tell me what you said to Chief Deputy Baker."

Coigne told her about the phone call from Misty the morning she died and Chief Deputy Baker's assertion he had the message and she'd asked to meet. "I knew she'd called and left a message, but I didn't even listen once I recognized her voice. I had no idea of any meeting. I swear it. And he may have been lying about a message anyway."

"What else?"

He told her about the knife's location, Misty's saying his name to Finn, and the whole mess about the "affair" the year before.

Norma didn't look up. "That's it? They must have more than that. Other than the phone call, they had all the rest of it when the body was discovered."

"That's the best I can remember."

She scribbled on her legal pad for a long time.

Coigne's knee shook beneath the table, and his fingers tapped along the top. "I need you to represent me, Norma. There's no one else I trust as much. I know you stop at nothing."

She glared at him.

"You know what I mean. You'll stop at nothing within the law."

She put her pen down. "Mine is a civil law practice, and I'm not trained to handle a murder case. I've never handled one. And stop fidgeting. You look nervous, and that looks guilty to everyone, including me." She continued writing.

"I was thinking I could take a polygraph test."

"Not admissible in a criminal case."

"I know it's not admissible in court. But you can give it to the prosecuting attorney, and maybe he'll drop the charges. I've seen that happen if the case is weak in other respects."

"I know the law, Coigne. But polygraphs aren't admissible for a reason. They aren't reliable."

"So you do believe me—you just worry I may not produce accurate test results?"

"It doesn't matter whether or not I believe you for these purposes. And the fact the test results aren't admissible is beside the point. They could be discoverable, and if they're no good for whatever reason, we can't take that chance. But The Fox will have to advise you on that. You know, despite his annoying and unsuccessful grabs for more office turf and support staff time, if The Fox believes in you, he's the lawyer for you." She stood and slid her legal pad into her saddlebag, never looking his way. She didn't want him to see her fear. She got ready to go.

"What will you tell Laney? She'll never want to see me again," Coigne said.

Norma stood at the door and knocked for the officer to let her out, then looked back over her shoulder at Coigne. "You underestimate your women—both your daughter and me, your co-counsel."

31

Norma contacted Laney after classes ended for the day. She wanted Laney home from school when she told her Coigne had been arrested, which assumed she hadn't already learned of it. The fact that she and her daughter were barely on speaking terms since "pizza night" would make their conversation so much harder.

If Laney didn't already know something big was going on, she certainly did once Norma led her out to the porch, their serious-talk zone, and sat down with her on the wide wicker rocker—the double-wide, as Norma called it. She gave Laney the news with a realistic view of what the next few months might hold and left unstated what could follow. She assured her she'd do all in her power to help Coigne, as would her colleagues Drew Fox and Jess Harper.

"How can you say you'll do all in your power when you're trying to divorce him? And by the way, why don't they arrest you? You were the injured party, right? You're the one who'd want revenge against Misty. Oh, God, how messed up this is. I can't stand it."

Norma answered her questions without reacting defensively. She explained that her own alibi had been confirmed by the sheriff's investigator. She'd been working at her office with Jess and The Fox at the time of the murder. And she acknowledged being an injured party, one among many, and it was among those many that the real killer would be found.

Norma held Laney while she sobbed and protested the injustice of Coigne's arrest and what a nightmare state they'd moved to, and if Norma had been a better wife, none of this would have happened. Laney vented for some time but eventually calmed down to ask more questions. Norma explained the prosecuting attorney would try to rush to trial, limiting the time the defense had to prepare its case. That meant Norma would be extremely busy over the next few weeks and months helping to get ready for the many proceedings they'd put Coigne through. "But The Fox will make sure you and Coigne will be able to talk on the phone pretty much anytime while he's at Eastern Regional Jail."

"Phone calls? Why can't he come home?" she wailed. "You've got to get him out on bail. We'll sell the farm if we have to."

Norma pulled Laney's damp hair back from her face and blew softly on her cheeks and forehead. "It's rare in a murder case that the Circuit Court judge grants bail. And we've got to face the fact that being retired law enforcement hurts Coigne's chances for bail more than it helps."

"Why?"

"Well, for one thing, he's knowledgeable about how law enforcement tracks down people who skip bail. For another, courts may be hard on someone who's supposed to engender society's trust. He's not supposed to be one of the bad guys."

Like many others, Laney was having a tough time understanding the justice system. "I wish—"

"You wish what? Anything, girl. You wish what?"

"I wish I hadn't been so mean to Coigne the other night."

Norma wrapped her arms around her and rocked their chair. "Bah. If you knew how many times I've said that very thing. Everyone knows I'm the Queen of Mean."

Laney grunted in agreement and squirmed out of Norma's arms.

"Besides, Laney, you had every right to be upset. And Coigne knows you love him, even if sometimes you get angry." Norma faced her. "But there's no time for wallowing in shame over things we can't change. We've got work to do, and you can help."

"I will. Of course."

"Good. I've made a short list." Norma pulled a folded piece of yellow legal pad paper from her coat pocket.

"Can I call Owen first?"

"Anything." Norma smiled. "I'll explain the list when you're finished."

Laney made it halfway up the stairs before Norma heard her turn around and slowly head back down to the porch.

"You know what you said about how Misty harmed a lot of people, and it's among them we'll find the killer? Well, I just remembered something Owen said. I don't even think it's so much what he said but just how it worried him that makes me think of it now."

"Good girl. Tell me."

Laney's forehead crumpled with worry. "I don't want Owen to get into trouble."

"Before I'd ever tell anyone about whatever you have to say, we'll evaluate whether it could hurt him. Let's hear it."

Laney leaned against the door frame, her legs locked in tree pose. She told Norma how disturbed Owen had been lately about Finn, someone he'd always looked up to and enjoyed hanging with. Owen said he saw his cousin differently now.

"Did Owen say he saw Finn differently now, or Finn acted differently now?"

"I don't remember. Does that matter?"

"Everything matters, kiddo. But go on with your story. What was different?"

"Like Finn didn't always tell the truth, or he'd hide things for reasons Owen couldn't understand." She gave the example of how Finn acted now like he barely knew Misty when Owen remembered from several years ago, Finn talked all the time about some big business deal he and Misty had going. "But you have to promise you won't tell the police about this. I don't want Owen—"

"I've been worried about Finn for a while, and nothing I learn allays my concern. Owen needs distance from his cousin, much as he might look up to him. And that goes for you, too."

"You think I'm stupid?"

"I think you're young, and your heart is wide open."

32

The Fox had just left the office to talk further with his newest incarcerated client. Their first meeting, the day before, had gone well. Coigne was smart enough to recognize The Fox, though just thirty-two, was plenty smart himself, and while he'd attended a "big city" law school, he was still a local boy, and that went over well in the county. Coigne relied on Norma's judgment to tell him whether The Fox's knowledge of West Virginia criminal law and procedure was top flight and whether he'd be surefooted in the courtroom. But The Fox had to do some of his own vetting and Norma had waited anxiously the day before on his assessment of Coigne as a client.

The Fox told her, "If I were to represent him, it would be tough enough, murder one. It'd also be tough leading a team with someone senior to me—you, that is—in a subordinate position who's as vested, knowledgeable, and, shall we say, assertive as you are."

"I promise—no micromanaging. I'm all those things you just said, but I'm also not an idiot."

"And finally, I understand from you that Mr. Coigne intends to plead not guilty. I don't need to believe one way or the other about his innocence, but I will do a better job if I have some facts that support that position, obviously." He snapped his briefcase closed. "Anyway, I'm off, and I'll bring you up to speed when you're free."

Norma surmised that if Coigne and The Fox ever ganged up on her, she just might not prevail. Was that a good or bad thing? At least she felt more hopeful now that they'd met than she had since Coigne's arrest.

Her best contribution to Coigne's defense would be to find out who the real killer was, and for that purpose, she'd need to round up some suspects: anyone who had a motive to kill Misty. The list would be long. Misty had burned many a hole through the hearts of Jefferson County. But what Laney had said about how Finn and Misty might have had a business together opened up a new front for exploration.

She also wanted to pay Sheriff Law another visit but hesitated. It was true they had history. She'd helped him find Dell Spenser's killers and save several lives in the process. Still, part of her felt betrayed, like he'd played her for a fool when they last met in his office because he must have known he was on the verge of arresting Coigne, yet he let her babble on, drawing her out, as she tried to convince him Coigne and Misty never had an affair. She'd think about it some more and talk it over with The Fox. For now, she'd take on the Finn angle, but not directly.

Norma drove alongside the Opequon on her way to the Fingerhuts. To get there, she had to pass what remained of the Chatte cottage. It was just a week ago the property had been overrun with emergency vehicles and the charred detritus of a household. That morning it looked much the same as it did a week ago. The local papers echoed her assumption that the cause of the fire was arson and the accelerant was gasoline from the cans she'd spotted near the shed.

She owed Marion Chatte a call. In fact, it was long overdue. In light of how worried Marion was about her son, it surprised her that Marion hadn't reached out to her again after their last call. In the Fingerhut driveway, she gave her a call but had no luck.

The Fingerhut farmhouse looked like a farmhouse should. Built in the late 1800s, it was white clapboard with red shutters in a Victorian style, complete with a wraparound porch with gingerbread trim. An enormous copper beech tree, perhaps the same age as the farmhouse, provided heavenly shade with its dense foliage as its elephantine roots destroyed the front walkway, a tidy illustration of the give and take of nature. The old bank barn, which allowed access on two different levels due to being built into a hill, was still used for a small part of their dairy operation, but the Fingerhuts had built a more modern structure farther from the house, just the kind of thing that excited Coigne. He'd see it again. She'd make sure of it.

Clad in her uniform of boots, baggy jeans, and a washed-out, cotton plaid top, Hilda Fingerhut invited Norma to have a seat with Jerry in their front parlor. "I know it's brag-talking and old-fashioned to say parlor, but that's what my daddy called it, and there wasn't a time he wasn't right." She removed a Burpee catalog from the camelback sofa and had Norma sit down. "I'll be right back with the coffee pot, and I hope you like peanut brittle."

Norma nodded in favor of the refreshments and removed her fishing hat. Hilda's kindness made her wish the visit were purely social.

"That's right," Jerry said, facing her from a wooden rocker stationed by the fireplace. Though no fire had burned there for some time, Norma caught a lingering whiff of smoke. "You're not at the office now. Make yourself at home."

They spoke of Coigne's arrest, and Norma tried to stay calm.

Soon, Hilda bustled in with a tray holding a large tin of brittle covered in wax paper, coffee mugs, cream, sugar, napkins, and toothpicks. Hilda served Norma, then Jerry. There was something about the curve of her back and her expression of concern that let Norma know how sorry she felt about Coigne's arrest.

Hilda confirmed it. "Saw it in the paper. And Skeeter Fox, Drew Fox's daddy, told us about it. He and Jerr hunt. We're so sorry, but we're sure Sheriff Law will get it straightened out because there's no one as kind as Mr. Coigne. Besides, Misty Bubb got what was coming to her."

Norma couldn't help but smile. "In a way, that's just why I'm here, Hilda. You've lived in Jefferson County a long time. You two know the folks around here, and that means you probably know a lot about Misty Bubb and her dealings. In particular, I'm wondering if you ever heard of a business deal between Misty and Finn."

"The main thing we know about her dealings is they were shady dealings. Right, Jerr?"

The brittle was delicious, but Norma had to take a moment to work a toothpick through her teeth while Jerry answered.

"Shady's right," he said. "I'm sorry, Norma. It sounds familiar, some deal between them, but my mind's grown hazy—it's as bad as my eyesight. I can't see worth a damn, pardon me, Hilda, and I can't remember back farther than a week ago."

"And speaking of Finn," Hilda said, "His mood wasn't too good last time we saw him. You see, he'd been pushed around or roughed up or something."

"Roughed up? Go on," Norma said.

Hilda turned to Jerry. "Shall I tell the story?"

He nodded.

"It starts before we found him on the floor, barely able to walk." She took Norma through the drive up to Finn's house, the way they were almost run off the road by an expensive sports car "driving like the devil was blowing hell's fire up his butt—Sorry, Jerr—So when we asked Finn about it, he told us his uncle had paid him a visit, that Spenser fella. Never smiles or says hello in town."

"Did Finn say what caused the fight?"

Jerr scratched his head. "I'm sorry. He didn't tell us anything solid. Did you make any sense out of how Finn kept telling us Mr. Spenser was a clumsy old fool, Hilly?"

"Sure, I did. Finn didn't want to tell us what happened, so he acted like it was an accident, but I could tell that wasn't the truth."

"Do you think his uncle's visit frightened him?"

"I don't think it was likely, Ms. Bergen. Not with his wife there with him. Finn said she was there too, didn't she?"

"He did, and he might have been scared, but he was also sore and angry, is the way I'd put it."

For a moment, Norma's attention was caught by a wren perched on the picket fence just beyond the Fingerhuts' parlor window. She wished she could just drift off and enjoy the moment. It would be a long time before such wishes would come true. But the physical altercation between Geoff and his nephew surprised her, especially since Evelyn hadn't mentioned a thing about it at the Marinoff Theater when she told her their son had made up his own mind to steer clear of Cousin Finn. Of course, maybe it hadn't happened yet.

"Do you remember which day he told you about the fight?"

"Of course we do. It was last Friday. Now, you want to know how I can be so sure? Sheriff Law had his deputy come out here and ask me when we last saw Finn. They asked me on account of I told him when they questioned me about the fire and Misty and all I was helping Finn with his dairy farm. So, I told him we'd seen Finn on our way to do grocery shopping, which is always Friday," Hilda said.

Norma did some counting of days too and determined she'd met up with Evelyn the Saturday after Finn had his altercation with Geoff Spenser. It was more than odd Evelyn didn't think to mention it. The mystery remained, why would Geoff Spenser have cause to beat up Finn?

When she'd eaten as much brittle as she could handle, Norma thanked her hosts for the wonderful treat and their time. But once she put a foot down on the front porch, something made her turn back. "If you don't mind my asking, what brought you to Finn's house that day?"

"We don't mind you asking, Ms. Bergen, but I don't think I remember." He turned to his wife with an embarrassed smile. "You, hon?"

Hilda explained they wanted to see how he was getting along since he didn't come to her farm as planned because of the fire.

"Of course. I'll leave you two to enjoy your afternoon."

Hilda washed up the dishes and got ready to return to the field as Jerry nodded off in his rocker. Dadburnit! Now she remembered the other reason they'd gone to visit Finn that day. She wanted to let him know if he was looking for his knife, she'd seen it at the fire. He must have dropped it. She knew it was his because they'd used it to cut through that old, frayed rope holding the fence together that day. That was the day they all visited his house, and that harlot Misty was there. She wanted to tell him he should ask Sheriff Law for it back. It looked expensive.

33

While washing up after dinner, Laney and Norma declared a truce on all outstanding issues "pending resolution of the Coigne crisis," as Norma put it. But she'd be willing to update Laney on what was happening with his case, something Laney desperately needed to keep her sane.

"I'd hoped to get information from the Fingerhuts," Norma said, "about any business dealings between Misty and Finn. I wasn't successful, but boy, Hilda's dislike—no, I have to call it hatred—of Misty is intense."

"Maybe she had something to do with her murder," Laney blurted. "The Fingerhuts live right there, and Hilda was on the scene."

"Right. Only we'd need evidence. The only evidence we have right now is bad evidence." Norma said nothing more. She busied herself putting dishes away.

"What's going on, Norma? Is there something new you're not telling me?"

"Sure. Plenty." She walked over and gripped Laney's shoulders. "Right now, I need us to visit Owen. This item was on the list I handed you the other night when Coigne was arrested—Assist as needed. Can you let him know we're coming? I promise—no third degree."

"Norma, no. I should never have told you what he shared in confidence about Finn and Misty."

Norma assured her she wouldn't go near that topic, but since Owen seemed to be the only person around who was close to Finn, she needed to explore what he knew about Finn. "Owen may not even understand the importance of what he knows. And may I remind you, you're the one who said you'd do anything to help Coigne. This is 'anything.'"

Owen had asked Laney over for lunch and a swim the next day anyway, but she wanted to warn him Norma would be coming. Norma asked her not to. "We can't give him a chance not to talk with me."

"At least tell me what you're going to say."

"No. I don't want your anticipation, anxiety, or anything else to clue him in to what to say or even color what he says."

Laney gazed at the looming Spenser home while Norma gathered her bag and locked up the Prius. She appreciated the fact that, unlike the big developers whose standard fortresses ate away at the county's forests and farmland, Owen's parents had preserved hundreds of acres of "unimproved land" behind their estate. As for the garish villa itself, which Owen called the Gar-illa, it was Mrs. Spenser's concession to her husband in return for his agreement to build their home in Jefferson County, where her people were from.

Owen had asked her over as soon as she told him about Coigne's arrest, but she'd stayed home a few days in case she was needed. He'd been so moody lately anyway, but even he'd agree she was the one with the bigger crisis now. As Laney mounted the final front step, she turned around and said, "You coming, Norma? All that huffing and puffing, they can hear you a mile away. You really are in horrible shape."

Laney wasn't usually so mean, but the last thing she wanted was her mother accompanying her to her boyfriend's house. She'd almost rather have stayed in school and faced the fallout from Coigne's arrest, but Norma worked it out with the principal so she could take some time off "until things settled down."

As Norma finally reached the top step of the Spensers' home, Laney said, "This visit of yours better be vitally important to Coigne's case."

"You think I'm going to enjoy horning in on your date?"

Owen greeted them in his old red jersey, dripping wet jungle design bathing suit, a towel around his neck, and blue Crocs on his feet. The aroma of grilled burgers Laney had whiffed when they first arrived assailed her senses now.

"Oh, hey, Ms. Bergen. My mom's not here. Hi, Laney. Where's your suit?"

Laney rolled her eyes. "Hi."

"Hi, Owen. May we come in?" Norma said, walking past him. "It's you, not your mother, I'd like to talk to, if that's all right?"

"Oh. Well, sure." He gestured for Laney to follow Norma out back to the pool.

"Sorry, Owen. I told you how she is," Laney said. "But it's for Coigne."

He shrugged. "You're good."

The Spensers always opened their pool early in the season. Owen once told her he suspected it was a ploy to attract his friends to his house where his parents could keep an eye on all of them. "Fuck. I'm old enough to die for my country," he'd said.

Not long after, Owen produced two plates with burgers topped with barbeque sauce, cheese, and pickles, and chips on the side. "I'll throw on a couple more burgers," he said. "You two start with these."

Owen grilled burgers to perfection—pink, no blood. They sat under an orange and red striped awning licking sauce off their fingers and drinking sweetened iced tea. Laney wondered nervously when *Dragnet* would begin. The TV show by that name was one of Coigne's favorites. Her eyes teared up, and she blinked rapidly.

Norma sat opposite Owen, so she'd pretty much make eye contact with him throughout the meal. Laney knew her subtle-pressure tricks. So far, she'd made Owen laugh hard by telling him stories about how his mother outfoxed some bossy, loud-mouthed board member on the Foundation she and Norma had established in honor of Owen's sister.

"I never knew this side of my mom. She's usually so, you know, stiff," he said.

"I'd say she's refined, but listen." Norma leaned across the table. "Your mom's versatile when the situation requires it. For example, you don't want to be on the receiving end when she's 'disappointed' with you."

"Trust me—been there." Owen wagged his head.

Laney'd observed Norma work people over before. She'd establish rapport, then elevate gradually to bosom buddies, at which point she could usually get someone to do or say anything.

"Goddam, that barbeque sauce you put on the burger was the best, Owen." Norma wiped her face and hands on a napkin.

"Must be good since you're taking some home on your shirt," Laney said.

Norma never even looked down. "Seriously, you guys, I appreciate your letting me join you this afternoon. I had some tough news about Coigne's case this morning—"

"What? I asked you before what was going on," Laney said.

"And I said 'plenty.' Now, just listen."

Just listen, she says. Laney gripped the side of the table. Norma could be so deceptive. Even now, Norma took Owen's hands, kept her eyes trained on his, and snapped the trap shut.

"Maybe we can get it figured out with your help, Owen," Norma said. "I'm turning to you simply because you know Finn better than anyone else around, so far as I know. You may be completely ignorant about the subject I'm about to discuss, but then again, if anyone could help, it would be someone close to Finn."

Owen pushed his plate aside. "Wouldn't Finn be the best one to talk to? I mean, it'd be more direct, right?"

Norma nodded. "Of course, you're right. And I'm no great judge of character, as Laney will no doubt confirm"—she glanced at Laney—"but my hunch is that you're more likely to be truthful in answering my questions than your cousin. Do you think I'm right about that?"

Owen shrugged, then nodded.

"You see, Coigne's knife was found in a place he swears he never was—Marion Chatte's living room. But there are so many innocent explanations for it having gotten there that I keep asking myself, why the big deal? And here's our problem." Norma explained to Owen how little information they had on why Coigne was arrested for murder. "All they needed to provide during his arraignment was enough evidence to establish probable cause to hold him while they dig around, find some more evidence, and pressure him to confess, save the state some money, or take him to trial. Probable cause is nowhere near as tough to establish as 'beyond a reasonable doubt,' the standard you always hear about in the trial portion of a criminal case. But, the point is, there's something they've got on Coigne that makes them sure he's guilty, even beyond what they needed to show probable cause. And I just know it has to do with that knife, combined with the other paper-thin bits of evidence they have."

Laney couldn't catch Owen's expression but felt his body tense next to hers. "So, Norma, how are you so sure the big thing they've got on Coigne has to do with the knife?"

Norma kept her eyes locked on Owen's. "Because every other piece of evidence they have is already about as bad as it can get: he can't deny he was there very close to the time she was killed, and there's no way, absent a clock breaking at the exact time she died, the prosecutor can be any more exact about it. And Coigne can't deny they had a relationship—"

Laney's face burned. Why did Norma have to bring that up? Surely, Owen already knew about it. But why confirm it? Give it a rest.

"And he can't deny she'd harassed him with phone calls, including one that very morning. Phone records are fact. So, my hunch is they have something more in their back pocket, and that's usually going to be forensics. Why? Because Coigne would already know what else they've got, but he wouldn't know about their forensic evidence against him. Anything incriminating Coigne would tell us about, so we could work on it until it wasn't a problem. We'd explain it away."

Owen finally spoke up only it didn't sound like him. This stranger's voice was reedy and hesitant. "Forensics—you mean like fingerprints and DNA and stuff?"

"That's right," Norma said. "Derived from the word *forum*, as in a court of law."

"Right. So why do you think the forensics have anything to do with the knife?" he asked.

Laney had this one. "Because Coigne's knife, just lying there on the floor of her living room, doesn't prove anything except he was probably in there. Do we even know if Misty was in the living room?"

"No, we don't," Norma said.

Owen nodded. He had paled, and his Adam's apple zipped up and down. If he was holding onto something, this would be the time for Norma to grab it.

"You see, Coigne wasn't the only one there at about the time she died. Finn was there, for example. Since he's your cousin, and I understand you guys might have hung around together since he came back to town, I have to ask if anything occurs to you now that might explain how that knife got to where the investigator found it, in a place Coigne says he wasn't."

The pool waves lapped against the sides of the pool even though no one was swimming. The gentle rhythm provided a strange accompaniment to the despair overtaking Owen's face. "I'm pretty sure Finn had Coigne's knife on him a day or so before the—before the fire," he said. "Finn had me use it to cut a tag out of the new shirt he was wearing."

"How did you know it was Coigne's? Had you seen Coigne use it?" Norma's voice was gentle. She lightly touched his clenched fist with her two fingers.

Owen glanced at Laney. "I hadn't seen it before, but Laney described it to me—the stars and everything."

They sat in silence until Norma spoke again. "This is very helpful, Owen. Is there anything else you can tell us?"

He shook his head.

"Did you ask your cousin about the knife," she asked.

Owen took his time before answering. "He said he had a lot of knives and didn't know where the one I described came from." He looked at Norma and then Laney. "I'm really sorry I didn't say something before. But, I mean, it's possible Finn was telling the truth, right?"

Laney and Norma headed home.

"Poor Owen," Laney said. "I hated to leave him like that."

"Stop worrying about him." Norma flicked her blinker. "Owen looked relieved to get it off his conscience. Unlike some people, Owen's the kind of guy who suffers when he's sitting on a bad secret."

"It was good the way you assured him his fingerprints on the knife wouldn't get him into trouble, but were you telling the truth? And why are you humming?"

"Am I humming? I guess I'm glad we may finally have something to buttress Coigne's defense. If we could just learn more about a prior relationship between Misty and Finn." Norma honked her horn several times at the vehicle passing her in a no-pass zone. "But, yes, I told the truth. Counting Finn, Coigne, and Owen, and probably me, there are at least four sets of fingerprints on that knife. And I don't know what kind of fingerprint smudging occurs when you shove a knife in your pocket. I don't think it's fingerprint evidence the prosecutor might rely on, though."

"What, then?"

"Evidence of Misty's blood, maybe? She was probably knocked unconscious before the fire was lit. Maybe that happened in the living room, and maybe that's when the knife fell out of Finn's pocket. That'd make sense. This is all guesswork, though. Please keep that in mind. We could be in for a disappointment."

"It sounds good, Norma. And..." Laney wondered if she dared compliment Norma when she was still so mad at her about other things.

"And?"

"I was going to say you're usually right—about this kind of thing. And thanks for helping Coigne. And Owen."

34

Norma was on a roll. She stopped by her office barely long enough to sling her saddlebag on her desk and phone Jess and The Fox and ask them to come to her office. She then briefed them on Owen's revelation about Coigne's knife, and The Fox agreed she should float the information by Sheriff Law.

"Normally, we might sow doubt as to who possessed the knife at the time of Misty's death in a more strategic way," The Fox said. "For example, there might be reasons not to show our hand until we have even more evidence to help make sense of it all. But, in this case, our priority is on getting Coigne out of Eastern Regional Jail fast. It also makes sense for you to talk to Law rather than let me approach the new prosecutor about it in light of Law's seeming willingness to barter with you for information. This new guy is still an unknown, but what is known isn't good. He gives up nothing."

"So you heard he's got chronic constipation?" Jess said.

"That'd explain it." Norma smiled devilishly. "Who'd you hear that from?"

"Who'd know better? His paralegal," The Fox said.

Norma stayed on good terms with so-called invisible people, people who did the hard, mind-numbing jobs, like housekeepers and lawn guys—people whom some regarded as unimportant—that is, until they left their jobs to go elsewhere. Sheila, Sheriff

Law's receptionist, might be considered by some as invisible and unimportant, but not by Norma. Sheila was smart, but she was also fun, with that kind of guffaw that makes people break into laughter with her even if they don't know what's so funny. Most important of all, at least when you're defending your husband against murder charges, Sheila could find the sheriff whenever she needed to, even early on a Friday morning. It turns out the sheriff had taken a few hours off. He was down at the town landing trying to catch fish.

"Now, you be careful, Ms. Bergen. Fishing time is sacred time for Sheriff Law. Says it's his only alone, quiet time."

"Then I'll make sure we're alone and quiet."

Norma got the belly laugh she'd hoped for.

The town landing was one of the best-kept secrets in Shepherdstown. It was, in terms of temperature, the only cool, outdoor location in the whole town between June 1 and September 30 because of the natural shade of its thick woods. To reach it, one rolled down a steep hill several blocks off the main drag, a hill so steep it felt like a chute. The town run, a waterway sourced from six natural springs that burbled and zigzagged its way through Shepherdstown, flowed alongside the hill and then gushed and thundered down the rock-tiered drop into the Potomac.

One can launch one's boat from the town landing or just stand along the bank to fish. On this occasion, Norma saw no one on the river or the riverbank. She passed picnic tables and giant, fallen oaks along the path heading east only to find Sheriff Bud Law, as still as a rock himself, in deep contemplation.

Until he turned her way and removed his fishing cap, she hadn't been absolutely sure she'd found the right man since, out of uniform and context, he could have been any old, balding fisherman. But the sprouts from his head, his broad smile, and the considerable stuffing beneath his fishing vest assured her she was disturbing the right man.

"Get any bites?" she whispered loudly.

Law's shoulders sagged in defeat. "I have a feeling I'm about to." Despite his answer, his tone was jovial, but within seconds his shoulders sagged. "I imagine you're here about Mr. Coigne. I'm sorry as can be. What can I do for you?" He reeled in his line and pointed toward a nearby picnic table. "I know you have a lot of questions, and I wish I could answer them."

They took seats on opposite sides of the table. The slimy green dampness of the benches didn't bother her. She inhaled the leafy, nutty atmosphere with deeply felt wistfulness. Sheriff Law reached over to his tackle box, pulled it closer, and began to organize, making eye contact from time to time.

"It's not so much what answers you can give me as I have a thorough accounting from Coigne. It's what I can tell you, Sheriff, which should convince you you've got the wrong man locked up."

He nodded curtly and crossed his arms. "Fire away."

"Finn Spenser arrived at the Chatte cottage a good half-hour prior to his scheduled visit at the Fingerhuts. No one has explained that, at least not that I know of. Ditto, no explanation for his jiu-jitsu moves on Misty's dead body."

No one spoke for a moment.

"That it?" he asked.

"That ain't it." Norma spent the next few minutes telling Owen's story about Finn's possession of Coigne's knife. "Now, why he had it and when he obtained it are unknowns," she acknowledged.

"And, I expect, when or whether he gave it back to Coigne before the murder is also unknown? Assuming it was Coigne's knife in the first place, of course."

"Fair enough. But you'll get answers now that you know the right questions to ask." She watched his face for signs of agreement. "You can't deny this new information shoots a big hole in the state's case."

179

"I suppose you've got a motive for Finn Spenser?"

"Sure. We're talking about Misty Bubb. The motive would involve sex and money. All you have to do is fill in some details."

Bud Law removed his cap, smoothed down his hair, and put it back on. "I appreciate the intel, Ms. Bergen. We'll look into it, of course."

"Can you at least admit this 'intel' is a lit stick of dynamite?"

A father with a fishing rod and his young son with his own passed by on the path and delayed Law's answer. It was further delayed when Sheriff's breast pocket buzzed and throbbed, and he got up. Courteous as ever, he lifted one finger to indicate he'd be a minute and turned away.

She was so lost in listing her next steps to prove Finn was Misty's killer she didn't notice how long Law's call was taking, nor that Law had wandered off a long distance from their table. When he disconnected and returned to the table, she did notice his face was tense, so unusual for Bud Law.

"I'm afraid I've got to go."

"But you haven't answered my question. Can you at least agree it's no more likely that Coigne killed Misty than that Finn did, and considerably less likely, wouldn't you say?"

"I'd say the chances Finn's our man have been drastically reduced. I'm afraid he's dead. Body just discovered. Now, if you'll excuse me, I've really got to go."

Sheriff Law hastily gathered his fishing gear and headed back down the path.

Norma followed him. "Too much of a coincidence to think Finn's death isn't related to Misty Bubb's. Whoever killed Misty killed Finn too. So doesn't that put Coigne in the clear? He's been locked up, for God's sake."

Sheriff Law stopped in his tracks and appeared to ponder something, which gave her time to catch up. He didn't look at her, just said, "It doesn't put him in the clear."

"What do you mean?"

Law kept moving.

"Sheriff Law?"

He still didn't answer, and she didn't need him to. Coigne was arrested four days ago, June fifth, for the murder of Misty five days before that, on May thirty-first. If he wasn't in the clear, Finn's death occurred on or before four days ago, even though it was just being discovered now. Norma thought back to her phone call with Finn when she asked to meet with him, and he blew her off. That call occurred on Saturday, June third—six days ago. So, Finn must have been killed at the earliest sometime between that call and Coigne's arrest, a two-day window. So, in Law's mind, Coigne could have murdered Finn before he was arrested.

The back of Norma's neck felt hot like it would break into large welts, a reaction that meant she was about to say something reckless. But this was not the time to offend Law. She slowed her pace. She needed to keep reminding herself this was just how it was going to be until they had proof of Coigne's innocence. Two steps forward, one step back, two steps, one step. But she'd been almost certain, what with the information about Finn and the knife, they'd be able to spring Coigne soon. Her disappointment was acute and almost made her forget The Fox's last words to her earlier that day on the subject of springing Coigne—something about the need to prioritize getting Coigne out of Eastern Regional Jail fast. Had he been stating the obvious, or had some specific need to get him out recently surfaced?

35

Evelyn knocked and peeked inside Owen's bedroom. There she found Laney on his bed with her knees drawn up and her elbows propped on them. Her fists supported her chin. She looked up and waved at Evelyn. Beside her, Owen had stretched out, his eyes fixed on the ceiling, which was covered in posters of lesser-known musicians and scenic nature shots. Her son hadn't budged since she checked on them an hour ago. They still had *Alexa* playing mournful, dissonant jazz.

Norma had delivered the incredible news about Finn by phone and had asked Evelyn to keep an eye on Laney, who was there visiting, while she attended to urgent matters concerning Coigne. She promised to pick Laney up as soon as she could. The police contacted Geoff about his nephew's death shortly after Norma's call, but Evelyn was glad to have an opportunity to talk to her friend. It confirmed no tension remained between them after their recent talk in front of the Marinoff Theater.

Evelyn now worried, as she looked around Owen's room, that he and Laney had had too much exposure to death over the course of their short lives. She worried they'd somehow hold themselves responsible for these unfathomable events, and she wanted to help them. Tending to her own feelings about Finn's death would simply have to wait.

"I was so wrong about him. How could I be so wrong?" Owen's words, spoken to no one in particular, could barely be heard above the soft music. Although his eyes looked bloodshot as if he'd been crying, Evelyn wouldn't embarrass him with a hug right then.

Those days of comforting with a cuddle or even a pat were long gone. But words were not the tool she'd need to help her son through this latest crisis either. There was no tool that could help. The best she could do was stand by and make sounds that let Owen know she was there with him always.

"I blamed him for Misty's death," he said, full of self-loathing.

Evelyn sought the right words. "Finn was not an easy person to understand, and though his death is so painful, it doesn't change the fact he had faults. In time, we'll have to accept he's gone."

"How can we accept it when we don't really know anything? It's so fucking crazy."

So like his dad. His mood could ignite into rage. She let the language violation slide. Hardly the time.

"I just want to forget about it all. Can you leave us alone, Mom? Just—you know, sorry."

Throughout the flare-up, Laney had said nothing. Evelyn told Norma she'd keep an eye on her daughter, and she would. "You okay, Laney?"

"I'm just sad. Even though I've known a lot of people who've died, I still don't get how a person you know can be so alive one minute and then not the next."

Evelyn took a chance and sat next to Laney and hugged her. "It's not easy for me to understand either." She stayed awhile longer, just in case—just in case she could help. Then, "You two take your time. I'll go see about some food."

"Forget it, Mom. I can't eat."

But it was all she could think to do. Food and warmth, all the things you'd do for a baby resisting sleep. And how Owen had resisted. Most mothers would have checked into a sanatorium to escape those crying jags of her colicky baby. If she could only rock him now, the way she used to. Sometimes it would take hours, but it never failed, at long last, to provide the tranquility her baby needed. Not to mention, rocking soothed her too.

Downstairs, she defrosted the chicken broth she'd made a month before, back when she thought she'd already experienced all the bad things life could afford. How innocent she'd been to think that nothing more could go wrong.

Geoff was sorting out his feelings about Finn's death with his blowfish, or so she imagined. She could hear him on the phone now, talking to the funeral home about his nephew's cremation. Was that what Finn would have wanted? Even if he'd been a mature forty-year-old, would he have thought that far ahead? Would his body even be released anytime soon? Geoff must have had some notion of the answer before making the call. She was used to his knowing things she did not.

"Mrs. Spenser?"

"Laney!" Evelyn spun around, startled out of her ruminations. The microwave dinged to make the point. "Call me Evelyn, hon." She smiled and removed the broth from the microwave, but she was so tired the small effort almost drained her completely.

"I wanted to ask you a question, but I don't want to upset you or anything. I just—"

"Let me have it, sweetheart." Evelyn wiped her hands on a dishtowel and pulled the girl toward her. "I may not have an answer, but I think we're all better off having some conversation about what's happened."

"Do we know how Finn died? I mean, there's all this stuff on the internet, but we didn't know what to believe. Even the network news isn't saying anything concrete. Did Norma give you specifics? Like, do they have someone in custody? Where he was when he was killed?"

Norma had told Evelyn on the phone more than she was willing to say now, but she needed to say something. "They don't have anyone in custody yet. Norma says he died by drowning in the Opequon."

"You mean near Marion Chatte's house?"

"Somewhere close to that, I think."

Disengaging completely, Laney scrutinized Evelyn's face. "Does this mean his death has something to do with Misty Bubb's death?"

"It's too soon to tell or to tell *us*, anyway. When Dell died, it took a while for the police to tell us her body had been moved from the place she was killed to the place where Norma found her and a lot longer to tell us exactly how she died. We'll hear some details about Finn's death in a day or two, I expect. Were you fond of him?" Evelyn hoped the answer was yes. So far as she knew, Finn had no close friends. She had cared for him, but even she wouldn't have wanted someone so spoiled, undisciplined, and unreliable as a close friend.

"Well, I—he was very cool. You know, he could be charming. He—"

"It's okay, Laney. We can all admit he had his faults."

Evelyn returned to her cooking. She added more seasonings to the broth as Laney took a seat at the breakfast bar and watched. She seemed entranced by Evelyn's stirring. The slow, steady process would give the girl a point of focus, allowing her troubled mind to settle for a brief time.

Geoff Spenser swung open the kitchen door and broke the brief tranquility. "Oh. It's Laney. Where's Owen? I need him a minute."

"I'll get him, Mr. Spenser," Laney said.

"Let him know we've got chicken noodle soup and sandwiches coming, and he's got to eat or else," Evelyn said.

Laney nodded and left.

"Laney's wondering whether Finn's murder is related to Misty Bubb's. I have to say I'm wondering the same thing," Evelyn said.

"How would I know? I don't have an *in* with law enforcement."

"Of course not." Evelyn removed the loaf of pumpernickel she'd purchased from the bakery the day before and began her sandwich preparations, poking through the refrigerator for dark mustard, deli roast beef, and some cheeses, then hoisting the heavy cutting board onto the counter. "It seems too much of a coincidence that he's tied to the time and place of Misty's murder, and now here he is, dead. Two murders in ten days? It's not like Shepherdstown is the crime capital of the Mid-Atlantic," she said, her usual serene expression now a puzzled frown.

"Of course, this isn't a crime capital." Geoff bumped into his wife as he crossed the kitchen to fill a glass with water. "And don't be ridiculous, Evelyn." He drank the whole glass and set it on the counter. "There's absolutely no reason to think they're related except that this is a small town, and everything is related to everything else."

Geoff had essentially agreed with her point. She'd keep that observation to herself, but she was less certain how to deal with the fact he'd also called her ridiculous. There'd been times in the recent past, as her friend Norma had pointed out, when she'd defied her husband's authority. She wondered if now was another moment when Geoff deserved some defiance and decided it was.

"Geoff, did you, by any chance, kill Finn and Misty?"

36

Norma arrived mid-afternoon to pick up Laney just as everyone sat down for soup and sandwiches, and she joined them. That is, everyone sat down except Owen, who stayed in his room. Norma had nothing new to tell them about Finn's death, but since they were Finn's family, they'd probably receive updated information before she did.

On the drive home, Norma filled Laney in on her conversation with Sheriff Law down at the town run and how he'd assured her he'd take into account the likelihood Finn had Coigne's knife at the time of Misty's murder. She didn't mention that Coigne could be charged, if there was evidence to support it, with Finn's murder as well as Misty's. Everything in its own time.

Now at home, she encouraged Laney to take a long, warm soak and come down for a movie and some brownies Evelyn had given them to take home. She told Laney she'd only be able to watch with her for a while, and then she'd have to get back to work. That news didn't go over well, nor should it have. What she couldn't tell Laney was she'd first head to see Coigne before heading to her office. Norma was probably being absurd, but she had a bad feeling something wasn't right. Of course, plenty wasn't right, but even putting aside the new complication of Finn's death, she was worried about Coigne's physical safety. All day she'd tried to catch The Fox and ask him whether he'd had something specific on his mind when he said the priority had to be on getting Coigne out of Eastern Regional Jail fast. But he'd been locked in talks all day, and still was, with the prosecutor's office on Coigne's case as well as that of other clients. She'd have to see how Laney fared after her bath and make a final decision about leaving her alone.

"Another reason it really sucks that you're going out," Laney said as if their previous conversation hadn't been interrupted, "is that I wanted to ask you about something." She cinched the belt of her terry cloth bathrobe with Rod Stewart's face plastered on the back and adjusted her towel turban. "I wasn't going to say anything, but I convinced myself in the bathtub I'd better."

"Whoa, kiddo. If you need to talk, let's talk." Norma unwrapped the plate of brownies and poured two glasses of milk. As they sat down in the breakfast nook, she prepared to use those listening skills Jess was always on her about.

"It has to do with Owen's dad," Laney began. "It's kind of awful, though."

Norma spilled milk all over the table as she reached across to grab Laney's hands. "What did he do to you? Did he try to touch you? Don't be afraid to tell me, Laney. I'll yank his dick off."

"God, Norma. What's the matter with you? Are you out of your mind?" Laney ran for paper towels and mopped up. "Of course, he didn't touch me. Not like that. What gave you that idea?" Laney stopped a moment. "You look like someone punched you in the gut. Are you okay?"

Norma had been so wound up in Coigne's case she'd forgotten to speak with Laney about Jess's experience with Geoff Spenser. Norma told her right then.

"That is disgusting. And I don't believe any of it. At least, I don't think I do," Laney said.

By now, they'd finished their snack, and Norma needed a change of venue. They headed to the double-wide on the porch.

"You're right to question it, Laney. Whatever happened, it was a long time ago, and Jess was young. Memory can be faulty. I only wish she'd felt like reporting it at the time when it could have been investigated properly. But true or not, we'll need to talk about ways for you to stay safe. Like maybe you and Owen should come here from now on."

"I can't do that. What will Owen think?"

Norma didn't particularly care what Owen thought at that moment on that topic. But she knew this wasn't the time to go into it, especially since Laney had something else troubling her about Geoff. "What did you want to tell me? This time, I promise I'll keep quiet."

"It's probably nothing. It just sounded weird. And I wasn't eavesdropping on purpose, so don't go all condemnatory."

"Con—never mind. Keep going."

"I'd been in the kitchen with Mr. and Mrs. Spenser. Then I left to get Owen for Mr. Spenser. Right outside the kitchen door, I could feel the back of my earring fall off, and I was on the floor searching for it. I could hear Mr. and Mrs. Spenser talking. More like he was arguing with her about the coincidence of Misty and Finn's deaths being so close together, you know."

"Right. Go on."

"And so then Mrs. Spenser asked him if he'd killed them both."

"Well, did he?"

"He didn't answer. He just stormed through their swinging door, and there I was, on the floor. It was awkward and scary."

"Awkward and scary. That about sums up Geoff Spenser."

37

Norma stayed home that evening. She'd finally reached The Fox, and he assured her he'd meant nothing specific when he prioritized Coigne's release from Eastern Regional Jail over waiting until the preliminary hearing to present evidence about Coigne's knife. Norma hadn't been able to reach Coigne by phone all day, and again, The Fox reassured her he'd seen Coigne earlier and could vouch for his good health and spirits under the circumstances.

Laney was too restless for a movie, so Norma suggested she get dressed and they walk around the property. Neighbors were taking turns helping with the horses, along with Laney and Owen, but Norma thought it best to check around, too. The sun had now made its daily crossing from the back to the front of their farmhouse, and they sauntered down the long slope of the front yard to the rill that flowed across their property. Norma listened hard for the gear shifting of Coigne's truck, hoping that by the strength of her imagination, she'd hear it groan all the way up their long gravel driveway. Instead, she heard only the soft conversation of some cliquish horses who'd gathered by the boundary fence.

Along the way, Laney talked up Owen's revelation that Finn had kept Coigne's knife. If she hoped Norma would confirm that bit of evidence would buy Coigne's release from custody, she was disappointed. Norma wouldn't give her false hope but instead emphasized the need for more discoveries like it. She just hoped Chief Deputy Baker wouldn't come up with more unhelpful discoveries of his own.

The two of them turned toward the grumbling protest of Judd Spud's pickup as he mounted the driveway. Norma never minded his rooster's wake-up call each morning. She was a little surprised to see him that evening. Feed time was in the morning, every morning, like clockwork. She stopped. *Wait a minute. Judd might have seen Coigne the morning of Misty's murder.* But as suddenly as the thought occurred to her, disappointment followed. How likely was it that Law's officers had failed to question Judd? Or had they just questioned the neighbors where the murder occurred, a good twelve or thirteen miles over in Marion Chatte's neighborhood? Coigne had been so befuddled the day of the fire, and then when he was arrested, he might not have thought of Judd as a possible alibi witness. Besides, The Fox said the police were downplaying any alibi defense. Misty's death had occurred sometime between eight-thirty, when she was last seen pulling out of her driveway, and 9:45 when Coigne reported the fire. She did a quick calculation. Judd would have had to see Coigne after 9:20 in order for him to have an alibi for the time she was killed.

Even if the police knew about Judd, they might not have reached him yet. He was out all day, and who knew what he got up to at night? Single guy, simple guy—probably wasn't home working his way through *Tess of the d'Urbervilles.* In fact, she'd heard rumors about him staying late at the Dandridge Tavern and raising Cain. But would he remember what he saw over a week ago, even assuming Coigne was within sight? It was a long shot, but in her experience, long shots paid off, and, she reminded herself, there was no such thing as a short shot.

"Follow me," Norma said to Laney as she raced up the hill, waving her arms and calling out.

Judd must have heard them coming as he spun around and dropped his stapler gun. "What's wrong, Miss Norma, Miss Laney? Who's hurt?"

"Everything is fine." Norma held a hand up and caught her breath.

"D-did a fox break through and get your chickens, Mr. Lamb? I see you've got a pile of wire fencing. Did a fox, you know…?" Laney looked ill.

"Oh, no, ma'am. And you can call me Judd. You're the one who finally got me to do something about overhead fencing. You were right. Them chickens fly right out of here no matter how high I build the fence. A wire roof will do the job. These here are free range. I have a theory—"

"And I want to hear it, Judd Sp … Judd," Norma said, drawing on her low reservoir of patience. "I hate to interrupt your fence project, but right now, I have an emergency." Sweat poured down her forehead and stung her eyes.

"You hold on, Miss Norma." Judd walked over to his truck and pulled out a wooden crate, emptied its heavy, clanging contents into the truck bed, and set it upside down on the ground for her to sit on. "Take your time, now." He leaned back against his truck, ready to listen for the rest of the evening.

"I need you to think really hard about something. What you remember may be very important."

He closed his eyes, and his mouth hung open. He nodded for her to go ahead.

"Can you remember coming here Wednesday before last in the morning?"

He opened his eyes and smiled with relief. "I don't have to remember that. I always come same time every day, and that would include two Wednesdays ago."

That was good news and bad news. He had a daily routine that others could vouch for. But Coigne had a routine too, tending to the horses, feeding them and letting them out, then checking fences around the property. How could Judd remember seeing Coigne on that particular day?

"Try to remember that morning, and not just your usual morning routine, because I need you to think about whether you saw Coigne that morning."

Judd removed his baseball cap, smoothed his oily, shoulder-length strands of hair, then put it on again more snugly. "Yes, ma'am."

"Are you saying 'Yes, ma'am,' meaning you saw him?" Her eyes bore into his.

"Don't push him, Norma. Let him think," Laney said.

"I saw him. I remember because I heard him talking—or yelling, really."

"You mean you spoke to him?" How could Coigne not have remembered a conversation with Judd Spud on the day of the fire? They'd always chuckle about the funny things Judd came up with. Coigne would have told her something about it.

"Well, no. I didn't talk to him. You see, he was pretty far away, and I'd a had to walk over there. I had this fencing to put up—I guess I'm not getting on with my story as fast as you—"

"No one can fault you for that, Judd." She wanted to punch him for not getting on with the story. "But are you sure it was Coigne, and when, exactly? *When* did you see him?"

"Well, let me see. I usually get here around seven, but it was closer to seven-thirty that day. I started putting up the fence on that Wednesday because I couldn't pick up the fence material until the Memorial Day sale started, and that was that Wednesday before the weekend, you see. So I must have been here an hour or so. I stopped working in the middle for a coffee-doughnut break. Mary Beth made me the jelly doughnuts the day before. I guess I saw Mr. Coigne off and on all that time until about twelve minutes of nine."

"How can you be so exact, Judd?" Laney asked.

"Cause my job at Subway starts at nine, and I give myself twelve minutes to get over there. Set my timer. It's easy for me to lose track when I'm out here with my buddies." He nodded at the chickens.

"How could you tell it was Coigne, Judd? I mean, you pointed like he was way out there."

"Who else would be riding his tractor? Everyone knows that ugly thing's his, with that flag of some Yankee state. And he'd get off and on and walk like himself, you know, leaning forward like he's gotta get somewhere."

Norma thought about his explanation. "What exactly did you see him do?"

"You know, go back and forth, repairing the fence that lines up with Finn Spenser's property, may he rest in peace. I don't like to say this, Miss Norma, but he let off a string of swear words. Threw his cap down on the ground. I thought he was going to stomp it. I decided not to bother him that morning. I never heard a man swear like—"

"What was he swearing *about*? Think, Judd. I want you to tell me exactly what you heard."

"I don't like to."

"You could be a hero if you remember—truthfully remember."

Judd cupped his hands and spoke in Norma's direction so Laney couldn't hear him. "He yelled out, 'Fuck it all, you cocksucker.'"

"Who was he yelling at?" Norma began to doubt her star witness. Coigne would never have yelled those words at someone.

"He was yelling at the fence. He must have been mad about whoever knocked it down. I saw it the evening before on my way coming home from work. Right where he was when I heard him. That's what I'd been fixing to tell him about when he was far away. Great big tire marks clear as—"

Norma finally got the story out of him. Coigne must have just discovered the breach in the fence was caused not by weather and not by a miscalculating deer or a spooked horse. It'd been a hog of a truck that backed into it, breaking two segments. Whoever it was kept right on going. Judd took the two of them to the ugly gap that, in her consternation over the last few days, she hadn't even noticed. And Coigne probably hadn't mentioned it to her for the same reason. She looked over at Judd, who was staring at her, probably looking for a thumbs up or down.

Norma thought hard. If Judd saw Coigne as late as 8:48 a.m., Coigne could have reached Marion Chate's cottage in time to kill Misty and start the fire. But that would assume he took no time to put the tractor away, wash up, and drive way across town. She recalled Coigne had been wearing a good pair of jeans and a short-sleeved polo shirt, not a T-shirt, when she saw him at Marion's the morning of the fire, so he had to have changed clothes after working in the field. Things were looking up.

"Judd, you are a prince among men. You'll be hearing from the sheriff's office soon. And why the hell hasn't he been around to see you already? You're a neighbor. He should have had someone over within twenty-four hours." She'd never been so disappointed in Bud Law. She'd always counted him as one of the good guys.

"Truth to tell, someone might have tried to call me. I don't answer if I don't recognize the number. And if I saw a cop car outside my house, I might have not—you see, sometimes things get rowdy at the tavern and—"

38

Saturday morning. Laney plopped down on her bed and landed on an envelope. She tossed it in the direction of three other notifications from UVA on her desk. She'd already received the same information via email concerning orientation, course selection, housing, and roommates. If anyone had told her a month ago she'd consider this information of little interest, she'd have scoffed in disbelief. Since she'd saved the emails, she must still have held hope Coigne would be released, her parents would love each other again, and she'd go back to being her normal self, full of ideals and only somewhat insecure. If those things didn't happen, she had no interest in attending college or doing much of anything else.

She leaned back against the headboard. At least they had more evidence in Coigne's favor about his whereabouts the morning Misty was murdered. But as she and Norma walked up the hill and back inside, Norma hadn't seemed her usual ebullient self when something good came her way, which led Laney to doubt the importance of what Judd had told them. She'd explained that Judd had narrowed the time Coigne had to commit the murder and start the fire and let it burn to the point where it could be spotted by others, but it wasn't proof he didn't do it.

At least she could count on Owen to cheer her up once he had enough time to grieve over Finn. But then what? Was she not going to be allowed to go over to his house because of Mr. Spenser? Why the hell did Norma have to "share her concerns" about Owen's dad anyway? It was outside the realm of possibility Mr. Spenser had molested Jess Harper. Sure, he was a creep, but not a scumbag. He wasn't warm and friendly, that's all. No sense of humor. He always treated Owen like he was six years old and had just done something wrong. Come to think of it, he treated Mrs. Spenser the same way. But none of that made him a molester. Norma was wrong.

And that meant Jess was either mistaken or had lied to Norma. It was weird the way Jess had seemed so happy to see Owen that morning she delivered the FedEx package and stayed for breakfast. She was all about those good old days with the Spensers. Then, suddenly, she tells Norma she was molested by Mr. Spenser. Maybe Laney couldn't solve the puzzle of Misty or Finn's murder, but she damn well could get the truth out of Jess Harper. And there was no time like the present. It was Saturday, but everyone seemed to work Saturdays at Norma's office. Worst case, she would have a nice drive.

Laney hoisted herself into Coigne's truck. She knew better than to make Jess suspicious by calling to make sure she was working Saturday again. She could lie about why she was calling, but that was another problem—Laney didn't lie well. She'd just have to chance it that she might arrive and Jess wouldn't be there. She gave a moment's thought to Jess's age, coolness, and superiority in all other respects, which almost made her turn Coigne's truck around and avoid the confrontation. Then she imagined Owen's face if he were ever to hear the disgusting rumor about his father. Suicide. That's all anybody talked about at school. It wouldn't be out of the question for a person to want to end it all, what with all he'd endured. Her course was clear.

"Whassup, girl? Your mom's not here. On a run, I think. C'mon and sit down before The Fox crawls out of his hole with work for me." As encouragement, Jess nodded toward the seat across from her. "You want something to drink?"

"No, thanks. I'm not bothering you or anything…am I?" Laney noticed that the top of Jess's desk was bare but for her computer, a Charles Town County Seat coffee mug, and a framed photo of a dachshund with a winner's wreath around his neck. Unlike the tidy desktop, the floor beneath their feet was carpeted in manila folders, and Laney had to maneuver herself carefully into the chair to avoid stepping on them.

"How's Owen Spenser? You taking good care of that boy?"

Shit. Laney hadn't planned to dive into such a tense conversation as soon as she'd sat down. She'd wanted to follow another of Norma's strategies for getting information under tough circumstances: "It's far easier to squeeze out the honey if you first warm up the little bear." But she hadn't thought it through. She had no small talk to warm up the little bear with. She felt it would be rude to notice out loud Jess's eyelash extensions or her black leather camisole, though she did wonder how it must feel to sweat in one of those. She'd just have to dive in. "I wanted to talk about something—or ask something, really. It's weird, though."

"I'm fine with weird," Jess said, hamming it up by crossing her eyes and grasping the sides of her desk.

"Here goes. Did you tell Norma that Mr. Spenser molested you when you sat for his kids?" She forced herself to look Jess in the eye.

"That's heavy shit, Laney."

Laney raced through all the ways she could undo what she'd just said, turn her question into a joke. Haha. She said mole tested, not molested. Jess clearly had no idea what Laney was talking about, or if she did know, she couldn't have wanted someone like her, practically a stranger, to know about it.

"I didn't think Norma would tell you about that. And I never said molested." Jess shook her head. "What a fuck-up." She rolled her chair backward until her head hit a low-hanging print of Charles Washington, the president's youngest brother and founder of Charles Town. "You want to take a walk?" she asked.

Jess let The Fox know she had to run out for a small emergency, and they left.

Traffic along Washington Street was slowing, as it was close to rush hour. The broad street teamed with F150s, windows down, radios on, bases booming. If you were waiting for a Tesla, you'd wait a long time. Laney admired the old mansions and municipal buildings, mostly federal style and Greek revival. The old buildings bravely held their ground, despite the overall decline of downtown. These were things Norma had told her, and she was shocked to discover she'd listened and retained the information.

On her own, Laney had read about poor old Charles, how daunting it must have been to be Washington's younger brother. But now Laney's mind was on Jess. Her distress was obvious, the way she barely spoke or even looked up as they walked that first block. Jess practically fell against an elderly man standing in front of City Hall. They couldn't keep walking block after block without a word or at least a destination. She was relieved when Jess said, "Let's head to the library. It's pretty this time of day, and we can sit on the steps out front. It's shady."

Laney was terribly hot, but at least she now knew what happened when you sweated in a black leather cami—she looked over at Jess—nothing good.

"Let me set you straight on the most important thing first," Jess said. "Mr. Spenser never molested me or anyone else so far as I know. And he wasn't weird, either. He was actually almost nice, most of the time—I mean, for a rich businessman. So, one night, just after I arrived to sit with the kids, he led me back out to the front stoop, handed me one hundred and fifty bucks, and said my services would no longer be needed. God, I bet he wished he'd had his Human Resources Department with him because I gave him a lot of grief. They'd promised me the whole month of August. And I'd miss those kids. Okay, Dell was tough, but I understood her. She wasn't so different from me at that same age."

"Did he give you any explanation? What did Mrs. Spenser say?"

Jess closed her eyes, and a strong cool breeze blew her gelled crest of hair.

"Mrs. Spenser wasn't on the stoop with us. But I had the sense she was very much involved in the decision because he was real light on details about why they were letting me go."

"What were the light details, then? What reason did he give for firing you?"

Jess turned toward Laney, her mouth twisted with fury, her eyes brimming with tears. "*He* accused *me* of 'interfering' with Owen. You know—*molesting* him." Her body began to quiver, and Laney instinctively threw an arm over her shoulders. "I don't know how he could say such a crazy thing."

"It sounds horrible, Jess. It's okay, now."

"It isn't okay. It was completely unjust. I'd never have harmed either one of them. I even fantasized I was a member of the Spenser family. They'd sure treated me like one before they fired me."

Laney wanted to believe Jess, especially as she'd developed a massive girl crush on her. She did believe her. But Jess had lied to Norma, so how could Laney know for sure whether or not she was lying now? "I need to tell Norma the truth before she makes matters worse. You know Norma. She could feel compelled to report Mr. Spenser for molesting you to some authority or something."

"Hell, no! The cops would be all over me."

"And Mr. Spenser. It could ruin him, even if it's too late to press charges against him. That family has—"

"I know. I'm stupid to think of myself. He doesn't deserve any of that."

A knot of small children burst through the library doors. Their mother, presumably, followed at a sedate pace, a grim, tired look on her face. Who could blame the children, though; it was late spring, and the sun was shining.

Laney waited until the hubbub had cleared before saying, "What made you tell Norma that lie? Was it revenge against the Spensers?"

Jess spoke so softly Laney had trouble understanding her. It seemed like Jess's shame had smothered her spirit to the point of muting her voice.

"I hadn't given the Spensers a thought for a long time. I'd finally put the hurt behind me until I saw Owen again that morning at your house. I kept it together until I got outside, and then all the old humiliation overwhelmed me. At your front door, I told you to tell Norma I needed to tell her something. In a flash, I'd plotted a pathetic attempt at revenge, to paint Mr. Spenser with the same brush he'd used on me."

All Jess's quirky-cute, I'm-tough-and-you-can't-hurt-me façade disappeared. She sounded so sincere and contrite Laney believed her story. But she still wasn't entirely satisfied. "Have you any idea why Mr. Spenser lied—about the 'interfered with' business? He could have just let you go without explanation. And I sure don't understand why he paid you one hundred and fifty dollars."

Jess chuckled. "Turns out he didn't. As he was closing the door, I flung the bills at him. As for why he did it, I've thought about it a lot. You're right—why should he make up something so vile connected to his son and then pay me an extravagant amount— extravagant for me, anyway? I've sometimes wondered if maybe the kids made up something about me or misunderstood a hug. I've tried to figure it out a thousand times."

"And I can't see Mrs. Spenser lying either. She's always so nice."

"That's because you're from the right side of the tracks, girly-girl. Of course, she'd be nice to you."

"We're from the same side, Jess. My bio-parents were addicts like yours, my dad tried to sell me, and my mom almost got me killed. Otherwise, I had a golden childhood."

Jess laughed raucously. "I forgot you were adopted. You *really* had it rough, kid."

No one said much while they let their common past misery solder together a new friendship.

"I always liked Mrs. Spenser," Jess said, picking up the thread, "but she never seemed completely present, like we'd all be hysterically chasing a runaway ball down a hill, and she'd be looking off, thinking of something else."

Laney stood up. Her leg had cramped, and she gave her muscle a few squeezes. "We'll probably never know the answer to any of this, but I can keep you from getting into trouble with your boss for being late. Come on."

Laney held out a hand for Jess, who said, "Are you going to tell Norma I lied?"

Laney weighed the pain Jess had already been through against the trouble Norma might cause for the Spensers if she reported Jess's case to the authorities or for Jess if Norma confronted Mr. Spenser and then found out the truth. Norma Trouble was something Laney could write a book about.

"Yes, I will tell Norma you lied. But she, of all people, will understand how everyone deserves one pass."

39

Norma put her feet up on the coffee table and let her head loll over the back of the sofa. She'd just arrived home from a five-mile run through Shepherdstown, then through the university campus and over the bridge to the towpath. She'd hoped the cardio workout would give her stamina for a long day's work ahead. She was anxious to hear what The Fox thought about Judd Spud's alibi for Coigne. She gave him a call and summarized what she'd learned.

"It's great you found out Judd Lamb saw Coigne the morning of Misty's death,

Norma. Be prepared, though. I can just hear the prosecutor refer to this as Coigne's 'sudden alibi,' although that doesn't mean Judd Lamb's testimony won't have weight."

"Why the hell wasn't Law's investigator out interviewing neighbors like Judd Spud? And will you please just call him Judd? I get confused when you refer to Judd Lamb."

"Of course. And I think I've got some notes on the interviews." Norma heard him scrolling through his computer. "Chief Deputy Baker canvassed a number of locations for witnesses, including Misty's neighborhood, the area of the crime scene, and over your way around the farm. If Judd doesn't actually live in your neighborhood, they might not have thought to contact him if we didn't inform them about him."

"And how could we know Judd had seen Coigne that morning?"

"Exactly. We couldn't have known. But I'll be over to nail down his statement in an affidavit. From what you've said, the best time would be chicken feeding time, right?"

"Right. You sound worried, Foxy. What is it?"

He didn't respond for so long Norma thought he'd hung up.

"One of the strongest facts the prosecutor has is the statement of Finn Spenser, who supposedly heard Misty say Coigne's name. Misty's statement, technically hearsay, would probably be admissible in court anyway under the dying declaration exception. But I have Jess researching whether Finn's sworn statement about Misty's dying declaration would be admissible now that he's dead, too, and can't be cross-examined. I'm not confident it is."

"Well, hell, Foxy. Keeping Misty's supposed naming of Coigne out of evidence would be good news, wouldn't it?"

"Sure, but the problem is, the prosecutor is obviously already inclined against Mr. Coigne because that sworn statement did exist. He'll find every way he can to challenge Judd's credibility, and from what you've said, credibility isn't Judd's forte. And, of course—"

"Of course?"

"Finn's statement and the evidential weight it would have carried had he survived could be viewed as a powerful motive for killing him. For Mr. Coigne to kill him."

Which made Norma wonder if the prosecutor might try to introduce Finn's sworn statement not to prove what Misty actually said but as evidence of Coigne's motive for killing Finn.

"Let's wait for Jess's research and talk again. You're scaring me to death," Norma said.

Norma had developed a new appreciation for Foxy's work ethic. He'd been working all day and night on Friday, and there he was at the office on Saturday. He was the right man for the job. At least they had that going for them. And there was no way, knowing he was hard at work, that she'd let up, tired as she was. She opened her saddlebag and got to work.

It was after noon when she next checked the clock. "Hot Pockets should do." She checked the freezer and grabbed a couple. "Filled with pepperoni pizza," she read. "Along with a little salad, that ought to cover the four food groups nicely." She turned on the oven to 375 degrees. And where was Laney anyway?

She removed her shoes and massaged her toes and dwelled on the fact nothing definitive had yet been reported about the when, where, how, or who of Finn's murder, except that he'd been beaten and shoved into the Opequon, where he'd drowned. Finn's body was found not far from the charred remains of Marion Chatte's house, where all the bad news of late seemed to originate. Norma considered another trip to see Sheriff Law, but she'd only get frustrated by his equivocations. He'd never give her a firm, "No, Mr. Coigne is not a suspect in that murder," so what was the point?

The grandfather clock in their front hall struck the hour once, which again reminded her she was missing a daughter. She'd seen Coigne's truck blast out of the driveway before she left for her run, but Laney had left no note as to where she was headed or when she'd be back, which made Norma worry. "Wretched girl."

As she went about setting a place for one and rinsing some lettuce, her mind pivoted back to the location of Finn's death and its proximity to Marion's property. Marion had returned none of her several calls since the day of the fire, and Norma had not yet told her where her son was. She hadn't told anyone where he was, even though she knew the sheriff's office was interested in finding him too. For reasons grounded only in her fertile imagination, she'd been afraid to pull on the Kaleb thread without knowing what else would unravel.

The front door slammed. "I'm home. Down in a minute."

Now that Laney was safe at home, Norma gave vent to her resentment for having to worry about Laney in the first place by slicing the daylights out of the tomatoes and cucumbers. She nearly broke the oven door yanking it open to shove in the Hot Pockets.

"I could eat five of those," Laney said, arriving just as Norma pulled the Hot Pockets from the oven. "Where's yours?"

"Oh, you want some?" Norma felt she should be a responsible parent and lecture her daughter on consideration, courtesy, and reliability, but thinking of her own record in those areas, she left it at "I'll get another plate."

"Hurry. I'm famished. I need to tell you about something, and I don't want you to overreact."

40

Five days. Coigne couldn't believe he'd been incarcerated just five days. He lay on a plastic-covered foam pad on the floor of his cell—no sheets, no blankets, and not enough cots to go around— with his head butting up to a stinking toilet. He'd almost gotten used to sleeping with low-wattage lights on all night and all the other features of the jail experience. With two cellmates who snored to wake the dead, it wasn't easy. Even in the short time he'd served, incarceration had changed him. As a Massachusetts State Trooper, he'd had no problem bringing criminals to justice and considered it a calling, although at times a soul-destroying one. But the regional jail that caged him imprisoned plenty of people who were guilty of nothing more than shoplifting a phone.

All along, he'd dismissed as bleeding hearts those who said the "tough on crime" policies did nothing to discourage crime, the same people who said those policies did nothing more than transform guys who needed mental health and rehab services into hardened criminals. At the time, Coigne thought they were not only bleeding hearts, they were flat-out wrong. He didn't think so anymore. The exposure to danger and deplorable conditions would turn just about anyone into a violent felon—if it didn't kill him first.

The Fox told him Eastern Regional Jail was supposed to hold three hundred inmates, and they were up to four hundred and fifty. A few of the guards were more sadistic than any inmate he'd met, but most of them were overwhelmed by the number and types of crises they were charged with keeping under control.

And it wasn't just the constant noise, black mold, rat feces, and spoiled food that got to him. It was the little things, like no toilet paper since he'd arrived.

He looked forward to Laney's visit. She was allowed one thirty-minute visit per month, and God willing, he'd be out before the preliminary hearing. Between Norma and The Fox, they kept him up to speed on new facts they'd dug up and the legal theories they thought worth a try. He tried to stay involved in his own case, helping to build his defense and find the real killer, but to preserve his sanity, he spent much of his time zoning out.

Coigne adjusted his position on the foam pad, but something in his cell had changed. He sensed it. The other two cellmates had stopped snoring. That worried him. He listened. One of his cellmates got up slowly. Something was happening at the cell door. Coigne couldn't see around the cellmate who stood.

Coigne fought for breath. A pillow pressed down on his face. He bucked and twisted and grabbed the guy's ears and pulled. He flung off the pillow and yelled, but a massive hand crammed his mouth shut. It was a gorilla, someone much bigger than the other two. He crawled onto Coigne's chest and pinned his arms down with his knees and punched his face, first right fist, then left fist, then repeat, like it was a punching bag.

"Here's what we do to cops." The gorilla rolled off Coigne's chest, took hold of his right arm, and yanked the shoulder out of its socket. A few more punches around the ears and nose, and Coigne gratefully lost consciousness.

They took Coigne first to the jail's infirmary, then to the hospital. Several hours later, with one eye open, he observed the frail, quivering guard at the door. He was more fully awakened by a familiar, welcome voice.

"You damn well better get out of my way."

"Listen, ma'am. I'm sure you want to see him, but I need to call the doctor and see if it's okay. You just wait a minute."

Norma could have taken that guard with the power of her rage alone.

The guard focused on his call to the doctor, and Norma slipped into the room. Loose security had its upside. Coigne had already learned its downside.

He reached for Norma's hand, his IV line getting twisted in the process. Every inch of his upper body burned with pain. She motioned for him to stay still. He smiled, hoping to allay her concerns, but God help him, he was thrilled to feel her concern.

"You didn't plan this yourself, did you?" she asked. "A ploy for sympathy, perhaps?"

He started to shake his head, and even that hurt.

"I knew something was going to happen, Coigne. I just knew it. I'm so mad I want to rip the head off the person who runs this place. It's a damn good thing there's nothing heavy and moveable around here to throw."

Without her hat, which she wasn't permitted to wear inside his room, her long, golden hair flew wildly with her every gesture of outrage and reminded him the sun still shone.

"Where were the guards? They seem to be all over the place now, so where were they before?" she demanded.

"It happened pretty fast. How long does it take to get two black eyes, facial lacerations, a fat lip, a concussion, and a dislocated shoulder? Could have been a lot worse." He felt his bandages. He didn't need a mirror. He knew he looked scary.

"How did it happen? Where'd this 'gorilla' who nailed you come from? Under the bed?"

"Under the bed would have been a tough one. This is my guess. One of my cellmates capped the door when the guard locked us up for the night."

"What do you mean, capped?"

"Put something on the door—even some fabric, a napkin—to keep it from closing. Then that gorilla charged in with the killer punches."

"You recognize him?"

"I'm not going to recognize him until I'm at least back on my feet."

"I assume you'll get new cellmates?"

Coigne studied his avenging angel, not sure she'd understand him now that he was, at the moment, anyway, not the confident, tough husband she'd married. He wasn't afraid—he just saw the world as a lot more complicated than before. His cellmates? They were a couple of addicts, probably caught peddling fentanyl for a dealer. They must have weighed the punishment the jail would mete out against that of the gorilla if they didn't go along.

"The Fox says they're in solitary, so at least you won't see them for a while. You know, you might be better off in solitary. I'm not joking. What do you think?"

Four concrete walls, dark, and cold. He'd have to think about it. "We'll see," he said. "How's Laney? I can call her today—or tomorrow, at the latest."

"She's worried. She'll be glad to hear from you, but Coigne, no Facetime. You don't want to terrify her."

Norma talked about the case and the Judd Spud alibi. Coigne smiled as if encouraged, but the truth was, he was disengaged.

"The neighbors are helping out with the farm. You'd be amazed, Coigne. Between the neighbors and Laney, the horse farm business is holding on. Isn't that good?"

He just wanted to go home.

41

"Well, she's going to know I know, that's for sure," Norma said in response to Laney's plea that she go easy when confronting Jess about her big lie.

Norma was surprised at how quickly everything snapped back to normal following Coigne's beating—or as normal as it could be with two unsolved murders threatening their chance for a reasonably happy future. Coigne was even back at Eastern Regional Jail, living the good life in the infirmary.

Norma wore her fitted black suit with a button-down, French blue blouse that morning. Back when she started up her new practice, Laney had insisted on going with her to buy her "court costume," the black suit. And she'd given her the blue blouse to go with it last Mother's Day. Norma had no court appearance that day, but she wanted to impress her young legal assistant with her somber bearing. Jess had lied to her, and that didn't sit well.

Despite heading straight to the office, no Starbucks side trip, Norma still failed to beat her assistant. Jess showed no sign she was worried about losing her job at the firm. The way she twirled her pen through her fingers like a budding Harlem Globetrotter and bounced her head to music flooding through her earbuds served to enflame Norma as Jess no doubt knew it would.

"Jess. My office."

Jess pulled out a bud. "Did you say something, Norma?"

"Get rid of the damn earbuds and meet me inside."

Their progress toward Norma's office was interrupted by a soft cough. "Uh, ladies?" Drew Fox stood at the doorway. He took a step into the reception area and started to say something but must have sensed the fraught atmosphere. He held up four fingers, then continued through to his own office. Four fingers, four days to the preliminary hearing. They had to get Coigne out of jail before that hearing.

Norma wondered what The Fox must think about her and the way she coopted their "shared" assistant so much of the time. But she had more pressing matters to consider now. She sat down at her desk. "Take a seat and start talking, Jess. I don't know what possessed you to lie to me, of all people, your employer and friend."

"We had drinks, Norma. Technically, we're not friend-friends."

Norma said nothing, just stared. The strategy always worked to get the other person talking.

"I already told Laney all about it and apologized." Jess took her time adjusting her rings and holding out one hand and then the other to admire all the metal.

Norma assumed the oblong blobs were made of silver, though they could pass for repurposed bullets.

"I was wrong to say what I said about Geoff Spenser, and I'm sorry. I should have corrected the impression I left you with—"

"Not an impression; it was a lie you left me with. A scandalous lie. You do understand you're in a position of trust here, right? Not only did you breach trust as an employee, but you also breached trust as a friend." Norma realized she was spanking the top of her desk with each mention of the word *trust*. She folded her hands. "But even more unbelievably, you're supposed to be helping me defend my husband, our client, against murder charges, and I'm having to take time out to deal with your breach of trust." Spank.

"You don't seem to think your lie is such a big deal. Well, let me ask you something. Have you heard anything from Kaleb lately?"

"Wait. What? What does he have to do with any of this?"

"He is a liar—that's what he has to do with this. His lies hurt you, am I right? You, of all people, should understand how wrong it is to lie, especially knowing the lie could harm an innocent person."

"Fine. Then you owe me the truth about where Kaleb is. Out with it, Norma. Boss or no boss, what's going on with Kaleb? The truth."

"Withholding information for valid reasons is not a lie." Norma realized she was skating on thin ice—on slush, really, but she wasn't ready to yield to her subordinate. "The situations are completely different."

"How?"

"I have to keep his location confidential. Marion is a client, and I have duties of confidentiality—"

"Oh, come on. I work here. I'm your agent, we're working on the same client matter, so it doesn't violate the Professional Rules of Santa's Dick to tell me. Besides, the police are looking for Kaleb. You told me so yourself." Jess pointed her longest, blackest fingernail at Norma's chest. "If you're hiding him from the police, you've got more to worry about than me."

Norma thought Jess really ought to get her law degree. What's more, she knew she needed to resolve their quarrel soon, or she'd be looking for a new legal assistant, something she couldn't afford to do, nor did she want to. On the verge of swerving her attitude from blame to reconciliation, she realized Jess was spurting tears. She handed Ms. Tough Stuff a tissue and gave her a minute to compose herself.

"Would you like to come with me to see Kaleb, Jess? In your role as my agent on a client matter, of course?"

By the time they reached her car, Norma had digested Jess's lie. Someday she'd figure out what was behind it, but not today. Today, all she needed was a miracle.

"You know the airbag light thingy hasn't gone off." Jess pushed random buttons on the console.

"Light thingy? Is that your biggest concern right now, Jess?"

"Sorry."

"No, I'm sorry. I'm wound up."

They drove a mile in silence. "I just keep thinking about how Marion's bungalow served as headquarters for a lot of activity the morning of Misty's murder, and Marion wasn't even home. Why was everyone there?"

"Everyone being Misty, Finn, Coigne, and Hilda Fingerhut."

"And don't forget, Finn wound up dead about a hundred yards downstream. Something must tie all those people together, and whatever it was, it drew them to Marion's cottage or thereabouts."

"Right. It's not as though Marion Chatte was some big shot, and everyone had to see her."

Norma turned to search Jess's face for signs of sarcasm. "Maybe not a big shot, merely head librarian at the university."

They traveled Route 340 up and down steep hills, past kayak rental shops, hotels, and strip malls along the winding highway, each woman lost in her own thoughts. Jess never even asked where they were headed or how long it would take to get there. Norma figured she was gripped by the hope she'd soon see the man she loved, and all the fears and suspicions of the last couple of weeks would evaporate. Norma had her doubts about that December wedding, but she kept mum on the subject of Kaleb. Coigne remained the focus of her worries.

"You know, all this time, I've been trying to find ways to cast doubt on Coigne as the killer, figuring that was the fastest way to spring him from jail. But I may have underestimated the pressure on Sheriff Law to find the killer—any killer will do?—and keep him in jail. Consider the mayor, the media, the new prosecutor, and the ghoulish public."

"Hmm?"

"I'm just saying we should be spending more time hunting down the real killer and less time wondering who had what knife and who's got an alibi. Let's focus on what was the common denominator that brought them there."

Jess said nothing—off in la-la land.

Norma considered several possibilities herself and rejected each one.

"Maybe it isn't a what question but a who question," Jess said. "Who was the common denominator?"

"Good point. By the way, we're almost there. Now, *who* could have drawn that motley assortment together so early in the morning? We know Hilda was holding a tutorial on dairy farming, which brought Coigne and Finn to the vicinity, but Finn was early. Why?" The answer suddenly seemed so obvious. It was Misty. She had, or at one time had, a business relationship with Finn. Could Misty have been Kaleb's financial backer, the one who threatened him into hiding? So, who among them hated her enough to kill her? Finn might have done it, but as a victim himself, it was an unsatisfying answer. Who else? But before she could come up with someone, they arrived at *chez* LaBomba.

42

It was almost eleven a.m. Norma assumed Kaleb's exotic hostess had left for work, the law firm just down the hill, some time ago. Before leaving her Prius, which she would need to park some distance from the house, she gave the neighborhood a closer look. No one was about, and no one stood in a window at Mimi LaBomba's house, but until Norma knew more, she and Jess had to stay hidden. After they parked, she guided Jess onto a path she'd observed during her last visit at the rear of the house next door to LaBomba's.

"You know it's always possible Kaleb finally called his mother, and they're both living temporarily at the university provost's rental unit while they get their cottage fixed up, but I doubt it." Norma was careful to keep her voice low. "If everything were tickety-boo, Marion would have returned my calls, if for no other reason than to get the calls to stop."

"Maybe they've left town for good," Jess said, the fear in her voice obvious.

"I wouldn't worry about that. Marion isn't independently wealthy. She needs her job at the university. A prolonged absence would be difficult."

The gods were on their side. They crept up to the back door undetected and peered inside. Amidst the shouting and swearing, Norma even saw spittle fly. They couldn't hear the words, but when Kaleb tossed a bright red dinner plate against the kitchen wall like it was a Frisbee, Jess jumped back as if it had hit her.

That was it. Norma rapped urgently on the door, causing both Chattes and a third person to freeze. Norma had to motion for Marion to come open the door.

"What's going on in here?" Best defense—good offense. "Ah. It's the fair Ms. LaBomba. Jess, let me introduce you. Ms. LaBomba is the owner of this lovely home, as well as that red plate, I suspect. Have the three of you been hiding in your aerie a little too long?" She glanced in the direction of the shattered plate, then at the dirty dishes on the counter, overturned chair, trash everywhere, and general disarray of the kitchen, and then at Marion. "What's all the fighting about, Marion?"

Marion opened her mouth to speak, but nothing came out.

Jess seemed dumbstruck, too, as her eyes drank in her lover's face.

Once Kaleb recovered from his shock, he chose a new target for his still-coursing adrenaline. "What the hell? Why are you two here? We're trying to hide, you know. Did you forget that, Norma? Now get the hell out of here."

"Back down, Kaleb, or I'll call the sheriff. He's been trying to reach you." As she said the words, she remembered Kaleb kept a gun. He remembered too.

He whipped his pistol from the back of his waistband.

"Oh, for God's sake," Marion said. "Give me that gun. If it were loaded, you'd shoot yourself in the—"

Norma sat down at the table. She was shaken by the gun and cursed herself for her thoughtless, aggressive approach. Even if the gun wasn't loaded—if—she was glad it was now in Marion's hands. "I'm glad to oblige you, Kaleb. I just have a few questions, and then we'll go. Oh, and Ms. LaBomba, may I introduce you to Kaleb's fiancée, Jess Harper?"

"His wha-what? Kale?" Marion sat down next to Norma at the table.

Ms. LaBomba scrutinized Jess from head to foot but couldn't have gotten much out of it. Jess had on her oversized army jacket. She stood in stark contrast to Ms. LaBomba in sleek black slacks, black patent heels, and a white silk blouse, unbuttoned from the neck down to her ribcage.

"So you do exist," said Ms. LaBomba. "Ms. Bergen mentioned a fiancée when we met, but I preferred to believe Kaleb when he said she was mistaken; there was no other woman, just me. He certainly likes variety in his women, I would say." She again took in the full measure of Jess Harper—down to the black lipstick and nails. "What do you say, Kaleb?"

"Can someone please clue me in? I thought Ms. LaBomba was your girlfriend, Kale. Isn't that why she's letting us stay here?" Marion said.

"What questions are so important you had to risk exposing us to get an answer?" Kaleb demanded, slamming his fist down on the kitchen counter.

Norma gave him credit. He did what she would have done in the same situation—ignored all their questions and asked an aggressive one of his own. But she worried about Jess. This wasn't the reunion her young assistant had expected. Kaleb barely acknowledged her. "What I need to know is why you're still hiding. Your benefactor, the one you hid from in fear of your life and that of your mother, is dead. Misty Bubb's been dead for days. I showed you the article about the fire last time I was here, and they named her." Norma was only guessing when she lobbed the Misty grenade.

"Wait a minute, Kale," Marion said. "I thought Finn Spenser was your backer. And he's dead too. Have I at least got that right?" She looked to Norma for the answer.

Even Norma's head had begun to spin. Kaleb had told her he'd led his backer on, which she'd assumed meant they were lovers—and maybe they were. Was Finn Spenser his lover and his patron and the one who threatened harm if Kaleb weaseled out of the relationship? Again, Norma glanced at Jess. She hadn't intended to cause the young woman so much pain with this visit, but by the looks of her, Jess wasn't hurt. Her eyes had now narrowed, and her jaw tightened. She glowered.

Norma continued to pursue enlightenment. "I'm trying to figure out which pieces of the several stories you've told the women in your life—and me—are true. My guess is that you've been hiding out to avoid the lover-slash-patron who threatened you, Finn Spenser, but since he's dead, you've continued to hide out from whom? Jess? Probably. As between Mimi LaBomba and Jess Harper, the former has this lovely place to crash with room for both you and your mother, so she's won you for the present. How am I doing?"

No one spoke. To add to everyone's discomfort, LaBomba's use of furniture polish throughout the house was excessive, enough to cause Norma a splitting headache. Couldn't she have tidied the kitchen instead? "Spit it out, Kaleb. You've harmed enough people, probably even bought yourself and your mother some more trouble for evading Sheriff Law."

"I'm not embarrassed if that's what you think. And I'm not gay," he blurted at Jess. "I just needed the money to get started. We're going to get married, Jess. I did this for us."

Norma studied Kaleb's ruby-red face. His tone didn't convey the same belligerence it had earlier. He was lying—about not being embarrassed. He hadn't denied he'd traded sexual favors for Finn's backing, and prostitution wasn't something to be proud of, even for Kaleb Chatte.

"You'll find your things in the front yard, Kaleb," Ms. LaBomba said. As she left the room, she addressed her final thought to Jess. "You are welcome to heem, *cherie*."

Before anyone could stop her, Jess grabbed a second plate off the counter and flung it at Kaleb's head. Marion screamed. Everyone threw defensive arms in front of their faces. The plate clipped Kaleb in the head and landed on the floor in pieces.

Kaleb bent over. He wasn't bleeding but seemed to be in some pain. Jess's face reflected a profound satisfaction.

"What the hell's the matter with that girl? Kaleb, honey, are you all right?"

Marion quickly loaded ice into a dishtowel and pressed it against Kaleb's temple, but he pushed her away.

"And you, Marion. Why didn't you answer my calls?" Norma asked. "I imagine you've avoided calls from the sheriff's office, too."

Marion put the dishtowel down. Apparently, outrage at the extent of her son's deception had just surpassed her maternal instinct to protect. "Kaleb asked me not to return the calls, any calls. Said he was in trouble and just needed a few days." She looked at her son, busy feeling the size of his knot. At least he hadn't lied to her about being in trouble.

Norma decided it was time to go.

They never did find out what made Kaleb hurl the first plate, but it had something to do with the big pile of dirty dishes in and around the sink, a problem both Kaleb and Jess had reduced in a small way.

As Jess followed Norma to the kitchen door, Kaleb reached out for her hand. Instead, she gave him the one-finger salute. The best that could be said about the Harpers Ferry excursion was that Kaleb's gun still had not gone off.

43

"Bring the sandwiches into my office," Norma said. "We've got work to do."

Norma reached for the broom from the corner of her office and prodded the window open as high as it would go. Jess gathered papers from the four corners of her boss's desk and put them in a single pile on the floor, annoying Norma no more than usual, and spread the feast onto the desk.

"You okay?" Norma asked, tucking a couple of oil-slick tomato slices back into their cushy bread roll. She had allowed Jess the ride home to pull herself together. She needed her in a high-functioning mode now.

"Of course, I'm fine. It's been a good forty-five minutes since my fiancé pulled a gun on me, and his mother revealed he'd been cheating on me, so, for sure, I'm chill." Jess pulled back the tab on her Diet Coke.

Norma realized Jess deserved some show of compassion for all she'd endured. "You saw for yourself the guy's a dick." She yanked open her desk drawer and pulled out a wad of napkins and handed one to Jess, saying, "Mayo—mouth—left corner. But I keep coming back to the question, does any of this have a thing to do with Misty or Finn's murder?" Her phone rang. She spoke to The Fox and agreed they'd stay put until he got back to the office for a powwow.

"Based on what you've told me," Jess said, as though they'd not been interrupted by the call, "Misty used men for money. Maybe that figures into it."

"Sex and money. You're right. Okay. Let's work with that." Norma pushed her sandwich wrapper aside and grabbed a yellow legal pad from her drawer. "Laney told me Finn and Misty might have had a business deal going, but Finn was acting like he barely knew Misty. She got this from her boyfriend, Owen, who's about as credible as they come."

"So, you're saying Misty got money out of Finn for her business in return for sex. If so, Finn's bi, right?"

"It's all conjecture, but to make this hypo work, the answer's yes. But we also learned, or at least no one denied the accusation, that Finn was also Kaleb's funding source and lover. So, the fact Finn distanced himself from Misty, according to what Owen told Laney—"

"Means Finn dropped Misty for Kaleb, and that made Misty mad."

"Real mad if he stopped investing in her business. You're good at this, Jess. I forgive you for every typo you ever made."

"Very little to forgive. You do your own typing. Those typos are yours."

"Nitpicker." Norma was enjoying herself because a picture had begun to form. "What if Misty decided to snitch on Finn's sexual preferences? Or threaten to if he didn't continue to fund her business?" Norma shook her head. "Oh, hell. Who would she snitch to? Who cares one way or the other about sexual preferences in this day and age, other than religious zealots and politicians?"

"Two words. West and Virginia. You seem to think you still live in Liberalsville, Massachusetts. Some folks in this state are so conservative they think even straight sex is deviant behavior."

"I've got two other words." Norma raised two fingers. "Geoff and Spenser. I think Finn cared more about what his uncle thought about him than we knew. The Spensers were his only relatives. Geoff Spenser strikes me as someone who would be quite uncomfortable—no, quite censorious—of sex in any context other than reproduction." Norma thought for a minute. "Also, Geoff and Finn had a physical fight shortly before Finn's death. That could've had something to do with Finn's affairs with Misty and Kaleb."

Jess crunched down on a chip, then another, and another.

"Stop that, Jess. Each bite sounds like a car backfiring."

"I'm just thinking. We've figured out how to put Finn and Misty together, but we haven't figured out how to put them together at Marion's house."

"Good point." Norma heard The Fox enter his office. "We'll have to pick it up later. My only thought off the top of my head is Finn didn't fall for Misty's threat, so Misty figured the first person she'd 'out' him to was Marion. As Kaleb's mom, Marion might do something crazy-harmful to Finn. Or, maybe Misty thought Kaleb was at home, and she wanted to spill the beans about two-timing Finn to lover boy. Listen, while I'm in with The Fox, I need you to find out if there's been any kind of corporate filings by Misty or Finn lately. That might at least give us a lead on whether Owen's hunch about a business venture between Misty and Finn has merit."

"Got it."

Norma dropped into the chair at The Fox's desk. "You don't look happy. I know we've got just three days before the preliminary hearing, but you look more woebegone than you did this morning. Spill it."

The Fox ran his hands through his hair, making it stick out in every direction like a crazy man. "It's that damn new prosecutor."

"Richard Mann?"

"They call him Tiger Mann. He plays golf."

"I'm going to think of him as Little Dickie. So, what's got you so upset?"

The Fox splayed his fingers across his desk as if physically laying out the dilemma for her. "He's got it in for your husband because Coigne's a lawman, and these days, catching a bad cop being bad is good. Furthermore, Little Dickie sure wants to make a name for himself. They all have the governor's office in their sights, and he's no exception."

"So, what does that mean in practical terms?"

"It means he's not going to let his schedule—or the judge's, if he can help it— delay the preliminary hearing."

"I see the upside. We'll be able to file a motion for bail after that, right?"

"Listen to me, Norma. It's tough for anyone to get bail on murder one, as we discussed, but because we're dealing with a prosecutor who's got to prove himself, there's no way, no how bail's going to happen. And I don't think the judge would think differently."

Norma got up and paced. "With three days left, there's no way we'll be as prepared as Little Dickie is for the prelim. So Coigne will likely rot in jail, unprotected, until the grand jury is called, and that will be—let's see, three months from now? Even assuming the grand jury doesn't indict him, and they probably will because the burden of proof—probable cause—is still low at the grand jury level—I know, I know, they'd indict a ham sandwich—Coigne will remain unprotected in that hellhole all that time until trial. That's the picture you're painting, isn't it? How soon does he leave the infirmary?"

"If he's lucky, or unlucky, depending on your point of view, he's out this evening. Different cellmates, though."

Norma considered the future and wondered not so much if there'd be another attack but whether he'd survive it.

Jess stuck her head in the doorway. "Bubbles, Barks, and Beauty," she said.

Norma and The Fox looked at her as though she'd lost her mind.

"It's the name of Misty's new company. Looks like she and Finn were the original officers, but now some other guy has taken Finn's place. The address for this other guy is the same as Misty's vet practice, so I figure he works with her."

"Thanks, Jess," Norma said. She felt her mood lift ever so slightly.

"We're on the right track then, right?" Jess asked.

"We just have to keep from running out of track," The Fox said, glancing at his wall clock.

44

Norma pressed down hard on the accelerator, heedless of the speed limit. She patted the top of the dashboard. "Time is of the essence, baby." She'd probably be interrupting Evelyn's preparations for Finn's funeral. The Spensers might have friends of the family coming to dinner. But what of that? She was worried about Coigne's dinner getting interrupted by a fork in the back of his neck, although he'd reassured her, they didn't use real forks. And she wouldn't call Evelyn in advance. Evelyn was her dear friend, but until Coigne was released and in the clear, she wouldn't allow herself to care about anything else. She had to know why Evelyn had essentially accused Geoff, her own husband, of murdering Misty and Finn. And, while she was at it, she'd find out why Geoff Spenser had gotten into a brawl with his own nephew. What she hadn't counted on was any objection from The Fox to her handling the interview with the Spensers by herself.

"What's the matter? You think I might strangle Evelyn and Geoff for holding out on me? You're damn right, I might. I've got to know why Evelyn didn't happen to mention the fight between Geoff and Finn when we met for coffee just one day after that fight."

"I should go with you. In some cases, two heads are better than one," he said.

"Two heads...better than one...Say, can I write that down?" But Norma relented. His presence would emphasize to the Spensers she was there as a lawyer defending Coigne and not as their friend. "Okay, let's go."

They decided to take separate cars, as The Fox had a meeting scheduled later that evening.

"I'll meet you in their driveway," he said. "We'll go in together."

Norma wasn't sure whether she was glad or sorry to find The Fox had enough backbone to argue with her on strategy. It gave her less elbow room. On the other hand, a little course correction for her now and again wasn't such a bad thing. He was, after all, a criminal lawyer, and she wasn't.

"Geoff's picking up some out-of-town guests—old friends of the family—at Dulles," Evelyn said, her bright blue eyes now bloodshot and her well-coiffed hair frizzy on one side as if she'd been lying on it. "Hello, Mr. Fox," she said. "Please come in."

Despite having to organize a funeral and play hostess to guests, Evelyn was gracious as she steered them into her "salon," as she called it, a room that ran the length of the first floor. Three enormous, tiered, crystal chandeliers hung from its coffered ceiling, and its bank of floor-to-ceiling windows overlooked a large corral, pastureland, and a stream that bordered the property.

Norma wasn't sure how to react to the fact Geoff wasn't home. Stick to the interrogation plan or come back later?

"We won't take up much of your time, Mrs. Spenser," The Fox reassured her. "We know you're busy, and may I extend my—"

And there went The Fox—taking charge by deciding to move forward with the interview without Geoff. She just knew it.

"Thank you." Evelyn gestured toward a pale blue linen settee and took the ivory-colored "bistro" chair across from him. Norma remained standing in front of a nearby armchair that matched the settee.

"And, please, call me Drew."

"May I get you some—"

"No time for tea and crumpets, Evelyn," Norma said.

"Or for manners, apparently." Evelyn winked at The Fox.

"It's about Geoff," Norma said. "And I wish to hell he were here, but so be it." She sat down and placed her fishing hat on the table next to her chair. "You'll have to forgive Laney, but she overheard you two arguing in your kitchen soon after Finn's body was discovered."

"Good grief. I hope you assured her that all married couples bicker, even in the face of—no, especially in the face of tragedy." Evelyn gave The Fox a look that said, "Here goes Norma again. Right off the deep end."

"Laney's well-versed in marital discord, of course. Coigne and I home-schooled her." Norma then recalled for her friend the overheard kitchen conversation, including how Laney had interpreted it. "Since you didn't tell me that Geoff and Finn had had fisticuffs, for God's sake, I can only assume you accused him of murdering Finn for the same reason he saw fit to take a slug at him, whatever that was. Why you would also accuse Geoff of killing Misty, I don't know."

Evelyn turned toward the bank of windows.

Don't stall, Evelyn. Don't cook up a story.

"Sometimes I wonder how our friendship survives," Evelyn said, finally, her lips betraying mild amusement. "But, I suppose I understand how you drew the conclusion you did. As a matter of fact, I drew the same one initially."

Norma glanced at The Fox. His elbows barely touched the arms of his chair, his hands were clasped on top of his belt, and his legs were crossed at the ankles. The man might have been waiting for a train.

"You might recall I told you the day I dropped you at your office that I'd started clearing out Dell's things. Oh, what a packrat. She had favors from childhood birthday parties and my old lipsticks from playing dress-up and a pair of special heels from her first prom. You get the picture. I was also surprised to find she kept a drawer for love letters, Christmas cards, report cards, and all manner of communiques from school."

Norma marveled at the positive, cheerful image Evelyn kept of her difficult daughter. She'd have to take care to do and say nothing to challenge that image.

Evelyn straightened her back and squared her shoulders like she was preparing to face something awful. "One envelope caught my eye because it had no stamp or return address on it. I hesitated to look. You know how kids are. I figured it would be something I wouldn't need to know. But curiosity got the better of me, and I'm still not sure I needed to know what I found out."

"Do you still—" Norma and the Fox had begun to speak at the same time, and Norma continued. "Do you still have the envelope and note? May we see it?"

Evelyn agreed and went in search of the document. While they waited, The Fox pulled out a pad and pen and made notes while Norma checked her phone.

"There's no envelope. I don't know how the note came to her. I also don't know how Geoff will react when he learns I shared the note with you and thereby let you know the background of the confrontation with his nephew, but I imagine it will all come out anyway. Shall I read it to you? It's from Finn to Dell. It's not long."

They nodded. Never had Norma felt so torn in her loyalties. She mentally rubbed her palms together as Evelyn began to read, hoping they'd learn something that would help Coigne. But she also feared she was about to hear something that wounded her friend deeply.

> *Dell-*
> *Don't show anyone this note. What happened yesterday was a mistake, but you shouldn't have taken off the top of your bathing suit. It never would have happened if you'd kept it on. I know you said your new suit was scratchy,*

but no guy can turn away from that. It wasn't my fault.
You can never tell anyone what happened. You'll get in big
trouble if you do. Tell Owen to keep his mouth shut if he
saw anything.

    Finn

Evelyn kept her eyes on the note for some time after she finished reading.

"I'm so sorry, Evelyn." Norma went to her friend and put her hand on her shoulder. "I can only imagine the anger and hurt you and Geoff must have felt reading that. I'm stating the obvious, but that's why Geoff fought with Finn before he died, right?"

Evelyn nodded, still not looking up. "I thought Geoff would kill Finn. I sure wanted to." She thought a moment. "Dell wore that 'scratchy' bathing suit the summer of her eleventh year." Evelyn shook her fists and shouted, "Her eleventh year, Norma."

Norma gave her friend some time before asking, "And Finn was how old?"

"He was about thirty years old. I can't remember any occasion he would've been here alone with her out at the pool. Now that we look back on it, we remember that was a bad summer for Dell. She was irritable and always had an upset stomach, and she lost weight, and I just thought it was hormonal. When we pressed her as to what was wrong, she came out with some story about Owen and our babysitter, a young gal whose mother taught at the school. We didn't really believe Dell's explanation but couldn't be sure. Now we know what was really bothering her."

Norma couldn't believe what she was hearing. Poor Dell. And unless she was badly mistaken, poor Jess too. She must have been the babysitter Evelyn was referring to. It all made sense now.

As The Fox continued to take notes, Norma took Evelyn's hands in hers. "Why didn't you tell me this the day we had coffee in front of the Marinoff Theater? Did you think I'd go off the deep end and report Finn? Or go after him myself?"

Evelyn said nothing at first. Then, "You might have felt it was your duty or something. We wanted to think about whether it was our duty to report him and what that might mean for the way people remembered Dell. I know we should probably turn over this note to cousin Bud, even now, but with Finn's death— well, it does sort of turn the spotlight on us as his likely killers, doesn't it? I guess Geoff's punching him in the face would have come out anyway since you learned about the fight somehow. Was it the Fingerhuts who told you? We saw them drive up as we left Finn's house."

Norma didn't answer the question as to how she found out. No need to drag the Fingerhuts into it.

Evelyn turned the note over to Norma. "Geoff will be unhappy with me for turning the note over to you, but nothing good ever comes from keeping secrets."

Norma was grateful Evelyn gave her the note. It might help Coigne since it gave Geoff and Evelyn a motive for killing Finn, but it wouldn't help Coigne in connection with Misty's murder. And Norma felt certain the two were connected.

The Fox hadn't budged an inch on his seat, and Norma wondered if he was thinking what she was thinking. He was.

"This background is very helpful, Evelyn, by way of filling in some blanks for us. And we may just have to wait for Mr. Spenser to learn more. Do you know when he'll be back?"

Evelyn shook her head. "I don't know. The plane isn't due until six, and you know how it is with traffic. You'll need to speak with him, though I doubt he'll have more to say than I've already told you."

Evelyn inched forward in her chair, evidently ready to conclude their visit. They all headed to the front door. At the last moment, Evelyn turned to Norma. "You're in a difficult situation, to put it mildly, and maybe this information has helped you as far as giving us a motive that's probably stronger than any motive your husband had for killing Finn. But I will warn you that as for

Geoff, he has an alibi for Misty's death. He was in the dentist's chair, shot full of God knows what, from seven-thirty until nine-thirty on the morning Misty was murdered. I don't know her exact time of death, but Geoff doesn't seem concerned. Thank you, Dr. Bennis."

"Was Geoff questioned about an alibi?" Norma asked.

"Bud's investigator, Chief Deputy Baker, spoke with both of us."

The Fox opened his mouth and then closed it.

"Bud is Sheriff Law. He's Evelyn's cousin," Norma said.

"Of course," he said. "Now I remember."

Norma thought she detected a wee smile on The Fox's face but rejected the notion—The Fox simply didn't have a sense of humor.

As they said goodbye, Norma studied the deep lines around her friend's mouth—new since she'd last seen her, she was fairly certain.

While they'd been inside, the sky had clouded over and the temperature had dropped to an unseasonable fifty-two degrees. Even the brilliant, trumpeting scarlet color of the redbud tree couldn't lift Norma's spirits much. Still, the fragrance of fresh, new grass reassured her that spring was here to stay.

She grabbed the car door handle and turned to The Fox. "I'm headed off to see Coigne. Can you get Jess to verify Geoff's dental appointment? What's his name again?"

"It's 'Bennis...the Dentist.'"

"Bennis the Dentist. Funny." So much for no humor. "Of course, Dr. Bennis may not talk freely to you. You may have to go armed with a good threat."

"Something with teeth in it?"

Before Norma could smack him, his phone rang. The interruption gave her a chance to check her own phone before she got underway. But the note of concern in The Fox's voice caused her to tune in to his call. He was speaking with Jess. Sounded like a scheduling matter. What was the big deal? Her gut sank.

"I'll be back in a flash," he said to the phone and hung up.

"Don't tell me," Norma said. "They've scheduled the preliminary hearing."

45

Coigne stood as Norma entered the meeting room.

"You've heard the news," Norma said.

Coigne nodded and wiped his hand across his face, hoping to rearrange it into a hopeful one.

Before Norma sat down on the metal chair across from him, she tore a sheet of paper off her legal pad and placed it over the dried brown splotches on her chair.

Coigne wanted to take her in his arms but feared the guard would burst in on them. He settled for a statement of the obvious. "It stinks in here. I've gotten used to it, but you—"

"Don't worry on my account. I live with horses, remember?"

He met her quip with a half-hearted smile. Half-hearted because she was probably just reminding him it was his idea to start up a horse farm in a place far from her home—and look how that turned out.

"I know what you're facing if you don't get through the prelim a free man. But I also know you can handle it." She paused. "We can handle it, whatever happens." Her voice then changed from something that bordered on emotional to her everyday swagger voice. "Now I want to get this out before The Fox gets here and claims credit for the bit of good news we've had." She brought him up to speed on all they'd learned from Evelyn and the disgusting implications of Finn's warning letter to a very young

Dell Spenser. "It's not that I hope for bad things to happen to Geoff Spenser. Had I seen that letter, I would have offed Finn myself. But coupled with the fact that Geoff punched Finn at his farm a few days before Finn was murdered, he's on the short list of Finn Spenser murder suspects. What do you think about that?"

Coigne closed his eyes as if giving the matter serious consideration, but that was not the case. "Does it matter? You say he has an alibi for Misty's murder, and that's the one they're frothing at the bit to pin on me."

"Some would say you looked good for Finn's murder too. He's the one who could have testified that Misty named you as she lay there dying. That testimony might have been admissible as a dying declaration. Whoever bumped him off did you a favor, and some might think that whoever was you."

Norma said nothing further. Instead, she pounded the table with her fist slowly, like a bell tolling. "Does it matter? Everything matters. Every word uttered by anyone associated with Misty or even Finn matters. This is your life on the line. The life of Laney's dad and the life of my—well, husband!" She was shouting now. "Goddammit, Coigne. Sit up and get involved in saving your life." She slapped the table hard and stood up.

The guard shoved open the door. "What's going on in there?"

"Everything's fine, but if it weren't, I'd've been dead by now," Norma said, her voice menacing with irritation. "And where were you when this man was being brutally beaten to within an inch of his life?" She resumed her seat.

As Norma and the guard swatted insults at each other, Coigne studied his raging beauty. God, she deserved better than him. But she'd chosen him, and even though the time was right for her to give up and take off, she stayed. Now, after all his failures, their separation, and his arrest, she still referred to him, with only slight hesitation, as her husband. He could do better. He had it in him. He needed to stop working against her and get on her side, no matter how long the odds.

The guard finally retreated and quiet reigned.

"I'm with you now. And thanks for the kick in the ass," Coigne said.

"Gotta stay in practice. You're going to get out of here, right?" Norma shuffled some papers. "Your alibi for Misty's death is strong—if we can just get Judd Spud to sound confident and intelligent."

A chuckle bubbled up between them at the notion Judd might ever sound confident and intelligent. But to Coigne, the chuckle felt foreign—good foreign.

"I'm glad you've stopped playing dead," Norma said, "because, with the hearing day after tomorrow, everyone's help is needed. Truth is, I wish we were working on this the usual way, as a team. The Fox is a good guy, but—"

Coigne took her hand and squeezed it. "So, let's work as a team. We'll do what we've done before. Something you taught me, as it happens."

"Naturally."

"Let's look for where we've made assumptions and maybe not realized it and see what happens if we un-assume those things."

"Like what? Where have we made assumptions?"

"The list is endless. We've assumed Geoff's alibi is good, and you said The Fox is checking that out. We've assumed the same person committed both murders. We've assumed we've got our arms around the world of suspects for both murders, yet both victims probably made more enemies, lethal enemies, than the rest of the Jefferson County populace put together. We've assumed Finn didn't murder Misty. Maybe Finn did murder Misty."

"What do you know? You actually are alive."

They continued listing assumptions, arguing about them, and assigning to one or the other the task of working through those assumptions. On Coigne's part, he'd have to do the best he could in light of his limited resources. The assumptions they thought were less promising they'd hand off to The Fox, which gave them another shared laugh.

When The Fox finally arrived, he all but tripped over himself, burdened as he was with apologies for his late arrival, the bad news about the preliminary hearing schedule, and an empty bag of tricks to delay it. But Coigne didn't share his dismay. He had his eye on Norma. A strange look had come over her face like she was trying to make sense of something or remember something. When he gave her a questioning look, she shook her head, and he let the matter drop, hoping she'd reveal what was on her mind when she was ready.

Norma got up to leave, and The Fox stayed behind with Coigne to go into detail about the preliminary hearing procedure.

"Where will you be if I need to reach you?" The Fox asked.

"Out looking for a talented actor to play Judd Spud on the stand." Norma left with a nod to Coigne.

46

The rain held off, and the temperature rose. Norma was ready to find a good omen wherever she could, and the weather would do.

Much as she enjoyed fantasizing about an actor to play Judd Spud, her time would be better spent looking for someone else who saw Coigne at the farm and could give him a solid alibi for the time of Misty's death. But no alibi was going to be a sure-bet get-out-of-jail card because Coigne couldn't deny he was at Marion's property at or close to the time Misty died.

That left pursuing Coigne's idea to challenge any and all assumptions they'd made concerning Misty's and Finn's murders. All that required hard thinking, and she knew where to go for that purpose. She double-checked her jacket pocket and located the list of assumptions she'd jotted down in the jail's parking lot.

Shepherdstown was rich with old—and some said haunted—cemeteries. Her favorite was downtown, spread out behind the Reformed Church of Christ on East German Street. The cemetery was established in 1774. Its ghosts were quite friendly, especially the ones who'd fought in the Revolutionary War because they received honors and well wishes from every visitor. That was not the case for those who fought in the Civil War and were buried at the nearby Elmwood Cemetery. Elmwood hosted Confederate soldiers who'd been rudely disinterred from the Antietam

Cemetery. Those ghosts were only too glad to bend your ear over the nasty comments uttered by certain passersby.

Norma believed in ghosts because she figured to deny their existence might bring trouble her way. Her reasoning was something similar to Pascal's on the subject of whether or not to believe in God. He figured it was best to stop wondering and place your faith in God because if you believed in God and he did exist, you'd go to heaven, and if you didn't believe in God and he did exist, you'd go to hell.

One assumption they'd all made could probably shift from their assumption column to their fact column. She and the rest of the defense team had focused on a short list of suspects, which seemed unrealistic in light of how vicious in life the two murder victims were. If anyone had many enemies, Misty and Finn did. But based on information The Fox had gathered through his network of journalists and unwittingly chatty employees in the prosecuting attorney's office, no witnesses had come forward to identify cars or trucks or other vehicles in the area of Marion's cottage at the critical time. Most any vehicle would have stuck out a mile in that rural area. And no pedestrian could have walked along those hairpin curves without winding up in an ambulance on the way to the hospital.

It would be dark soon, but she could still wend her way through the family plots she liked best to visit. Thus occupied, she figured she'd now eliminated the world-at-large from her list of suspects. That left her with a mere handful, and it was time to whittle that list down even more by eliminating those individuals who could not possibly have killed Misty. Marion was hardly likely to have burned down her own home in the course of murdering Misty, so she crossed her off the list. And Hilda Fingerhut was the one to call the fire department as soon as she saw smoke. It was most unlikely she would've put out a fire that was doing such a good job of destroying evidence if she were the one who committed the murder. Geoff may have an alibi, depending on the outcome of The Fox's visit to Bennis the Dentist, but that still left Evelyn and Owen. But no one had ever placed Evelyn or Owen at the crime scene, so far as she knew. And she couldn't imagine either one letting Coigne take the blame for a murder he didn't commit. It was possible, and she'd have to keep them on the list of possibilities, but somehow, they didn't fit.

Kaleb for Misty's murder? He might have snuck back home and killed her, but he was supposedly hiding out from Finn, his ex-lover and financial support, not from Misty. Neither he nor his mother had a motive to kill Misty that Norma was aware of.

"Ah," she said to the spirits assembled. She had arrived at her favorite spot in the cemetery, a comfortable wooden bench overlooking the Barton family plot—an area full of weather-worn gravestones, some old, some faded, some facedown, some no longer there. The souls of Barton parents and other relatives kept close, steady watch over the single row of young Bartons—she counted twelve—buried side by side, each before his or her first birthday. Their stones, just markers really, reminded her of so many white-gloved fingertips pushing up through the cold, hard ground. High above the Barton clan, red cedars had lent their shelter and beauty for over two hundred years, as they did that evening.

One bit of evidence the police held over Coigne still troubled Norma. The charge sheet referred to a phone call from Misty asking Coigne to meet her on the morning of her death. Coigne had lied about listening to the call, and when he finally admitted to picking up the message, he said he erased it as soon as he heard her voice. The prosecutor's position would be that he met with Misty because of that call, whether or not he listened to the whole thing or not. Why else would Misty have been in that neighborhood? The prosecutor would reason she was there because he was there. Why the hell did Coigne lie about listening to the message? As a former member of law enforcement knows, or as any reasonably intelligent person who watches television knows, it's real hard to hide the truth when it comes to cell phones. Thank you, AT&T.

Another assumption was that Finn was telling the truth about the one word Misty uttered before she died—"Coigne." Finn was the one who had motive to kill Misty. While Norma had no proof of his motive, she was sure it existed. She knew Misty's *modus operandi,* and if Finn had harmed her financially and emotionally by transferring his affections and checkbook to Kaleb, she'd try to blackmail him until he was penniless, so he'd have to deal with her, as indeed someone had. And if anyone suggested that Finn would never have lied about Misty's dying words, Norma would laugh until she cried. In light of the note Evelyn had just read out loud to The Fox and her, nothing was beyond that man's treacherous self-interest.

It would be foolish to consult a grave on this question, she told herself, and yet she did just that. Every single Barton agreed with her that Finn was up to the challenge of murdering Misty, but since that didn't explain who killed him or why, Norma still hesitated to embrace that theory. And yet...

And yet, if she jettisoned her assumption that both victims had to have been killed by the same person, it was possible Finn Spenser killed Misty and his uncle, Geoff Spenser, killed Finn. After all, same gene pool. Maybe murder was a family trait. She thought back to what Evelyn said about Geoff's and her motive for killing Finn. "You're in a difficult situation, to put it mildly, and maybe this information has helped you as far as giving us a motive that's probably stronger than any motive your husband had for killing Finn. But I will warn you that as for Geoff, he has an alibi for Misty's death." Finn was killed early on Monday, The Fox had told her, a "school day." Geoff was an employed executive at a well-run Fortune 500 pharmaceutical company. Someone had to have known where he was at all times. It would not be hard to learn if he had an alibi for Finn's death. No doubt the prosecutor wouldn't jump for joy at having to prosecute someone like Geoff

Spenser and would have much preferred to prosecute Coigne for a double murder, but we can't always get what we want.

She had to remember Coigne had not been accused of Finn's murder yet. Amazing what she considered good news these days.

It was getting late, and Norma was tired of testing assumptions with no one around except the Bartons to say she was right. The fact the clock was ticking for her to help gather together a convincing defense before the preliminary hearing made the pressure unbearable. Her strength was giving out, but she couldn't let that happen.

She said goodbye to her friends and asked them to think of Coigne over the next few days. When she reached her car, she called Laney to ask her to stay put for the evening and not head off to Owen's house, her daughter's most likely destination. Maybe Norma needed a chance to view all the Spensers dispassionately, and that meant keeping them at arms' length, even from Laney. In any event, Laney didn't answer her call, so Norma headed to the grocery store to pick up something for dinner. She'd call Laney again from home, check in with The Fox, and then try to get some sleep before the final stretch.

47

Norma sat in the parking lot of Food Lion. She kept her head bent over the steering wheel so shoppers would think she'd passed out on drugs and leave her alone. She knew her tears were the result of fatigue, but the phone call she had just had with The Fox didn't help. She'd shared with him her assumption-busting idea about separate killers for Misty and Finn, but he was way ahead of her on confirming Geoff's alibi for the time of Misty's death, which she'd expected, but also Finn's death.

"You know, I figured so long as I was alibi-checking—"

"Okay, so you're a go-getter, Foxy. What did you find out? And how did you find it out?"

"Bennis the Dentist was easy, the reason being he's a big mouth, and that's not a joke. He was ready to violate all state and federal common and statutory laws requiring patient confidentiality without qualm."

"Someone needs to report him," Norma said. "Go on."

"He pulled Geoff's record from his files and not only told me when he treated him and when they sent him home, he told me what the problem was. He was having a tooth removed—it was infected, impacted, and it made his mouth stink. Because his gums are so sensitive, they had to put him good and out."

"They put him out because he's a spoiled baby who likes blowfish."

"What's that about blowfish?"

"Never mind, Foxy. I'm just not liking the way this call is going."

"I get it. If Geoff had been trying to establish an alibi for the time of Misty's death, he couldn't have done a better job. It almost sounded like Bennis had been paid off; he was so certain and so enthusiastically precise about every detail, including the fact Geoff Spenser insisted on wearing two of those protective aprons."

"You said you checked out his alibi for Finn's murder, too. Seems to me that would be more difficult since we don't know precisely when Finn was killed unless you've learned new news."

"No new news, just more bad news. Geoff Spenser chaired an all-day event on marketing developments called—get this—Pharma Faculty Forum—at which professors from area universities present papers on the drug industry today, referencing challenges, opportunities, et cetera."

"You mean a SWOT talk: strengths, weaknesses, opportunities, and threats. They still talk like that? But anyway, go on. You can't mean he was there all day. There had to have been times he could have ducked out for a final showdown with his troublesome nephew. Please, Foxy. Tell me he could have."

"He introduced every speaker. And did I mention the full name of the conference? Pharma Faculty Forum of Phoenix, as in Phoenix, Arizona. Norma? Are you still there?"

"I don't suppose the conference was on Zoom?"

"Whether or not it was Zoomed, he was on the dais all day, behind each speaker, and ate lunch and dinner with the conference attendees, introducing the keynotes. In sum, Geoff Spenser is out-of-town alibied for almost forty-eight hours around the time of Finn's murder early on that Monday, the fifth," he said. After a pause, he said, "I can hear you breathing. If you don't want to talk, just listen. I have found something that might, and I emphasize *might*, help Coigne, but you won't like what I've found." He had her on speakerphone, and the noise he made organizing his documents sounded like the crashing of waves at Nazaré.

"I'm back," The Fox said. "I don't know about you, but I've been focusing on Geoff more than Evelyn Spenser for the obvious reason that Finn was his nephew, and he just seemed, from all you've told me, the more aggressive party. But after today's meeting with Evelyn, I started thinking about her differently. Not that she's more of an aggressive type than we thought. It's just that anyone, including the most genteel woman in the world, could have killed Finn after seeing that note about Dell in her scratchy bathing suit. Then it struck me as a little strange she didn't offer up an alibi for herself when she was telling us about her husband's. My sources tell me she has no alibi for either murder."

"How'd you get that information?"

"It helps that Chief Deputy Baker goes deer hunting with my dad and some other guys. The thing is, they don't suspect her of anything, so they're not as careful as they should be with information about her. I'm frankly surprised they asked her or Geoff for an alibi for Misty's murder. There must have been some gossip about Geoff and Misty."

Norma speculated that cousin Bud Law might have said something about Misty's failed attempt to seduce Geoff and the fact Misty told Evelyn she'd succeeded with her seduction even though that wasn't true. Norma explained to The Fox that she didn't believe Evelyn was capable of allowing Coigne to sit in jail for a crime she committed, even assuming she could kill someone.

"I know she's your good friend, Norma, but you have to admit, she has more motive than Coigne or anyone else to murder both Misty and Finn. That's assuming, once again, one person killed them both."

"But what evidence is there against her other than motive?"

"Aha. Here we go. Geoff drives a black Aston Martin. They're hard to miss in Jefferson County, West Virginia. Someone finally came forward and reported seeing an Aston Martin in the area of Finn's murder on the day he was murdered."

Norma wanted to laugh. The thought of petite, refined Evelyn Law Spenser subduing, then throwing Finn, that hunk of manhood, into the Opequon was too much. "How is that poss—" Before she got her sentence out, she thought of Owen. Could he have overheard Geoff and Evelyn talking about the scratchy bathing suit incident? "Where did this information come from?"

"Same source. I'm embarrassed to say I've gotten pretty good at weaseling information out of people without their realizing it."

"Don't try it on me, weasel. Listen—I need to go home, spend time with Laney, get a little rest. Then I'm coming down to the office. Putting in an all-nighter will remind me of the good old days when I was just starting out. And who knows what we might come up with."

"Who knows? See you then," he said.

She tried to reach Laney again but without luck. She picked up a gallon of milk and headed home. Thinking back on the call, Norma admitted The Fox was right to consider Evelyn and/or Owen as possible killers. Still, as much as she wanted Coigne out of jail, she couldn't summon any enthusiasm for either one of them being the guilty party. What worried her was that by offering up such an unlikely culprit as Evelyn, The Fox was out of ideas, and this was his Hail Mary.

The drive home was one of her loneliest.

48

It was almost dark when Norma drove up her long driveway. Two surprises met her when she reached the top. The first was a sighting of Laney, in silhouette, all alone at the paddock. She was leaning over the fence and stroking Durham, a buckskin quarter horse stallion Coigne had been thrilled to board. Durham's owner must have called to say he was on his way over. Otherwise, the stallion would have been fed by now and back in the barn. Knowing Laney, she was explaining to Durham the reason for the disruption to his normal schedule.

While Norma didn't know why her daughter had failed to answer her phone despite repeated calls all afternoon, she would understand if Laney's need for quiet and solitude were the reason. On that assumption, Norma tooted her horn as gently as she could and left Laney to commune with the stallion.

The second surprise was the arrival of Jess, or at least she thought it was Jess. The young woman who emerged from Jess's beat-up Miata wore collar-length dark hair tucked behind her ears, a jade halter top, an ankle-length, flowing black skirt, and caramel wedge sandals.

"Who are you? Or am I in another remake of *Invasion of the Body Snatchers*?" Norma asked as Laney sauntered over to join them.

"Hey, Laney," Jess said. "I know, you didn't think I had clothes like these. Thought I might air them out and take 'em for a stroll.

But you are probably wondering, both of you, what brings me here since I should be burning the midnight oil with that sadistic taskmaster at the office."

"Can we go inside?" Laney said. "It's chilly out here. C'mon, Jess."

"You look like you've got news," Norma said, searching Jess's face. "The only news I can bear to hear right now is that someone's confessed to Misty and Finn's murders. Might that be why you're so dressed up?"

Uncharacteristically, Jess grabbed Norma's hand as they headed for the farmhouse. "I wish that were the reason, but at least what I have to say isn't tragic."

"As hints go, 'isn't tragic' isn't helpful."

"Lighten up, Norma," Laney said, grabbing Jess's other hand. "Sarcasm is for idiots. Now who is it who said that? Oh, it was you, Norma."

Norma wondered if Jess and Laney had been drugged or hypnotized, the way they both were so steadfast in their sunny-side outlook.

In the kitchen, Laney insisted on pouring everyone, including herself, a glass of white wine "to provide the right conditions for receiving news that's not tragic." She led them out to the screen porch and bestowed the place of honor, the double-wide, on Jess.

Norma gave everyone three seconds to settle in and take a sip. "Now, what is it, Jess?"

At the same time, Norma couldn't get over a new look of mischief, delight, even sparkle in the eyes of her young colleague.

"Hear ye, hear ye. To those who've been privy, the kind of privy that's not *a* privy—air quotes—but *is* privy—"

"Is she drunk?" Norma asked.

"No. I think I get her. Just listen," Laney said.

"No interruptions, please, ladies. You've both been privy, indeed very privy, to my—how shall I put it—my lies, yes lies, that's the word, about Geoff Spenser and my explanation as to why I lied, am I correct?"

"Do we need to answer that?" Norma asked, enjoying herself despite all she had on her mind.

"No, not at all. I'm only here to hear myself talk. Also, I had visitors this evening, as I was supping—"

"Even I have to object to 'supping,'" Laney said.

"But isn't that what the Spensers do? They sup?"

"Yes, so what do the Spensers have to do with it?" Laney asked.

Norma finally caught on, but she let Jess tell it her way and have some fun.

"As I was saying, the Spensers arrived as I was supping, and they brought with them glad tidings. Any eye-rolls about the term 'glad tidings'? It wasn't exactly glad tidings, anyway. It was an apology—and it was about damn time they got around to it—for having fired me so many years ago in the belief I'd done something unspeakable with their son Owen."

All of a sudden, Jess choked up, and Laney flew to her with a warm, long-lasting hug.

Norma had to tread carefully. She wasn't sure Evelyn and Geoff had told Jess the entire truth about the contents of Finn's note and what probably happened to Dell. In fact, no one would ever know the whole truth about what happened, but what they suspected was abominable. "Did they tell you what brought this on, Jess?"

"Wait. Don't say a word until I get back with tissues." Laney rushed into the kitchen and returned with white napkins for Jess.

After a thorough nasal honking, Jess continued. "They didn't go through chapter and verse but did say they had proof that what they thought had occurred years ago that led them to fire me was a lie. Now that they had a better idea of what really happened, they couldn't forgive themselves for not trying harder to get at the truth."

Norma caught the look of joy that passed between Jess and Laney. She only wished she'd understood the depth of pain Jess had endured, knowing that the Spensers, the family Jess had admired and trusted and perhaps fantasized as her own family, had turned on her so suddenly and for such an awful, mistaken reason. If Norma could garner one lesson from her legal assistant's suffering, it was that everyone experienced deprivation, disappointment, cruelty, lies, and all the rest of it so differently. What for Norma might have been just another day in the life of Norma Bergen, for Jess, it was a sudden, dramatic loss of self-worth.

The evening could have ended with several more toasts and burgers on the grill. Instead, Marion Chatte showed up, and Norma led her back to the porch with the others. She wasn't sure she felt up for enlarging the party, especially not with Marion after the showdown at *Chez* LaBomba. Jess looked even more unhappy with their new guest.

"Don't worry, Jess," Marion said, apparently sensing Jess's discomfort. "Kaleb is not with me. He's packing. We're both on our way to the airport. We'll be staying with an old friend, Kaleb's high school history teacher, as a matter of fact. He lives in Asheville now. We'll be there for the foreseeable future until we get the cottage rebuilt—or not."

Marion's news floored Norma. Last time she checked, the history teacher had barely escaped Marion's clutches, or that's how Norma had interpreted their strained relationship and his departure from town. But the couple went way back with a history that long preceded Norma's arrival in West Virginia. In fact, Norma had once speculated that Kaleb was the teacher's son. To find they would be staying with him made a great deal of sense. Maybe he could do something with Kaleb. She knew what she'd do with him.

"Come in, Ms. Chatte," Laney said. She introduced herself and offered to get her some wine. Norma felt her heart flutter, seeing how poised and mature Laney had become.

"Okay, everyone, into the kitchen," Norma said. "We're having a patty party—a hamburger patty party, that is. I'm making burgers. Can you stay, Marion? Jess?"

"Sure, I'm staying," Jess said.

"I won't stay, but thanks," Marion said. "I had something else I needed to speak with you about. Umm, privately?" She brushed her thick chestnut hair out of her eyes and looked around as if a private corner for their talk would present itself.

"You guys can talk here. I'll show Jess my room. You didn't see it last time, did you, Jess?" Laney asked.

Norma waited to hear them pound up the stairs, then turned to Marion. She wondered if an apology was due from her for their last meeting. On reflection, she felt both of them were equally right and wrong in how they'd handled the colossal mess Kaleb had caused, mixing finance with romance. She'd leave things alone and let Marion have her say.

"Have a seat here in the nook. I'd offer you a plate of something, but I'm afraid of what you might do with it, and I only have the set of eight." Norma couldn't remember if Marion had a sense of humor. She hoped so.

"I think enough plates have been 'offered,' and I'd like to pass on a discussion of my son's obvious faults. I've done my best parenting him, and now it's up to Kaleb how the rest of his life goes."

"Here, here." Norma got to work at the counter making burger patties. "It seems like you've got something else to tell me. Shoot."

Norma had brought the wine and a clean glass to the breakfast nook, and as she'd anticipated, Marion poured herself a glass.

"I've discovered something that may or may not be helpful to you. Information, that is. It has to do with a phone message I received while I was at Union Station in D.C. looking for Kaleb."

"Go on."

"It was from Misty Bubb. I didn't know her. We've never had pets, so our paths wouldn't have crossed. In her message, she introduced herself as a friend of yours and the Fingerhuts, I guess by way of saying we had friends in common. She went on to say she needed to talk to me in person about something important, and would I be home that Wednesday? Turns out that Wednesday was the day of the fire and the day she died. Well, I did listen to her message, but not until the day after the fire. You see, I didn't recognize her number, and finding Kaleb was my first priority."

"I assume the police asked you about the call?" If the police had Misty's call to Coigne that morning, they probably had Misty's call to Marion as well. Norma was beginning to feel a little excitement. Misty had a reason for going to Marion's that presumably had nothing to do with Coigne. She'd just bet it had something to do with spilling the beans on Finn and his dealings with Kaleb, sexual and otherwise. It was the same kind of trouble-making Misty had tried with Evelyn Spenser.

"The police did ask. I could tell them nothing more than I've told you. I have no idea what Misty wanted to see me about. Do you?"

"None at all."

Marion nodded. "I just hope this information is helpful."

Norma maneuvered her elbows to turn on the water faucet to get the gummy slime from the patties off her hands. "Did the police have anything more to say or ask about Misty's call?"

"I'm afraid not."

Norma thanked Marion for the information. She wasn't sure how it helped or if it did. Obviously, Misty had phoned Coigne and Marion the morning she died, asking to meet with each of them. Norma might never know what Misty wanted with them, but it was one more bit of confusing evidence that she hoped would serve to confuse the Circuit Court judge at the preliminary hearing and the grand jury if, heaven forbid, the criminal proceedings against Coigne would get that far.

As Marion stood to leave, Norma said, "You have a new haircut. Looks nice." It wasn't something she'd normally notice, especially not at a time like this, but there'd been a time when she'd hoped she and Marion could become good friends. Maybe that was still a possibility. She needed good friends.

After Marion left, the younger women returned to the kitchen, and their youthful chatter kept Norma steady through dinner. Afterward, Laney was more understanding than one would have expected when she learned Norma had to return to the office. At least she'd have company, as Jess made no moves to leave, which suited Norma just fine.

The monotony of dishwashing gave Norma some headspace to ponder an idea that had been forming throughout the day, something to do with their list of assumptions. It concerned an assumption they'd left off the list, but more than that, she didn't know.

49

For the second time that long day, Norma set out for her office. She'd been methodically making a mental list, once more, of all the assumptions she and Coigne had come up with together and many more she'd thought of on her own relating to the killer or killers, the different combinations of possible killers, and their respective motives, means, and opportunities to carry out one or both murders. She reached assumption number twenty-eight and was on the verge of giving up the exercise when she spotted a woman seated on a bench close to the Jefferson County Courthouse. The landmark building was most famous for hosting John Brown's trial for treason. The old-fashioned streetlamps weren't all that bright but bright enough to catch the waves in the woman's long, luxurious jet-black hair.

And then the woman stood. Except, it wasn't a woman. It was a man. Other than the long black hair, there was nothing effeminate about him, yet Norma had been sure she was looking at a woman, and she'd seen a woman because the long hair raised that expectation.

This event at the courthouse led her to the missing assumption, the one assumption about the murders she should have challenged but failed to do so. Because Misty was murdered, they'd all assumed Misty was the intended victim. What if she weren't? What if the owner of the home where the murder occurred—innocent, responsible Marion Chatte—was the intended victim, and killing Misty was a mistake? Norma considered the question for the rest of her drive, by which time she had a good idea who Misty's killer was. It seemed so obvious. All she needed now was the proof.

50

Norma found The Fox seated at his desk, gripping a pencil with his teeth and running his fingers through his hair with evident frustration.

"What's new?" she said.

"Motions, motions, motions. You?"

"Just make sure one of those motions concerns bail. But hold on tight. I've just been to see my old pal, Sheriff Law."

"This late? He met with you this late?"

"We're like the United States and the United Kingdom—we have a special relationship. He and I have worked out a plan, and, I'm glad to say, I didn't need to threaten to broadcast his drinking on the job to get him to agree to it."

"Everyone knows about that, Norma. The word is they couldn't afford to pay him a decent salary, so they made up for it in benefits. On-the-job drinking's one of them. But go on. What's your plan?"

Norma laid out her theory about the murders and how she'd prove she was right, and even if it wasn't sufficient proof of who killed Misty and Finn, it would provide enough evidence to get the sheriff looking for the real killer. Norma felt gratified not only by The Fox's rapt attention but by his vigorous note-taking, which showed he took her theory seriously and would follow up as needed.

When she finished summarizing, she leaned back and closed her eyes. "What do you think?"

"I'd say your theory sings a sweet tune. And you say Law is willing to follow through?"

"He said he would if I deliver. I'm going to go home and get some rest and then confront the killer in person. I'll need to be smart."

"You'll need to be careful. You going to tell Coigne? We should, you know."

"Here's the problem. We've got to keep him informed, so he can participate in his defense. That's our duty. His best interests are served by going forward with the plan, right? In this instance, if we told him the plan, he'd be worried about me, so he'd nix the plan that's in his best interest. Therefore, we shouldn't tell him."

"You're a sorceress. You can flip things upside down without moving a muscle."

"Let's compromise. You tell Coigne—sometime tomorrow afternoon. That work?"

"Hold on. You're forgetting about another client's best interests, aren't you? That's a real sticky wicket. Why don't we take a couple of minutes to do some legal research?"

"No point. Even if I were certain there was a conflict of interest, even if I faced disbarment, do you think it would change what I need to do?"

Norma left him to worry about the ethics of hanging one client out to dry in favor of another.

As feared, she slept fitfully. She was worried if she failed to get the desired reaction, it would be a long time before Coigne saw daylight outside a prison—if he made it out.

Morning broke too early, too hot, too humid, and too gray. Only June fourteenth, and it felt like a late afternoon in August. Despite her caterwauling, she loved her new home state, but that morning the fact that West Virginia was a proud sponsor of global warming chafed more than usual.

Norma said her regular goodbye to Laney but didn't quite make it out in time.

"What's happening, Norma? You seem weird. Is Coigne okay?"

"Yes. So far as I know, and I'll see him this afternoon to confirm it."

"Nothing's screwed up my scheduled visit, has it? I swear you're acting cagey."

"Nonsense. Did Jess get off before midnight? Seemed like she was hunkering down here for a siege. You guys get along. I'm really glad things are working out for her, aren't you?"

"You're pathetic, Norma. What's with the small talk about relationships? 'I'm really glad things are working out...' That's not you. What's going on?"

"Stop worrying, will you? You're making me jittery. See you later."

Norma wanted to wait a while before heading over to the Opequon. She drove along Route 230 with the sun rising over her left shoulder and the Blue Ridge mountains. She felt reassured by that imposing barrier, safeguarding her from whatever lay beyond, like urban sprawl. This morning, the ridge was a smokey French blue. Could she look forward to a drive like this with Coigne soon?

At last, it was time to head toward the Fingerhuts' farm, where she passed Hilda Fingerhut heading in the opposite direction as Norma had hoped. Hilda didn't seem the type to swim laps almost daily at the university's new health center, but then, people surprise you. Norma planned on at least an hour with Jerry Fingerhut.

She swung around the curve, and with the remains of Marion's cottage now in view, she checked on the progress of the cleanup. The calamity along the creek occurred two weeks before, yet already the sodden sheetrock and charred remains of a home had been hauled away. Soon the grass would grow back tall, and there'd be no evidence the site was scarred by hatred so intense it started a fire.

She pulled into the Fingerhuts' driveway and got out. Sweat seeped through the fabric of her sleeveless white top. At least the warm weather provided an excuse for so much perspiration other than the real reason—fear. Could she dare to hope that a killer who'd shown no mercy toward two human beings would turn on a fan if she asked?

Jerr met her at the front door. "Well, now, hello, Ms. Bergen. Norma. I'm sorry you just missed Hilda. It's Tuesday, and this is her swimming time."

"Hi, Jerr. That's all right. You can pass on to her what I wanted to talk about." Norma made herself casual and accommodating.

He invited her in, his disposition kind as ever, his movements slow as ever.

"Make you some coffee? I seem to recall you favored Hilda's peanut brittle, and you're in luck. She made a fresh—"

"Thanks, Jerr. It's a bit early, but sure, that'd be nice." She wandered into their living room and sat on the sofa. "I just had a few follow-up things to talk about, if you don't mind." She pulled out a pad and pen, just another day in the life of a busy lawyer.

"Sure. I'll be right back with a plate."

"Don't forget the toothpicks."

He laughed and teetertottered into the kitchen.

She almost felt remorse for acting like she didn't know the truth. Then she remembered he'd killed two people and was willing to let Coigne pay for it with the rest of his life. Forget the remorse.

When he returned, he placed a plastic plate full of brittle and a bunch of toothpicks wrapped in a paper napkin on the coffee table. He took his seat on the rocking chair.

"I guess you saw Marion Chatte had her property cleared. Looks like she'll be rebuilding soon."

"Where's she getting the money to rebuild? I'd a thought she'd be scared off anyway, what with everything?"

"The money? I guess you inherited your farm here, Jerr, but Marion probably has a mortgage, and that means she has insurance. And I'm sorry. She told me she intends to take the opportunity with all the construction going on to take down the fence and move forward with her building plans. I wanted to tell you in person. Maybe we should talk some more when you and Hilda can come into the office. New strategies, things like that. It'll start costing, I'm afraid."

Norma studied the impact of her words and wasn't sure they'd made any. His gaunt face had always been gray, and his wattle couldn't get any looser. He was the very image of Pa Joad in *The Grapes of Wrath*.

"More brittle?" he said.

"Sure. I'm using the brittle to celebrate, and, by the way, you're the first one, other than Drew Fox and Laney, to hear the news. They're releasing Coigne. Seems they've come up with new evidence that points a finger in another direction. Oh, they're making him sit through some processing. They'll drag it out because that's what they do. But, yeah, they've found more evidence that exculpates him."

"Hmm. You don't say."

Jerr reached for some brittle. As he leaned back and crunched down, his rocking picked up speed. "What evidence, I wonder?" He sounded like he was making conversation, half-bored, but she wasn't sure.

"Apparently, it's a number of things, but now this is just gossip The Fox—Drew—overheard, but one of the things they found is a bit of wool—red, black, I'm not sure—they missed it first time around. Careless." She shook her head. "When you think of all Coigne's had to suffer because of it."

"Now, wait just a minute. I hear they went over that cottage, what was left of it, and there couldn't have been much of anything like that because of the fire. I think someone's pulling his leg."

"Looks like our killer slipped up just like Chief Deputy Baker, the investigator, did. The shed didn't burn, and that's where the gasoline came from. And that's where the wool was found. It was just a small bit, but you'd be amazed what they can find out from a thread under a microscope."

"But I hear Mr. Coigne got ahold of those cans. Even Hilda saw him standing there with them. Probably Finn Spenser did too."

She grabbed another small piece of brittle. She didn't want to run out of it before she'd laid it all out for him. "There's no evidence Coigne or Finn went into the shed, and that's where the evidence was found, in the shed. Coigne might have touched the cans outside the shed. You didn't have cause to go in that shed recently, did you?"

"Hell, no. And besides, why are they coming up with this evidence now?"

She didn't see the longed-for beads of sweat across his brow, but a crimson patch appeared on each cheekbone.

"Damn good question. I asked the same thing—here's Coigne getting beaten up in jail while they take their ever-loving time still poking around for evidence. But that's how it is in rural America. They may find something that could be evidence, like the wool. Then it takes a long time to see if it means anything. They have to get ahold of an expert, apply all these chemicals, do computerized studies, and then there are DNA tests to run, and then you have to wait for the results. Then they go house to house asking likely people for their woolens to see if there's a match-up. The good news is that both Marion and her son Kaleb break out when they wear wool. They don't own any. So, whoever left that bit of evidence is likely the one who killed Misty and burned down the cottage to hide the evidence. Surprising, isn't it, that the killer hid all other bits of evidence—fingerprints, shoe prints. Should have burned the shed too."

Neither one spoke, but she noticed Jerr's hands gripped the rocking chair like he was going to catapult himself into the fireplace. Or maybe she imagined it. Maybe he thought she was just pulling the wool over his eyes, a pun The Fox would appreciate.

She wanted to give him plenty of time to think about what it would cost to build another fence to keep his cows from wandering off into the creek. Only time would tell what he'd do about that wool. Her hope, the one she'd expressed to Sheriff Law, was that he'd run get his buffalo plaid birthday coat, the one he'd worn to her office a couple of weeks ago when it was still cool, wad it up, and throw it away somewhere. Anywhere. No warrant was needed to search trash.

"Anyway, I just wanted to let you know we'll need to get on old Marion again before she starts on your fence. I hope you meant it when you said back in my office you could handle a Rottweiler because she sure is one. It's going to start costing real money, too, but a lawsuit is what it's going to take. I don't think this is a case for a contingency fee arrangement either—you know, where the lawyer doesn't get paid unless the plaintiff wins money damages because I don't think there's a real good chance you'll win." At last, all color, even the gray, drained away from his face. She prayed he was saying to himself, "All that, and for nothing."

"I'm so sorry, Jerr."

Norma prided herself on knowing when to quit, a talent that didn't extend to curbing her appetite for sweets. "May I?" She folded two large pieces of brittle into her napkin and told Jerr she'd be in touch.

The trap had been laid—she could almost hear the first eight notes of Beethoven's Fifth. She only hoped the *Ode to Joy* would follow. That would be up to Sheriff Law.

51

Peanut brittle notwithstanding, Norma felt she deserved an additional treat, having endured a most difficult hour setting Jerry Fingerhut up for murder charges. It didn't concern her that she'd ruined his future, but Hilda's would be ruined too. That did bother her. But she wasn't Jesus Christ—she couldn't take on the sins of the world. Hell, it was a full-time job keeping her family alive and intact. Having disposed of the irksome moral qualm about Hilda, she pointed the Prius toward Eastern Regional Jail with a stop off at the mall nearby for some Baskin-Robbins ice cream. The one advantage of being close to six feet tall was she could eat an unlimited number of scoops without weight gain. As for how it affected her heart, probably not at all. Most people weren't even sure she had one.

She was glad to get in and out of there fast. They kept the room temperature as cold as the ice cream. She'd parked her car in a corner at the back of the parking lot where there was shade and a breeze, and she now regretted that. Even more so as she reached for the door handle and felt a slender metal pipe at the base of her spine. Her ice cream cone, piled high, slipped from her hand and landed upside down on her shoe.

"Don't move, or I'll pull the trigger. No one will notice around here. Believe me, not with this traffic noise."

Norma was furious with herself. How dumb was she not to have considered he'd follow her and not dispose of his wool coat first? He must have seen right through her. And where was the sheriff, anyway? He was supposed to have someone tailing Fingerhut the moment he left his house.

"I'm sorry, Norma. It looks like you weren't as clever as you thought."

"I'm on all fours with you on that, Jerr. So where to? Not the Opequon, I hope."

"Just get in the car."

She stalled for time, futzing around with her saddlebag. "You understand Sheriff Law and my office know where I was headed and the reason why. You're not going to get away, Jerr. Don't make it worse than it is."

"I've run out of time for talking, Norma. Get in the car, or I'll shoot you right here."

A family of four she'd seen inside made their way to their car and fumbled with a car seat. The baby started to cry as he was buckled in, and Jerr was beginning to lose it. His breath and body odor confirmed it. Surely someone would see them in the back of the lot and notice something was wrong. Here goes!

She flung the bag at him. The gun fired. Norma screamed. The family turned around and stood there, staring.

"Get in the car. Get in the car. You're driving," Jerry ordered.

Shocked by the gunfire, Norma got in.

"Is everything okay back there?" The family man finally found his voice.

Thunk. Thunk. The doors of the Prius closed, and they sped off.

The car lurched and swerved. It leaped the curb and bounced down again. She was going to vomit.

"Go faster," he said.

She felt too scared to think of a plan and instead focused on steering, unaware of where she was headed. Surely someone would stop them. They were going over ninety on a busy highway with four-way stoplights. His directions were taking them back to Shepherdstown, but why?

"Rumsey. Head to Rumsey Park."

What can he be thinking? What kind of getaway is that? She got a mental image. There's nothing there but trees and a statue of James Rumsey at the top of many stairs, and a low stone wall between the park and a long, steep drop into the Potomac. "Jerr—this isn't the way to go. There's always hope if you're alive."

"*I* plan to live, Ms. Bergen."

He kept the gun stuck to her rib, and she kept her foot on the pedal. *Think. Think. Keep your wits. Keep breathing.* She figured his plan was to prod her with his gun up the steps to the plinth on which the statue stood and give her a good shove. She'd either break her neck on the way down to the river or wind up in the river, where she'd drown.

She needed a plan. As she mounted Mill Street to the park's entrance, its massive wrought iron gate wide open, she began to speed up and twist and turn like crazy.

"Hey, slow down. You'll hit somebody."

"I can't help it. You're making me nervous."

She had no intention of hitting anybody. Early in the day, no one was around. She did intend to make an adjustment, though.

She said a prayer and said goodbye to Coigne and Laney. Then, pedal to the metal, she headed straight to the low stone wall—

"Hey!" he roared.

—swerved at the last second and rammed it. The wall held. The gun went off. Her airbag inflated, but Jerr's didn't.

And thank you, Jess, for letting me know the passenger airbag was faulty.

52

"There's this one thing I don't get," Laney said, turning to Sheriff Law. "You say you knew Coigne was innocent, but you didn't let him go. Why not? That's so unfair."

The family had gathered with Coigne's defense team and a few friends and neighbors on the screen porch to celebrate Coigne's release. Coigne had his arm wrapped around Norma's waist where he'd planted it the moment he arrived home and where he'd kept it ever since. The Fox and Jess were whispering nearby at the dessert table. Owen and his parents were the only ones who looked less than totally happy, which Laney understood. Norma had explained to her all the rotten things Finn had done. Maybe his death made things easier for the Spensers, but they still had to live with what he'd done to their daughter.

Sheriff Law had accepted the invitation to join in the celebration, and Laney wasn't going to lose the chance to get all her questions answered.

"Fair enough," Law said. "I knew your dad was innocent because I know him. I also knew the source of some of the evidence surrounding Misty Bubb's death wasn't always credible."

Sheriff Law was referring to Finn's lie about Misty's final word. Geoff Spenser merely shrugged at the reference, but Evelyn turned away and wandered to the dessert table. Standing next to Owen, Laney grabbed his hand and squeezed.

Though Sheriff Law had not asked permission to smoke a cigar on the porch, Norma looked the other way, which shocked Laney. His big smile made the job of puffing out the smoke very difficult.

"But it took your mom and Mr. Fox and Jess here, and you, young lady, from what I understand, to put the pieces together for me. It took time, and I had to be sure."

Law sat back on the double-wide and flicked his ashes in the saucer Norma handed him. "Remember, against your dad was the troubling history between Ms. Bubb and your family, the fact his knife was there in a place he said he wasn't, the fact he'd received a call from Ms. Bubb asking him to meet her there, and the fact Misty had allegedly said his name before she died. Add to that his alibi wasn't great. You may not like this idea, Laney, but it happens sometimes. A person will be arrested even before the state can prove beyond a reasonable doubt he's guilty. And while he's in jail, the search for more substantial evidence continues. And before your mom came up with her theory about Jerry Fingerhut, that old fool, no one else 'looked good for it,' as they say on TV."

Owen raised his hand, which had a soda can in it. "I've still got a question if it's okay to ask."

"Sure, son. Fire away. This stuff's been in the news already," Law said.

"It's about Mr. Coigne's knife. I figure Finn had it on him the day he showed up at the cottage, but I don't understand how it got inside the house or why it was so important."

"Thanks for asking, Owen," Laney said. "I never got that either."

"Well, everybody, sit back. This is gonna take a while. This is what happened, and it will explain the whole knife business. Misty Bubb decided to pay Marion Chatte a visit. The women didn't know each other, but Misty knew something about Marion's son. She knew that Finn Spenser had pulled out of his romance with her and pulled out his investment in her doggie spa, and then he connected with Marion Chatte's son, Kaleb. He set Kaleb up in a studio, and they became a secret couple. When Finn came back to town and bought his farm and was acting like he was some big shot, it was too much for Misty, and she decided to blackmail him. She threatened to reveal to Marion what Finn was up to with her son. Turns out Finn didn't care and wouldn't pay Misty since his relationship with Kaleb wasn't going well anyway. In fact, it was kaput.

"But Misty wasn't one to take things lying down. If she couldn't blackmail Finn, she could at least cause him trouble. That's why she went to see Marion—to stir the pot. Unfortunately, Marion didn't get Misty's phone message about a visit in time, but Misty decided to take a chance and see if she was home. It was on the way to her clinic anyway.

"So, Misty shows up at the Chatte cottage and, lo and behold, Mr. Fingerhut, who's got a grudge against Marion Chatte about property boundaries, spots Misty at the door of the cottage and thinks it's Marion. His eyes aren't so good, and the women are about the same height and coloring. He'd been clearing a fallen tree from a path through his woods when she showed up.

"The sight of her infuriates him. He sneaks up behind her and hits the back of her head with a nearby large stone. When she falls, he decides to move her, finds the front door key under the mat where the real Marion Chatte keeps it, and drags Misty into the kitchen. On the way, blood drips on the living room floor. That's why the fact Mr. Coigne's knife was found in the living room where Misty's blood had spilled was so important. It put him with the decedent before she died. She died of asphyxia in the fire."

Some guests took that moment to get some dessert, but Laney still had questions. "But now that we know Finn had Coigne's knife, and we know he got it when Coigne gave it to him to cut some knotted rope at his farm, how did Finn wind up dropping the knife in the living room of Marion Chatte's house?"

"I'd like to know that myself," Coigne said.

"Fair enough. Finn had arrived early, much earlier than anybody thought, for the visit with Hilda at her house. As he drove by and saw strange goings on at the Chatte cottage, home of his former lover, Kaleb, he pulled over—believe it or not, onto the Fingerhuts' property in their woods. He recognized Misty but not the man with her at the front door. He watched as Jerry Fingerhut exited the house, got the gas cans out of the shed, and lit the place on fire. Once Jerry left, Finn ran in." Sheriff Law turned to Evelyn and Spenser. "I like to think Finn ran in to see if Misty was okay and to get her out of there. He must have dropped that knife on the way out. That was kinda typical for his bad luck, I'd say. And, of course, he came back a second time when Mr. Coigne showed up, acting as if he'd only just arrived.

"It's a shame that fire was so fierce—made it hard to detect evidence of Jerry Fingerhut's presence or anyone's really. And Jerry was wearing gloves from chopping that tree."

Sheriff Law slapped his kneecaps and stood up.

"Are you able to answer one more question," Laney asked, worried that he'd said all he wanted to and would prefer to eat some more food.

"Of course. I owe your family that much." He nodded at Coigne and sat down.

"Well, I thought you were supposed to follow Mr. Fingerhut once Norma warned him the bit of wool from his jacket had been found in Marion Chatte's shed. He was going to throw it away somewhere, and that would show guilty knowledge, like he'd worn it in the shed the day of the murder, and you'd catch him red-handed."

"I hate to tell you this, especially in front of everyone," he said, hanging his head. "Truth is, we were late. I know in the movies and on TV things like short-staffing, having to stop for gas, waiting at the wrong house, all those things don't happen. But in real life, they do. I'm just glad your mom had the good idea—"

"And remarkable presence of mind," Norma threw in.

"To crash the car with Mr. Fingerhut sitting there airbagless. And it's a good thing Jerr's practically blind and didn't see the 'airbag off' indicator light on, or he might have guessed what she was going to do. Oh, and for your mom to have the driving skills to brake just right so she didn't go over that wall was downright—"

"Spectacular?" Norma suggested.

"Exactly," Law answered.

"Will Mr. Fingerhut be well enough to stand trial?" Laney asked.

"I hear he's having trouble walking. Shot himself in the foot, literally," The Fox said.

"It is so, my man," Law said. "That's what he did."

"I've got a question for *you*, Norma," Evelyn said. "How did you know Jerry Fingerhut had worn that wool jacket that day of the fire?"

"I was there when he came to pick up Hilda. He had it on," she said.

Evelyn gave her a thumbs up. "Clever woman."

"My turn again," Laney said to the sheriff. "When Norma told you her plan, weren't you worried she'd get Mr. Fingerhut mad enough at Marion Chatte for supposedly planning to take out his fence and build he'd go after her again? Oh, wait. I've got it. She'd already left town for Asheville with Kaleb."

Coigne, beaming and full of pride, turned to Norma. "I thought you were clever to realize Jerr was the only person who could have come to Marion's house, committed the murder, and set the fire without getting there by truck or car or something and without being noticed. He had the woods for cover. Of course, Hilda did too, but she was the one who called nine-one-one about the fire, making her an unlikely suspect. How'd you get so smart, Ms. Bergen?" Coigne nuzzled her neck.

"It's a skill one develops when one's husband will go and get himself arrested for murder."

Laney laughed with abandon, not so much because her parents' lovey-dovey repartee was clever or sweet—actually, she thought it was gross, but she'd take it. She'd never seen Norma show so much warmth toward Coigne. Toward anyone.

"So how did no one spot Finn's Denali?" Owen asked. "You say he showed up while Mr. Fingerhut was there at the cottage."

"When I say he got there early, it was real early, and he was good and tucked into those woods. I'm sort of surprised Hilda didn't see his car when she came running toward the smoke, but she didn't."

Laney continued to pepper Sheriff Law with questions that were both insightful and a little resentful. It all should never have happened.

Norma turned her attention to her assistant as Jess shot a gumdrop into The Fox's mouth. "Ahem. You all should know I owe many of my amazing deductions to our matriculating law student, Jess Harper. Three cheers for Jess!"

They all shouted, "Hurrah! Hurrah! Hurrah!"

Owen cleared his throat and addressed the sheriff. "I saw in the paper Mr. Fingerhut confessed to killing Finn, but they didn't give his motive."

"A few days after the fire, Finn tried to blackmail him. Now, how Finn saw Jerry Fingerhut messing around the cottage, and Hilda did not, I can't say. Hilda came through those same woods when she smelled the fire, so maybe after Jerry got away. Maybe she did see Jerr, but that's not something we'll hear from her.

"So, later on, Finn demanded to meet Mr. Fingerhut and old Finn was foolish enough to let Jerr choose the place, the woods behind his dairy farm, which back up onto the Opequon. It was a simple matter to sneak up on Finn while he was waiting—Jerr's a hunter and knows how to sneak—knock him in the back of the head and push him into the creek."

At last, all the questions had been answered, and even if they hadn't, the night had turned chilly, and the party—everyone except Coigne and Norma—went inside. "What happened to The Fox and Jess?" Coigne asked. "They were here a minute ago."

"Don't try to find them," she said. "Just follow me."

"Anywhere."

The End